THE ASCENT

THE ASCENT

by Carmela Cattuti

Author of *Between the Cracks:*
One Woman's Journey from Sicily to America

Three Towers Press

Milwaukee, Wisconsin

Published by Three Towers Press
An imprint of HenschelHAUS Publishing, Inc.
www.henschelHAUSbooks.com
Milwaukee, Wisconsin

ISBN: 978159598-717-4
E-ISBN: 978159598-718-1
LCCN: 2019901639

Printed in the United States of America

Alice came to a fork in the road.

"Which road do I take?" she asked.

"Where do you want to go?" responded the Cheshire Cat.

"I don't know," Alice answered.

"Then," said the Cat, "it doesn't matter."

Lewis Carroll, *Alice in Wonderland*

In memory of Duane Hess

Table of Contents

Chapter 1

August 1932

Angela spread the white tablecloth over the dining room table and placed a white linen napkin at each setting, along with a freshly cut white lily. Today was the day the Blessed Mother rose to heaven. Angela had felt Mary's intervention in her life throughout the years and enjoyed honoring Her with an afternoon lunch for all her friends. She never mentioned her Friday candle-lighting ritual. The altar she kept to honor Mary was in her bedroom, out of sight from visitors and family.

"Angie," called Franco. He came into the dining room dragging one leg behind him.

"What is all this?" Franco asked, pointing at the table.

"I am having friends over. It is the feast of The Assumption, Mary ascending into heaven," Angela said.

"OK." Franco turned around and went into the cellar. He never liked anything to do with religion, as he thought the church never cared much for poor people. There was never any benefit in praying to the saints or any of the other figures in God's hierarchy.

"I will leave lunch for you on the kitchen table," called Angela.

Angela heard voices outside her front door before the doorbell rang. It was a demanding ring, as if a tantrum was about to ensue if not immediately answered.

"Angelina," called Paolina, Salvatore's sister, entering the hall and followed by other women. Angela greeted her, but with underlying resentment that Paolina had encouraged the marriage between her brother, Salvatore, and Speranza.

All the women carried pocketbooks hanging off their arms like padlocks. These were substantial women, both physically and socially, within the immigrant Italian community. Paolina dressed in a floral pattern that was too young for her age, her ample shoulders concealed with a crocheted shawl. She was the leader of the pack. Second in command was Ramina Galluci, whose husband Gianni was a local tailor and Angela's chief competition. Angela enjoyed letting Ramina know how successful she was as a designer. Ramina was the only guest who wore makeup, applying thick powder to her face that highlighted deep lines, but no one would dare tell her that it made her look old.

"Hello, hello," called a shrill voice from the doorway.

Angela had invited Claudia Cerverci, whose voice often preceded her physical presence. Compared to Angela's other friends, Claudia was a renegade. She was outspoken, outgoing, and funny. She wore a gold cross, and it often nestled between her large breasts that protruded from every outfit she wore.

"Angela, how are you doing?" asked Claudia.

"Do you have to be so loud?" asked Amelia.

"I don't have to, but I like it," said Claudia. "It's good to put a little life in this beautiful summer day."

She handed Angela a bouquet of white lilies.

"For the center of the table," said Claudia.

"Thank you," said Angela.

When Italians immigrated to the United States, they did so in large numbers—all from the same village and sometimes entire neighborhoods—so when they arrived in America, there was already a relationship between people. An orphan, Angela came to New York without any personal connection to the Italian community—just her naturalized husband. Franco had come to America with his mother and brother in 1901 from Palermo and returned to Sicily in 1912 to look for a wife. He went to the convent, where Angela was one of the most eligible young women, and married her in 1913. Angela had been in the United States for 19 years and everyone coming to this luncheon had been in America for a long time; however, the conversation would still be in Sicilian. Angela had navigated an unknown landscape and made a life in the new world.

Paolina kissed Angela on both cheeks.

"It is a beautiful summer day," Paolina said. "God has blessed us with perfect weather."

Directly behind Paolina stood Sadie Malaci. She wore elastic stockings that bagged at the ankles. She carried a needlepoint pocketbook that she had purchased in a thrift store. Her grey skirt was bunched together with a belt, the hem undone on one side. She too kissed Angela on both cheeks. When Angela first met Sadie over 15 years ago, she had assumed that Sadie was quite poor because her appearance was consistently unkempt. A few years ago, Sadie had buried her second husband. Her first husband was a steel worker in Sicily, and when he died, she married his older brother in America—even though his brother was engaged to be married to a woman in Sicily. A few years later, he met his end and Sadie inherited the house in America and the houses he owned in Sicily. She turned away the Sicilians who rented the seaside properties and invited rich vacationing Americans at double the rent. Her appearance belied her astute business acuity.

Angela showed the ladies into the dining room.

"Paolina, you sit next to me on the right," Angela said. "Sadie, sit on my left, and Amelia, sit next to Sadie."

Amelia Saldi prided herself on being the wife of an artist. Her husband was a tombstone designer, and whenever a member of the Italian-American community died, they were obligated to use his services. Amelia could carry on a conversation beyond their community and spoke English with the faintest Italian accent.

"Amelia, next to Sadie."

"Claudia, take any other seat," Angela said.

Angela offered her arm to Elena Domenico, who walked with a cane. The oldest of her guests, Elena emigrated to the United States in the 1890s. Now at 86, she had seen the Italian community develop into a social and political force along the Hudson River Valley. Angela felt Elena was the wisest of her guests. She had lost relatives in the 1908 earthquake, had been kind to Angela when she first came to America, and introduced her to many of her friends. Her husband had passed and her children had moved away, so Angela looked in on her periodically and made sure she was seen by the local doctor on a regular basis.

"Elena, you will sit at the end of the table," Angela said, assisting her to her seat, "directly across from me."

"Where should we sit?" squealed one of two women who were dressed alike and stood arm in arm.

Angela had invited the Venzetti twins at Paolina's behest. They were the youngest among the visitors, and Angela felt they were not earnest in celebrating The Assumption. They were distant cousins of Paolina and were questing for husbands. Paolina seemed to think that an invitation to Angela's house would expedite the process. Angela and Franco lived in one of the most beautiful homes in Nelsonville, so Paolina felt it would attract the most eligible men.

Lastly, there was Paolina's younger sister, poor Nancy Caputo. Nancy was the relative that no one talked about. The family and the Italian community considered Nancy a lost soul. She had moved to New York City when she was 15, and she now lived in a rooming house and worked as an elevator operator at the Park Plaza Hotel. She was reclusive, considered slow minded, and rarely had contact with family. She wasn't even considered a gossip fodder. Occasionally she would come to Nelsonville on the train to visit her sister, and this was one of those times. Paolina did not want to bring her to the lunch, but Angela had insisted. These were Angela's compatriots.

"You cannot leave her home alone," said Angela. "That is not nice." She thought that Nancy was treated unfairly. She also enjoyed annoying Paolina.

Paolina had conceded and brought her, grudgingly.

"Angela, you are looking well," said Ramina. "I saw you at mass on Sunday. Did you enjoy the sermon?"

Angela had attended mass every Sunday since she arrived in the United States, primarily because she could not risk gossip. In a small Italian-American community, gossip could slaughter one's reputation. She was tied to the idea that she needed to outwardly comply with the teachings of the Catholic Church—not that she believed she would go to hell, but because she feared isolation. The community tended to ostracize anyone who did not attend mass, especially someone as respected as Angela, so Angela walked between her inner mystical and exterior worlds with as much balance as she could.

As a child, Angela had unseen friends who would come to play with her in dreams. They showed themselves as children with long curly hair, and as Angela grew older so did her unseen friends; their voices and appearance matured. Angela would speak to them in her mind during the day and receive guidance and advice. She never received heartfelt connection and advice in church, so Angela kept her beliefs and experiences to herself as she traversed both her inner and outer landscapes. She hoped to one day openly share her inner experience.

Angela wanted to stay connected to her Sicilian culture, so she did not share her connection with the unseen friends of her inner world. They were part of her life journey and had influenced her major decisions. Attending mass was Angela's quiet meditative time to connect with her unseen friends and listen to what seemed like a distant voice from her past. She never paid much attention to the sermon, especially if she had a strong connection to her unseen friends that day.

"Yes, it was lovely, although sometimes I find it difficult to understand. At times there is an echo with the microphone," she would say when pressed. Even if there was clearly no echo, no one would outwardly challenge Angela. Over the years, she had become proficient at expressing her opinion with absolute certainty.

Angela had communed with the divine most of her life without the intermediary of a priest. Ever since she was a young girl, she felt her unseen friends were there to ensure her survival and success.

"Thank you so much, Angela," said Nancy, her fire engine red lips smiling. Her lipstick reached outside her lip line, not quite at clown proportions. "I am so rarely invited to parties." She hugged Angela. "Why are you so good to me?"

"I am good to everyone—and you are family, so why would I not be good to you? Please come in and sit next to your sister. I am sure you will want to enjoy this experience together. Our Blessed Mother values sisters."

Angela delighted in Paolina's failed attempt to disguise her true feelings about the seating arrangements; her lips drooped at the end and her eyes looked away as she took a deep breath.

"Julia and Louisa Venzetti, sit anywhere."

Angela stood at the head of the table.

"Let us say grace," Angela said and folded her hands.

Everyone bowed their head as Angela led them in prayer that thanked God for his bounty, and she also thanked the Virgin Mary for bringing His Son to earth, because without her there would be no Jesus.

"Amen," everyone said.

"That was an unorthodox prayer," said Amelia. "Did you create that one yourself? You are so creative, but I am sure the church would not like it."

"Oh, we think it was a lovely prayer, Angela," said one of the twins.

"Oh, yes," said the other, nodding her head.

"We are honoring our Blessed Mother today," said Angela, "the church has nothing to do with it."

Angela glanced at Nancy, who sat nervously with her pocketbook in her lap.

Nancy was prone to paranoia and was often paralyzed with fear. Angela wondered what happened to her to create that situation.

"Tell us, Angela, why do you celebrate The Assumption every year?" asked Amelia. "The church only suggests that we celebrate Our Lady's feast day. It is not required. Christ's ascension is the important celebration."

"She did not tell you?" interjected Paolina. "Angela almost died a few years after she came to this country, and she feels the Blessed Mother saved her."

Angela was not going to discuss her relationship with the Virgin Mother. It was personal, and it was something she kept for herself. She never told anyone about her unseen friends, and yet she spoke to them in times of distress. Angela could discuss anything with them—there would be no judgment, and she could use any language. If she spoke Italian in her mind, then they would respond in Italian. If the conversation required English, then they conversed in English. There were no limitations in content or language. She believed they her kept her safe after the earthquake, especially when she was alone and searching for her sister.

"Mary's assumption is just as important," said Angela. "I said the church has nothing to do with this celebration."

The room quieted, and all the guests looked at one another waiting for someone to speak up. No one did—except Claudia Cerverci.

"What difference does it make?" asked Claudia. "It is a nice day to celebrate the Blessed Mother. After all, many of us here are mothers; and if we are not, then Mary is our mother, so let's eat."

"I agree, and I would like some wine," said Sadie. "We should have a toast to the Blessed Mother to celebrate her ascension to heaven."

It was common knowledge that Sadie favored wine at lunch, dinner, and into the evening. Most of the husbands made their own wine, so not only was it in abundance, but it was as strong as turpentine. She would go around and visit friends who were peppered around the city of Nelsonville and have wine at each house. Most of the hosts would give her one glass and send her on her way. The worst thing was to see Sadie Malaci walking up your front stairs swinging her pocketbook, her elastic stockings falling to her ankles.

"Sadie, you do not need wine," said Amelia. "You need a dressmaker. Why don't you ask Angela for help? I am sure she would alter your clothes and make them more presentable. She is an artist, like my husband, and has done wonders for my wardrobe."

"Oh, leave her alone," said Claudia. "She enjoys it."

"I am sure Sadie can make up her own mind about her wardrobe without help from us," Angela said.

"Well, if you ask me, it is not appropriate for her to come to a luncheon dressed like that, even if the Assumption is only a minor holy day," said Amelia. "How is Franco doing?"

"He is doing well," Angela said.

Since his stroke several years ago, Franco was viewed by the community as a bombastic person with a propensity for unprovoked outbursts. Prior to his stroke, he was strong and self-sufficient, never needing anyone's help. Angela had struggled with this change in his character. She made dinner one night and told Franco it was ready.

"No, not hungry."

"But I made dinner, and you need to eat," said Angela.

"Not hungry!" He slammed the cellar door and spent the rest of the evening in the basement.

When she first came to America, Franco had slapped Angela when his pasta was not to his liking.

"I don't need to stay here," Angela told him. "I always have a home at the convent. I will leave here."

The slap never happened again.

"Amelia, maybe you should mind your own business," said Sadie.

"Let us all remember why we are here," said Angela, "to honor our Blessed Mother, who is the mother of us all. Enough arguing. Pour the wine and toast to Mary."

An opened bottle of red wine sat on the table with silver salt and pepper shakers at its base. Angela had earlier arranged the condiments, so they looked like a still life painting. She felt that a table setting was just as important as art in a room. She wanted her guests to feel like they were in a work of art.

"I told you I like the way I dress," Sadie said. "It is comfortable. Not like the rest of you, dressing like you had someplace to go. You just sit around in each other's houses and gossip."

Amelia picked up her linen napkin and snapped it as if it was a towel aimed at someone's buttocks. She placed it neatly on her lap.

Angela thought Sadie's timing was impeccable. Whenever one in the community criticized her, she rose to the occasion.

"I think you look very comfortable," Nancy said. She blinked as if someone was about to hit her. "Oh my, I am sorry."

The twins giggled. Age-wise they were well past the giggling stage, but until they were married, they would act like teenagers.

"What are we talking about?" Elena said. She could barely hear anymore, and table conversation eluded her.

"We are not talking about anything of any consequence," Angela said, filling her wine glass. "Now we will pass the wine for each of us to enjoy a sip, so we can salute Mary the mother of Jesus Christ and to her ascension."

Angela raised her glass. Each guest dropped a small amount of wine in her glass for the toast. Sadie filled her glass to the brim.

All the guests stood and raised their glasses. Nancy snapped to attention and splashed red wine on the white linen tablecloth.

"Oh Angela, I am so sorry." Nancy said, teary eyed. She tried to clean it up with her white linen napkin. "I have taken advantage of your hospitality."

"Accidents happen," Angela said. "I will take care of it later. Everything needs a good washing anyway." Angela had not put on the protective plastic she used at family dinners because no children would be at the table.

Nancy whimpered.

"I have spoiled our lunch. I always do." She blew her nose on her linen napkin.

"You are ruining our lunch with your crying," said Amelia. She reached into her pocketbook, pulled out a fan, and snapped it open like a switchblade. Angela thought she was going to thump Nancy.

"Nancy don't worry about it," said Claudia. "Angela will take care of it."

"I would like to drink my wine in peace," said Sadie. She took a sip.

"We have not toasted yet," Paolina said. "You drink when we have toasted."

Sadie lifted her pinky finger and continued to sip.

"To Mary, the mother of Jesus Christ, and to her ascension to heaven," intoned Angela.

"To Mary, the mother of Jesus Christ, and to her ascension to heaven," everyone repeated.

"Salute!"

Sadie drained her glass.

Angela was thankful for silence as they drank. She had often wanted to share the joy of her experience of the Blessed Mother, but she had failed to realize that it was her relationship with the Virgin that she celebrated, and that others did not share the depth of her experience. She wanted to convey the devotion she felt but realized it was only particular to herself. They did not share her reverence for the mother of Jesus; for the others that was reserved for God.

"Bring out another bottle, Angela," said Sadie. She wiped her mouth with the linen napkin and hiccupped.

"I have prepared chicken to represent Mary's flight into heaven," Angela said. She put down her glass and started to go into the kitchen.

"I will help you," said Paolina. She jumped up and turned to Sadie. "And do not drink all the wine."

"Angela is a good woman," Elena Domenico said. "She looks after me. If I need anything mended, she doesn't charge me."

"Yes, we have heard she is well-connected," one of the twins said. "She must know a lot of fine men."

"What?" asked Elena.

"Angela," shouted the other twin into Elena's ear, almost knocking the frail woman off the chair. "She knows many fine men."

"Angela is well-respected," said Elena, "so she knows many fine people." Both twins giggled.

Angela opened the oven door and pulled out a pan of golden- brown chicken breasts, thighs, and potatoes. She placed them on the stove. Paolina drained the pasta, put it on the serving dish and covered it with steaming red sauce that was made the night before.

"Make sure you mix the pasta with the sauce," instructed Angela. She picked up each piece of chicken and placed it on an antique platter.

"So," Paolina said, "have you heard some of the younger women in our community are socializing at night without a chaperone?"

Angela stopped what she was doing and gave Paolina her undivided attention. Paolina had been Speranza's sister-in-law and was instrumental in bringing her brother, Salvatore, and Speranza together. Angela had despised the match from the beginning. He was ten years older, had infantile paralysis, walked with a limp, and couldn't hold a job.

"Paolina, life is different now. Young women have more freedom."

"Well," said Paolina as she folded her arms across her ample chest. "I have it on good authority that some of the girls have been stepping out and going to dances unchaperoned— and some without their husbands."

Angela knew what kind of "good authority" she was talking about: gossipy women who had nothing else to do but spy on people and make up lies.

"That is ridiculous," Angela said. "Besides, that is none of our business."

"You say that because that is what Speranza did to my brother Salvatore."

"My sister-in-law is dead, leave her to rest," said Angela.

Speranza had a chronic heart ailment and had passed a few years earlier.

"Many of the women in your own dining room have knowledge of her behavior," said Paolina. "They are just being kind by not mentioning it. Speranza is no longer with us, but she was not the saint you thought she was."

"I will not discuss such gossip on Our Lady's Assumption day," Angela said.

"She was not as innocent as you think. That is all I am saying," Paolina said. She picked up the pasta and walked over to Angela. "Everyone knows this but you."

"Paolina, do not bring this up at the table, and stop talking about my sister-in-law." Angela looked at Paolina as if she were about to throw her out of her house. Paolina turned and quickly went out to the dining room.

Stupid woman, thought Angela. Paolina had nothing better to do but spread gossip. The truth was, Angela did not care how Speranza lived her short life while she was on earth. People should be happy, and if they found themselves in a situation that prevented happiness, then it should be rectified. As soon as Angela immigrated, she went to work for St. Mary's School, sewing priests' vestments and making clothing for the students. Angela felt she had lived a multitude of expectations since she came to America. She tried to fulfill as many as she could, but after a while she decided to only fulfill the important ones: raising Speranza's young children, making money, and taking care of Franco. She could not remember a time that she did not work. As soon as she came to America, Franco and his family expected her to go right to work. They both supported his mother and sister.

She'd had to find her own way to make a life in America. Franco did not have the patience or the time to assist Angela in adapting to her new home. Speranza helped Angela learn English, and in turn, Angela shared her knowledge of the social graces and sewing. She had not known what to expect when she came to the United States, but she never envisioned anything like her experience. She did not expect the street to be paved with gold, but she envisioned that she would have more support from Franco. Instead, she was expected to take care of Franco's mother, the house, and make money in a strange new culture. With no one to guide her, she often turned to her unseen friends; they had guided her along the desolate landscape after the earthquake, as they guided her in her American journey.

By the time Angela got back to the table, Sadie was pouring the last of the wine into her glass.

"Oh Angela, we need another bottle," burped Sadie.

"You have had quite enough," said Amelia. "We only had one glass. You had the rest."

"I will get more," said Paolina. "You have had enough," pointing at Sadie.

"You can have mine," Nancy said, blinking constantly. "I do not drink."

"Elena, would you care for more wine?" asked Angela.

"What?" Elena asked, cupping her ear.

"Would you like my wine?" shouted Nancy.

"Don't shout. I am not deaf."

"Yes, you are," said Nancy. She pushed the wine glass toward Elena.

"Thank you," Elena said as she lifted her glass.

It was not the reverent lunch for the Blessed Mother Angela had planned, but it was a comfort that, regardless of the outcome, she had celebrated Mary's ascension.

"Pass the chicken," Angela said. "Let us be grateful for Mary's presence on earth."

Chapter 2

December 1934

Angela looked forward to the company of her first client of the day, Mrs. Sarah Einbinder, who had emigrated from Germany a few years before. In Germany, Sarah had been a successful playwright and was interested in Angela's story. Sarah found it intriguing and encouraged Angela to recount every detail. She still had family in Germany, and they kept her informed about the political situation. Angela and Sarah would discuss the most recent information coming out of Europe from those who were experiencing it first-hand.

"Mrs. Bellini, you are a marvel and an alchemist," said Sarah Einbinder. "I am the best-dressed woman at all my social gatherings."

Angela saw what she brought to her community and her customers. Many of her customers said that she worked magic. She felt more than a seamstress—she was a magician of sorts. When her customers tried on her garments, they transformed into whatever the dress or suit suggested. That was the mark of a successful artist.

Sarah was a tall woman with wisps of gray hair framing her face and a bun at the nape of her neck. Angela wore her hair similarly. Both women did not like the new haircuts, as they seemed unfeminine. Angela was fitting her client with a navy-blue suit, a pattern she had altered many times for various figures. Sarah Einbinder had a small waist, so the fitted jacket flattered her form beautifully. For most of her Italian clients, she had to let the jacket out. Angela made her garments with intention, so when her clients wore her clothing it transformed the person into the intention. Mrs. Einbinder's blue suit projected intelligence and focus. Angela thought that maybe she actually was a magician. It gave a new dimension to her work. She would not share this with her friends, because they would consider making magic against the teachings of the Catholic Church. It would be considered the work of the devil.

"What news do you have from Europe?" Angela asked. She pulled on a sleeve and pinned the hem. "We have not heard from my husband's cousin in Sicily, Roberto, for several months." She had also written to the Mother Superior at the convent in Palermo over two months ago but had not received a response.

"Well, I'm not surprised. You had mentioned that his poetry was politically motivated, and he had to flee Sicily at one point?"

"Yes," said Angela. Roberto was a recognized Sicilian poet who made his political beliefs known in the most public places: piazzas and churches.

"My sister and her husband refuse to leave Germany, even though every day more freedom is taken away." Sarah Einbinder paused and peered into the mirror at Angela. "Haven't you heard? There was a skirmish at a place called Wal Wal in Africa. I am sure Mussolini will invade Africa. They say he wants to have a great military victory to signify Fascism's success."

Roberto would certainly have spoken out against such an invasion. The last letter they received from him was uncharacteristic of his correspondence. It was cryptic and dry, lacking the poet's emotional voice. He usually included his latest brush with the authorities or the mafia, and sometimes he included a poem. He was their only link to Sicily and the political situation. The nuns were not as reliable, since they rarely left the convent and would do whatever was necessary to survive. Angela contributed money every year to the convent to help the orphans. She hoped it would ease any hardships from the political situation. She was fortunate to have survived the earthquake and then found a stable home with the nuns.

"It is dangerous to be a Jew in Germany," Sarah said. "Some of my sister's friends have disappeared, but she and her husband refuse to leave because her husband's parents are ill. Catholics are safe in Italy because the church is powerful, and Mussolini does not want to anger the Pope. There would be an uprising. But if Mussolini could rid himself of the church and replace it with Nazism, he would. None of these so-called leaders can be trusted."

"Where did your sister's friends go?" Angela asked. She stopped working and met Sarah's gaze in the mirror.

"We are not sure. But we do know the Nazis are killing people, Angela, for being Jews," Sarah Einbinder said. "Hitler plans to take over the world. No one is safe."

"My sister was lost in the earthquake in 1908, but I survived. I still do not know if she is alive. We went to Europe to find documents about her fate. There were none."

Angela remembered when her sister, Maria, was born. She was only four years old at the time, but she remembered her sister's dark hair and strong cry. After the earthquake, she kept going back to what was once their home and shouting her name, hoping that she would hear a cry in the rubble. Angela went onboard an American rescue ship, but she kept telling people she wanted to look for her sister. They would not let her return to the city but said they would put out the word about her. Angela was relieved to hear that there was an orphanage in Messina. This way she and her brother could continue to look for their sister. To Angela's dismay, she was told she would be sent to a convent in Palermo. She never knew why that decision was made or who made it.

Angela knew what it was like not knowing a loved one's fate. She had grown up feeling unsafe. The feeling was all-consuming and never really went away, even if she found herself in a stable environment. She had felt safe in America, but any talk of unrest in any part of the world brought back memories of the earth's anger. The very planet they stood on was unpredictable. She and Franco did not find her sister when they returned to Sicily to search and had to give her up for dead. A dictator did not take her away—it was an internal explosion of the planet swallowing her whole, never to be seen or heard from again.

Angela had never spoken about the details of her days following the earthquake. Most people were in their beds asleep when the earthquake hit, so the citizens wandered the city in their night clothes. There were a series of tremors after the earthquake, so the remaining buildings that people took shelter in fell, and many more died. Angela had wrapped a blanket around her shoulders and had been wandering around the ruins of her house shouting for her grandmother, brother, and sister. A man appeared from the ethers. She had not heard or seen him walk from the street; he seemed to manifest from the ashes.

"There is no one left alive here," said the man.

He was dressed in a dark suit and wore a fedora. He couldn't have experienced the earthquake, thought Angela. He was tall and thin with blue eyes, and he was immaculately groomed. He did not look Sicilian.

"Who are you looking for, little girl?"

"My family—my brother and sister—this was my house."

He is not here to help me, she thought. Even though Angela was just 13, her unseen friends had always spoken to her in her mind, and they were telling her to be wary.

"Everyone is dead," said the man. "You should leave this place, little girl. Earthquakes make people do strange and awful acts."

Angela didn't see his mouth move, even though she heard his voice. It was strangely calm.

"I want to search for my family." Angela said. He was not going to run her off from her home.

"There is no one to search for. Leave this place while you can."

Angela continued to call for her family by name, ignoring the man's presence. He seemed surprised that she did not obey him as she continued to move around the rubble and shout louder and louder. She noticed that the man became progressively confused and agitated. The more adamant she became in her determination to find her family, she saw fear appear in his face. She turned her back on him and when she turned around to face him again, he was gone.

She sat on a stone that was once the structure of her sitting room and felt the presence of the unseen friends. They would be her only company for the next few days. It was here that she had made a firm connection with her unseen friends. Even in all the chaos, their communication was clear. She would take their voices with her wherever she went.

A few days later, another child recounted a meeting with the same man. The boy was with a friend when he encountered him. The friend went to the man when he was beckoned. The child was never seen again. Angela was grateful she listened to her unseen friends.

* * *

"I am done, Mrs. Einbinder," Angela said absently.

"I am sorry about your sister, truly I am. I hope someday you will be at peace with her loss." Sarah stepped down from the platform and looked at Angela.

"My brother died of pneumonia a few years after the earthquake, so I was truly alone in the world."

"You know, you really should have someone write your story," said Sarah Einbinder. "I would like to do that someday if you'll allow me. Very few people know how devastating that earthquake actually was to Messina."

"I would be honored, Mrs. Einbinder."

"Your story is extraordinary, Mrs. Bellini, but there is one character who does not quite fit, and that is the Princess of Palermo. Why did she lavish attention on you? What was her name again?"

"Principessa Giulia," replied Angela.

"That's right. Why do you suppose she singled you out?"

Angela had asked herself the same question over the years, but she had no answer. The Prince and Princess of Palermo had given one of their buildings at the Palazzo Butera to the nuns to help the orphans and open a school. When she was a young girl at the convent, she never questioned why the Princess was concerned about her well-being. It was only as the years went by that she began to question why she deserved the Princess' favor. Angela tried to remember when she first met Principessa Giulia, but it seemed like she had always been there.

What was even more unusual was that the Mother Superior had encouraged the relationship. Convent policy stated that everyone was to be treated equally, and under no circumstances was any girl to be favored. For some reason, that policy did not apply to Angela. She told herself it was because the Princess bought the linens she sewed, and the convent made money.

"The Princess loved my sewing," Angela said.

Sarah turned and looked at Angela.

"You had your wedding reception at her palazzo? The connection had to be more than that. Friendship is one thing, but allowing you to have your wedding reception at her palazzo is another."

"She felt sorry for me," Angela replied. "She was like an older sister or an aunt."

"It seems that she was motivated by more than just sympathy," said Sarah.

There's no point in thinking about it now, Angela thought.

"Do you regret leaving?"

"Sicily? I do not think so, but sometimes I wonder what my life would have been like if I had stayed." Angela's current friends had never asked her any of these questions. Her friends were not interested in Angela's past or her story. They saw her as part of their community whose life began when she came to America.

Relaying her story to people like Sarah Einbinder was revelatory. It added a deeper dimension to her journey that she could not access when she shared it with her Italian friends. They tolerated her story, but Sarah saw her history as poetry or a great epic. She would also be able to keep her sister's memory alive through Sarah Einbinder's words.

* * *

The conversation with Sarah and other clients stirred Angela's long-forgotten memories and feelings. This was where she balanced her American life with her European past. From the beginning, Angela was able to walk between those two worlds. Her relationship with her Italian friends was different from her clients. She also navigated between her spiritual life and the physical world. She instinctively knew how to traverse the terrain of all three and became more adept over the years. Now she adapted to each social landscape with acuity.

Principessa Giulia had been unable to attend her wedding to Franco. This was another disappointment to Angela. She looked to the Princess as a model of what life should be: a loving nature combined with culture and position. Angela received a telegram from the Principessa, apologizing for not being able to attend her wedding. To this day, Angela kept the telegram and would occasionally read it.

She remembered sitting on the edge of her bed at the convent reading the telegram that told her the Principessa was on important business in Rome with her husband. The Princesses' husband's last name was Lanza: Pietro di Trabia was his full title. Angela's maiden name was also Lanza. Lanza was a common Sicilian name, so no one ever mentioned the coincidence; not her fellow students, not even the nuns. She had thought that she might mention the unusual circumstance to the Mother Superior, but she sensed tension between the Mother Superior and the Principessa, so Angela kept silent. She noticed that when the two women passed each other, either on the grounds or in the hallways, they would nod to one another without smiling or speaking.

Angela had secretly harbored thoughts of being part of the Principessa's household. She thought that Princess Giulia would bring her on as seamstress, or in some other capacity. When that did not happen, she chose to marry rather than become a nun. If her brother had lived, Angela would have left the convent to live with her brother and resettle in Messina. Together they would go on a quest to find out what happened to their younger sister. Whenever she felt alone and needed a boost, Angela would read the telegram; reliving the past was sometimes better than the present.

Angela wondered what it would be like to see her history on stage. She had loved going to the passion plays at the convent, and now she longed to see more modern plays—but that was for the elite of the world. But now she had an actual playwright in her house. If you take chances, like coming to America, life does change.

"I can't promise anything, but we should discuss this further," said Sarah as she came out of the bedroom buttoning her white blouse. "I am approaching a few theaters in New York to put on my plays. It's way off Broadway, of course, but it's a start."

Sarah Einbinder had been teaching playwriting at the local college to support her creative and political activities, and Angela had admired her since they first met. It was a relief for Angela to connect with other immigrants with unusual histories. Sarah had fled from Fascism, and Angela fled from not only the isolation of convent life, but memories of her lost family. A change of country did not mean it would wipe out dark experiences. They had both survived major disasters with grace and with their culture intact.

She was honored that an educated woman like Sarah Einbinder considered Angela her equal, but more than that, Angela believed herself to be Sarah's equal. This made for a harmonious creative collaboration. Angela felt she did not have to explain herself to Sarah. Angela had heard that her friends thought she had embellished her earthquake and convent story.

"I will see you next week, Mrs. Bellini, to talk about a gown I would like made for a function."

Angela assisted Sarah with her suit jacket, one that Angela had made at their first fitting. A well-designed and sewn garment always appeared new, regardless of its age. She used the best fabric, whatever the cost. If a client did not want to pay for more expensive fabric, she sent them to another dressmaker. Her only advertisement was the clothes her customers wore.

"I always look forward to seeing you, Mrs. Einbinder."

After Mrs. Einbinder left, Angela remembered a conversation she had with Sadie Malaci years ago about the Principessa.

"You know, I knew Franco before he married you. When he came back from Sicily the first time, he seemed enthusiastic about your relationship with the Principessa. You never talk about her."

"That was a long time ago, Sadie," Angela said.

Angela had shrugged it off as unimportant. Sadie had had too much to drink as usual. But she had felt that Franco wanted her to stay connected to Princess Giulia.

Angela was pleased with the turn of events the day offered. She started to imagine her life portrayed on stage with the audience transfixed on the drama taking place. *This way, people will know what I went through and what happened to my city.* Angela wondered if she should tell Sarah about the level of desperation and fear that plagued the remainder of the population. She had never described the details of the days following the earthquake to anyone.

* * *

Angela hung Sarah Einbinder's dress in a closet reserved for garments in progress and proceeded to get ready for bed. The conversation she had that day with Sarah encouraged Angela to look at her past with some detachment so she could look at her history from a more receptive perspective. Angela sat at her vanity. There was a picture of Speranza and Angela sitting in a flower garden, a brush, comb, and perfume bottles. Staring at the photograph, she brushed her long, fine hair from the roots to the ends with slow, deliberate strokes. She had not cut her hair in years, and spots of grey started to appear. At age 39, her skin was smooth, and her high cheekbones were prominent. She had worn the same bun since her teenage years. She embraced the new fashion as much as she could, but not its hairstyles.

Tonight, she was feeling grateful that she had the experience of having a younger sister through Speranza. She touched he photograph, then draped her rosary over the picture. Angela got into bed and pulled the bedclothes up to her neck.

She heard Franco's rhythmic breathing next to her. He had spent most of the day in the cellar, doing small repair projects. Angela was his caretaker, an in-demand dressmaker, and ran the house, so when she was able to completely rest, she was grateful. Angela closed her eyes and imagined her sister-in-law as a healthy, fun-loving young woman. That image faded as she drifted off to sleep, relieved from the day's stresses.

Images ebbed and flowed. Angela saw visions of Speranza as a child, teenager, and adult. Angela found herself in Speranza's bedroom, where Speranza was in bed surrounded by her three children. Angela found that she could hear Speranza's thoughts and feelings and was a complete observer to Speranza's experience.

Speranza's first child, Nunzio, had just turned 11, Alicia 10, and Joe, six years old. Nunzio and Alicia played on the floor, while little Joe slept next to his mother on the bed. Angela sensed she was near death, and Speranza's need to be near her children was overwhelming. Speranza focused on her children, but her thoughts entered Angela's mind: she wanted her children to know who she really was in life—not just a memory that they would have to conjure up when they thought of her. She did not want them to have to fill in the blanks. She also did not want them to have to ask relatives or her husband what she was like. That would be the worst legacy to leave for her children—the task of pulling different opinions and memories together to know their mother. It would be like a patchwork quilt with many holes and disjointed pieces.

She told Angela she had tried to be the best mother she could possibly be. She loved all her children but felt the most connection to the youngest, as even as an infant he seemed to understand her frailties. She surmised that he was very much like her. When she held him close, their two hearts beat as one. She loved him because he oozed compassion from his eyes and body. Her favorite thing to do was dress Joseph in Alicia's baby clothes. There was something so soft and feminine about him, and it comforted her. She never left him with her husband, Salvatore, because it angered him that she gave baby Joseph special treatment.

"I will always watch out for your children," Angela whispered to Speranza.

"Ma, look! My doll has beautiful clothes," said Alicia. "Aunt Angela made her a pretty dress." Alicia held up her doll so Speranza could see it. Angela was pleased that Alicia was a dolly girl. Not only was dressing her doll in frilly clothes her favorite activity, she also loved to dress up. Angela had made most of Alicia's clothes, as she had done for Speranza—even for Alicia's dolls.

"I will kill your doll with my gun," said Nunzio, pointing the toy gun at the doll's head. "Bam, bam!"

He blew on the barrel.

"Ma, he's gonna kill my doll!"

"No, no," whispered Speranza. "Love each other." Speranza became extremely tired and told the children she would lay back and rest. She no longer had the strength to shout or intervene when her children argued or fought.

"I want to rest my eyes," said Speranza. She asked Nunzio and Alicia to come up on the bed. "Always take care of your little brother." She looked down at Joseph and stroked his hair. He opened his eyes and smiled at his mother.

"Always look after each other."

Angela smiled. *You are a good mother*, she thought. *And I will look after the children*.

Speranza closed her eyes, and her breath started to slow down. Angela could see she wanted to take a deep breath but could not. She could hear

Speranza think about shouting but realized that she no longer had the desire to make her presence known. She did not mind leaving this world. Speranza wanted peace. She had married a man who disappointed her, and, in the end, she did not love him. Aware her marriage displeased Angela and her brother Franco, she was ashamed she had made such a choice. She admitted to herself in this moment that she was wrong in her choice.

The wonderful part was that she would leave a legacy through her children. All three of her children were with her now and would experience her death. Speranza marveled at how loving and tolerant they were. Out of her three children, she felt in her heart that Joe would be the most tolerant, because it would be through his differences and uniqueness that he would encounter adversity and transcend it.

Her faults had been many: smoking and drinking wine and going out dancing without her husband. Salvatore had complained to Angela about her behavior, but Speranza told Angela he was lying—and of course Angela believed her. It made Angela dislike Salvatore even more. Speranza kept these activities secret from Angela and Franco. In their eyes, she was the perfect wife and mother; she did not want to taint her image. She made choices to anger people whom she thought were attempting to control her, but not because these choices were what she wanted. She told Angela that she and Franco had given her their best, so she should have done better in life. She was determined to give her children the space to express themselves and build their own lives based on their differences. She was at peace. Her children knew everything about her, and they would keep her secrets.

In her dream state, Angela understood that from Speranza's perspective, her death was a gift to her children; she was with them at their birth, and they were present at her death. As Speranza slowly left her body, a door opened for her to step through. She did not want to leave her children, but it was her time and she welcomed it. She hadn't noticed, but she had taken her last breath.

Joseph rubbed the sleep from his eyes. "Ma, are we making cookies today?" Speranza did not respond.

"Are you sleeping, Ma?" asked Nunzio. He enjoyed the rise and fall of his mother's chest, but it had stopped. "Ma, are you sleeping?" he repeated.

"Mommy?" asked Alicia. She shook her mother's arm. Her mother's skin, usually warm, now felt cold.

"Mommy, wake up! Wake up!" She shook her more vigorously and then took her mother's head in her hands and peered into her glassy eyes. They looked like her doll's eyes.

"Papa, Ma won't wake up!" screamed Alicia. Nunzio ran out of the room crying.

"Papa, Ma won't wake up!" She repeated. There was no response. "Pa!"

"What now?" yelled Salvatore as he came into the room. "How are you spoiling the children now, Speranza?"

His wife's head fell to one side, and one arm hung off the bed. He found his daughter peering into her mother's eyes, pleading for her to wake up while Joseph cried.

"Speranza! Speranza!" Salvatore cried. He shook his wife. Salvatore's sister, Paolina, came running into the room.

"Dear God," Paolina said. "I will get Angela."

The dream morphed to Speranza's wedding day. Angela tried to appear happy and buoyant as Speranza walked out of Angela's bedroom in her wedding gown. The eggshell color against Speranza's skin added a glow that was both ghostly and illuminating.

"Remember me like this," Speranza said.

When Angela awoke, she remembered every detail of her dream. Throughout the years, her unseen friends had encouraged her to pay attention when she dreamed—because people who had passed over could communicate with the living.

Whenever Angela dreamed about Speranza, she would wake up in a sweat with her heart pounding. Today she felt oddly calm. Maybe her sister-in-law was showing her that she had accepted her own death. It also gave Angela clarity about the trajectory of her own life; she had committed herself to Speranza's children's welfare. Since her sister-in-law's death over two years ago, keeping up her spirits was a gargantuan ordeal—but after this dream, Angela felt a renewed sense of purpose.

* * *

"Franco, Alicia is coming today so I can fit her new dress."

"Down the cellar," said Franco.

He pointed toward the cellar door. Sometimes it was difficult for him to speak in complete sentences.

"Won't you say hello?" Angela asked.

Franco paused as he touched the doorknob, then turned toward Angela. "No."

Angela could see the grief in his eyes, but behind the grief was an anger that he released in spurts like the sputtering of a volcano. When Franco and Angela were first married, he spent a lot of his time drinking at the corner bar with his friends. She did not speak English at the time and felt isolated. When she told Franco that she did not come to America to sit alone every night, he told her she better get used to it because he would continue to do what he wanted. Having no children to care for, she had spent many hours making her own dress patterns and damning the Mother Superior for introducing her to Franco. In retrospect, all the signs of his discontent were there when they met.

Angela had thought Franco met with the Mother Superior a few times, but one of the girls at the convent saw him enter the building on several occasions followed by Principessa Giulia. Angela did not think it was important and dismissed the information. The Princess was most likely there to discuss convent business, since the convent was on the Princess' land. After Angela arrived in America, Franco insisted that she write to Princess Giulia and maintain her connection. When she explained to him that she would be writing to the Mother Superior only, he would become angry and sulk—as if he had been cheated out of something that was rightfully his. Angela repeatedly reminded herself that she would not have the life she had created without Franco.

The hall clock chimed. Alicia, age 13, was late for her fitting with Angela. She picked up the phone to call Immacolatta, Salvatore's wife. A woman with a thick Italian accent answered, saying "hello" as if she were clamming a hammer. Talking to Immacolatta was like walking through a minefield. Subtlety was not Immacolatta's strong suit; neither was speaking English. The rest of the conversation would be in Sicilian.

"Immacolatta, I am waiting for Alicia. I must fit her for her new dress. She needs a new dress for mass on Sundays."

"I need help cleaning the house," Immacolatta said curtly. "She will not be coming."

Angela shifted her weight and lifted her chest. This was unacceptable. Standing in front of her mirror was a joy for Angela and her customers—especially her family. Many joys had been lost or taken away; this was one she controlled. Angela had the idea that when she no longer made clothing, she would take the mirror to the backyard and smash it along with all the images and memories trapped in it. It was a miracle that Angela had permitted a full-length mirror in her home. She had transcended much programming the day she purchased the looking glass.

At the convent in Sicily, where she grew up after the earthquake until she was 18, mirrors were viewed as entrapment by the devil. Vanity was only a venial sin, but the Mother Superior banned full-length mirrors from the convent except one outside her office door. There were rumors that the real reason the Mother Superior banned these mirrors was because a mirror of that magnitude revealed the dark side of a person's nature. It was also believed that it was a portal to other realms that should never be accessed by humans. The Reverend Mother's office was in a secluded part of the convent, so there was very little foot traffic. Sometimes during the day, Angela would escape to view her full form in the mirror. One day, the mirror took on a life of its own.

Angela had just cut out the pattern for her own wedding dress and needed a full-length mirror to see how it fit on her body. Usually she let other girls pin it and then give their opinion about alterations—but this was an important garment, and she felt the only valid opinion was her own. After Angela had pinned the pattern on her form, she began to turn from side to side to see how the seams fit. She turned her back to the mirror and looked over her shoulder to view the back. As she peered into the mirror, an amorphous shape began to coalesce. She blinked, thinking it was a late afternoon shadow or a smudge on the glass, but it continued to ebb and flow. It took on human form, then morphed into an animal-like presence. When she turned to face the mirror, it seemed to recede into the space of the mirror. Angela reached out to touch the looking glass. The tips of her outstretched finger lightly glazed the mirror. The image quickly receded into a pinpoint as if it reacted to Angela's touch.

At times, Angela wished she could disappear into the world of the mirror. She imagined she would be able to look out at the material world. She would be invisible to everyone, but she could see everything. All the pain and ugliness of the earthquake and losing her family would be absorbed by the magic of that mirror. She would be able to change her environment with her intention.

"Did you hear me? She will not be coming."

Immacolatta woke Angela out of the distant past; to her it had felt as real as the present.

"Listen to what I am telling you, Immacolatta. Alicia has a fitting today because she is dressed shabbily in church. I will not have her dress sloppily because you cannot care for your own home and children. Immacolatta now had two children, Anthony, age two, and William, six months. Because of the close familial relation, both children were born with dwarfism.

"Have her here as soon as you can." She slammed the receiver.

Angela had not thought about her experience with the mirror at the convent in years. She had not felt frightened by the figure in the mirror, because it was not the first time she had encountered other-worldly beings. Memories came streaming back from other experiences and dreams from her childhood, and she remembered details from some. In one childhood dream, she experienced two figures who appeared to be twins. Both were female, had red hair and lips, and were draped in white cloth. Angela's immediate thought was that they were angels, but their energy and appearance did not project lofty ideals or Godly messages. They were there to be with her as equals. They did not move their lips to speak but projected images and words. They reminded Angela that there was always another way, nothing was predetermined, and she could change things whenever she wanted.

These two beings encouraged her to call on them and conveyed they would be there to guide her. After the earthquake, they guided her to walk down certain streets to avoid unsavory characters who would do her harm. Some spoke of disembodied spirits who were lost in time. From Angela's perspective, her visitors were as present to her as her friends and family. She experienced them as even more genuine, since time and distance did not matter; if she thought of them, they were there. She was not abandoned or alone, because she felt and trusted her unseen friends' presence. Since Speranza's death, she thought of them more often and the role they played in her inner life. If they were part of her, how did they affect her perceptions and choices?

* * *

Lately she had found her mind drifting while in church. The truth was, she did not have anything more to say to God or to priests, His representatives on earth. She never said this out loud, just to herself. She assumed her unseen friends heard her thoughts, but she felt no judgment from them. Angela still held a great deal of reverence for the Sicilian nuns who raised her after the earthquake, but now it was a more realistic admiration for their ability to survive in a tumultuous world. She still corresponded with the Mother Superior, but it felt like a world gone by. The Reverend Mother inquired about Franco's health in every letter, but the body of the correspondence was about the convent and Angela's life in America. How was she doing? How was life in America? Would she ever come back to Sicily for another visit? It was unlikely she would ever see her homeland again. Angela was happy that she had maintained the connection with the elderly nun since all her blood relatives, except her brother, had perished in the earthquake.

She now had the responsibility of Speranza's children, and in her view, they were not being cared for properly. They looked disheveled and unkempt. Their hair always needed combing, and their clothes needed ironing. Angela's greatest disappointment about her decision to come to America was her inability to have children. If she had stayed in Sicily and become a nun, she would not have felt that disappointment. If she had a message to give Speranza's children, it would be to follow your heart and it would never lead you astray.

"Aunt Angela," shouted Alicia, slamming the front door.

"Alicia, how many times have I told you not to slam doors? It is unladylike."

"Sorry," said Alicia, out of breath. "I ran here trying to get away from my stepmother. Thanks for calling." Alicia's light brown hair hung straggly around her face and shoulders, and her shoes had not been laced.

"I will get the comb for your hair. Please lace up your shoes."

"I don't feel like it. These are old shoes, so it doesn't matter. I need new ones."

Angela noticed the holes in Alicia's shoes. She tried not to show displeasure in Alicia's appearance, but it was Immacolatta's job to make sure Alicia was presentable before she left the house. It pleased Angela that Alicia looked like Speranza, but she felt her personality was different from her mother's. Alicia was not receptive to Angela's sensibility and social awareness. It displeased her that Alicia tended to sass back when told to do something. Angela assumed her niece's attitude was learned from Salvatore's side of the family. Speranza's children would never have acted like that without Salvatore's influence.

"I want to meet my friends after," Alicia said.

Angela brushed Alicia's hair from the roots to the ends. As she languidly moved the brush, the shine returned to her niece's hair. The sunlight streamed in through the window and magnified her blonde highlights.

"Why doesn't your stepmother remind you to do this?" Angela asked.

"Because she's busy all the time. And every time I try to do something for myself, she says 'Tend to your brothers. They need you.'"

Angela was silent. She would speak to Immacolatta about this situation. Alicia should not be caring for her siblings.

"It is not healthy to not take care of your body and appearance," Angela said.

As far back as Angela could remember, she was conscious of her health. It was not just the serious illness she suffered at 18 that took away her childbearing abilities—it was because when she was a child, people died without explanation. Both her parents had died suddenly, and Speranza died without warning. They were alive one day, and then the next they were not. To Angela, it was like people disappeared without acknowledgement that they were once here and lived lives that expressed sadness, joy, and anger. The strangest thing was that no one talked about the departed. Her unseen friends told Angela that the people who left earth were still alive somewhere else and that they tried to communicate with the living all the time. Angela felt that Speranza tried to communicate with her all the time through her thoughts.

"I do my best. Anyway, I want to have time with my friends," Alicia said. She popped up on the platform in front of the hall mirror, wearing a pale pink linen dress Angela had made for Speranza. It had been a bit large for Speranza's slim figure, but it was snug on her daughter. Alicia had started to develop earlier than most girls. She turned her back toward the mirror and looked over the shoulder.

"Can't you make this dress lower in the back? It's a summer dress and it's far too long."

"The length is fine. It will ruin the design if I lower the back. Besides, a low back is too mature. You are too young to think like that," Angela said.

She remembered Speranza as a young girl wanting to look older, but her figure was so slight that it did not worry Angela.

"I will get your dress," she told Alicia.

Angela brought back a light green dress made of taffeta, gathered at the waist with a diaphanous material over the entire garment.

"I wish I didn't have to do housework and take care of my brothers. She's only eight years older than me, and I have to do what she says."

"I will talk to her," said Angela with asperity. She tried to conceal her anger that Alicia was treated like the help.

"The other girls at school have better homes where fathers pay attention, and mothers take care of their daughters."

"I will speak to Immacolatta. You have nothing to worry about. You will have a new beautiful dress to wear. This will brighten your day."

Angela loved creating beautiful dresses for those she loved, especially those garments that would be worn in church. When she created garments for her Catholic clients, they would usually wear them to mass. It was the best calling card for her talents.

"Ma said a boy was looking at me at church and I should pay attention to him."

"Why?" asked Angela.

"I told you last week," Alicia said. She stamped her foot. "No one ever listens to me."

"Ma? Your stepmother," Angela said emphatically.

"Yes, she said I should call her Ma now. And why can't I wear black? Ma wears it. She says it looks nice on me. She says you dress me like a doll and that you are trying to keep me a child."

Angela grasped Alicia's shoulders and peered into her eyes.

"Listen to what I'm telling you. You are a child, and I will continue to make dresses that are right for your age. Your mother appreciated the clothes I made for her. Now take the pink dress off, and let's see how the green dress fits."

Angela lifted the pink dress over Alicia's head and dropped the green dress onto her well-formed figure. She placed a chalk dispenser at the hem, pressed the bulb, and a chalk mark was left to indicate the hemline. The dress had transformed Alicia from a disheveled child to a delicate young woman.

"Do you see how you look?" Angela asked. "Your mother would be proud." Angela sensed the social landscape was changing for young people—but without direction, it was not for the better for young girls like Alicia.

"Well, my mother is dead, and I'm me. Besides, people say she wasn't the angel you say she was," said Alicia smugly.

Angela cringed. How could she know about this gossip?

"Who is telling such lies?"

"My stepmother said so."

Rumors had circulated within the Italian-American community about Speranza's behavior, and it seemed they had reached Immacolatta. Angela was sure they were started by Salvatore's sister, Paolina.

"You should never listen to rumors," said Angela. "Step down, Alicia. I'm finished."

Alicia jumped down from the platform.

Angela thought about having all Speranza's children live with her, but because of her husband's limitations, she did not think it prudent. At times his behavior was volatile.

"Come on, Alicia. I will give you a crochet lesson."

"I want to go into town to see friends," said Alicia.

Angela gingerly lifted the dress off Alicia and hung it on a padded satin hanger. She handed the pink dress back to Alicia.

"You look wonderful," said Angela. She stepped back and admired her work. Angela could turn any garment in a work of art. Sometimes she tried to reproduce a silhouette of the dresses worn in a 19th Century or Renaissance painting she had seen in Rome when she and Franco visited in 1929. The paintings had impressed Angela more than she had thought. One could go into any church and find a Caravaggio or a painting by a Renaissance master. She also wanted to preserve her perceptions of what she saw in the art world. Many of the colors in the paintings informed her choices of material and colors in her garments. These patterns were especially useful when she made wedding gowns.

"What friends are these?" asked Angela.

"Just friends," Alicia said. "We get together and talk."

"Alicia, you do not want to fall in with the wrong crowd. You need to pay attention to your studies."

Angela had tried to prevent Speranza from marrying at 16, but she had failed. She was determined that Alicia's life would be different.

"What was my mother really like?" Alicia asked.

"She was someone who helped me adjust to American life," said Angela. "Your mother was very thoughtful and sweet. We were good angels to one another."

"What do you mean, good angels?" Alicia asked.

"She helped me with my English, and I made her clothes and made sure she was groomed properly. Like you, she liked to do things her own way, but there is a right way and a wrong way. I taught her that."

"But what was she *like*?"

What was Speranza like? thought Angela. Her mind was a blank. Why didn't she have an answer? Angela reached deep into her memory. This was like asking Angela, "Who are your unseen friends?" She felt that her unseen friends and Speranza were ethereal creatures that could never really be known. Angela's clients added a revenue and sophistication to her life, but what Speranza and her unseen friends brought to her life was intangible and could not be summed up into a neat package. Angela had to be careful not to paint the present with the past.

"Your mother was an individual and she loved you children very much," she said. Angela never thought about what Speranza thought or felt as an individual. Angela felt that Speranza was her creation, so when asked about Speranza, Angela felt she talked about herself.

"Well, I'm an individual too," declared Alicia.

This new generation of Italian-Americans did not have the same moral compass; moral relativism was the norm. When Angela had immigrated, one's life was dictated by one's family—in her case, Franco's family. There was a strong Italian community, and there was support. The newly emerging generation was individualistic and determined to create their own lives, without forethought about the future and regardless of the consequences. Given the state of the modern world, simply living in the present suggested danger to Angela.

"Can I go, please?" Alicia folded her arms over her chest.

"All right," Angela said. "Remember to pay attention to your studies."

Angela went out on the front porch to water her plants. Her neighbor, Mrs. Mabel Martens, waved to Angela from her porch.

"How are you, Mrs. Bellini?" asked Mabel. "Thank you for the home-made rolls."

"I'm so glad you liked them," said Angela.

"Oh yes, we had a dinner party the other night, and my housekeeper served your rolls. Everyone asked where I got them."

Whenever Angela made rolls, she shared them with Dr. and Mrs. Martens. Mabel Martens had been a concert pianist, and Angela often heard her play when the windows were open. Her husband was a general practitioner who had his office in his home. Angela admired them for their talents and generous dispositions.

"I told them the beautiful Sicilian woman next door made them," said Mabel. "How is Franco doing?"

Angela was considered exotic by her neighbors. She enjoyed the experience of being different, but it often set her apart from her neighbors. They all seemed to thrive in modern America. Mabel Martens' family arrived from England in the 1600s and claimed that they came over on the Mayflower. The Martens home was passed down between generations, as were many of the houses on Morning Glory Avenue. Angela and Franco were an anomaly in a neighborhood that was established long ago. She developed her relationships with neighbors through friendly chatter and in a giving manner.

"He is doing fine," said Angela.

"Well, if you ever need my husband's assistance, please let him know."

"I will, thank you, Mrs. Martens."

Angela's fresh rolls bought her many favors.

Chapter 3

Late Spring 1935

Angela heard her husband's labored gait in the kitchen. Since his stroke, his memory had slowly returned, and he could participate in simple conversation. He got himself up and down the stairs without a problem and had even contemplated repairing furniture again.

"Angela," called Franco.

"I am coming," Angela said. She folded the sewing machine back into its cabinet and placed a linen runner on top. She went into her bedroom and took a small vase of flowers off the altar to the Blessed Mother and placed it on top of the sewing machine cabinet, smiling. Pretty things should be in every corner of a house.

She found Franco sitting at the kitchen table, gazing out the window and sipping a glass of wine.

"I will fix the yard soon," Franco said. It was almost time to plant the garden, and he loved the smell of freshly overturned earth. The physical act of planting a garden would strengthen his muscles. He had become stronger from going up and down the stairs several times a day.

"Yes, that will be nice," Angela said.

There was nothing like making pasta sauce with fresh tomatoes, basil, and garlic. At the convent, they grew their own vegetables year-round, and bread was baked daily in large ovens. In fact, Angela had never tasted anything from a supermarket until she came to America. She now frequented Italian specialty shops instead of grocery stores as much as she could.

"I am going to the cellar," said Franco.

He opened the back door and began the arduous descent into the basement, where he could be alone with his thoughts, dragging his left leg down one stair at a time. Once he reached the bottom, Franco sauntered over to his worktable. All the tools he used to construct furniture and make household repairs hung on the wall. He recalled that these were the tools he used when he made furniture before he married Angela. The refurbished chairs required all his screwdrivers and wrenches.

It was a relief to be alone with his memories without Angela's opinions and suggestions. An oak china cabinet he had been making for Speranza stood in a corner like an ancient ruin. He had started to make it a few months before she died. Now it sat in a basement, decaying a little every day.

Franco would never have met Angela had it not been for his cousin, Roberto. It was Roberto's sense of adventure and insight that made Franco boldly go to the convent and ask the Mother Superior for a bride. Roberto was a risk-taker, while Franco enjoyed his comfortable life in America. The poet still dealt with his country of origin, while Franco looked on and felt relief that he did not have to participate in the sinister force that now enveloped Europe. Franco hoped that wherever his cousin was, he would survive the turmoil in Europe.

* * *

"Franco, I have invited Speranza's children for dinner," called Angela from the top of the cellar stairs.

"Sure, ok," said Franco. "Coming up."

He slowly dragged his left leg up the stairs until he reached the top.

"I don't like the way the children are being treated," said Angela, picking up a pot and wiping it dry. "Alicia hardly takes care of herself, and Immacolatta and Salvatore are encouraging her to socialize with the wrong people."

"Why do you always bring these things up?" Franco said. "What can I do about them?"

"I want to make sure the boys are eating properly and that they are doing well in school," said Angela. "Maybe they can go to college one day." Many of her customers sent their children to college. Most of her clients were European, wealthy, and had been educated in Europe. Their children were going to the best universities in America, and she wanted this for Speranza's children. Her conversations with her customers were a welcomed breath of fresh air to her home environment, which often felt bleak and lacked intellectual vitality. The quality of interchanges she had with her customers opened realms of possibility. Conversations ranged from art to politics to family. Every chance she got, she imparted this energy to her niece and nephews. "Mrs. Bernstein's son is going to college in Boston," she would say to Alicia, Joe, and Nunzio, or, "Mrs. Goldsand's daughter will be attending college in New York next year."

Angela set the table for dinner. She hoped the children were getting along. They were all so different that sometimes they clashed.

"The children will be here soon," said Angela. "Come and get washed."

"What time are they coming?" Franco asked. He went over to the sink to wash his hands.

"Any moment," said Angela. "They will be staying the night."

Franco preferred that they go home. They only lived a few blocks away, so it was an easy walk. The children's neediness irritated him. He had a short temper, and an overnight visit made him more anxious.

"We're here," called several voices from the hallway. The front door slammed.

The children rushed into the kitchen and embraced Angela all at once, nearly knocking her over.

"Oh, my goodness. You'll topple me over if you're not careful," Angela said. She relished this kind of greeting.

They hugged Franco. It was less enthusiastic but respectful.

"I hope you are all hungry. I have prepared your favorite meal," Angela said.

"Cheese ravioli," said Joe. "I could help you."

His face was bubbling with the enthusiasm of a child who had received few surprises. Since he was five years old, Joe had displayed a love of cooking. Angela nurtured his interest.

"I'll eat it all," Nunzio said. He had a cap gun tucked into his pants that were bunched at the waist. His pants were held up by a belt that was far too long.

"Nunzio, where did you get those pants?" Angela asked. "They are too big."

"Ma bought them from Good Will. This is Pa's belt."

Nunzio's voice was becoming deeper; he even had hair on his chin. *A young man should not be dressed like this*, thought Angela.

"Well, we will fix those pants," Angela said.

Angela restrained herself from speaking her mind. *This needs to stop*, she thought. She touched Nunzio's head and ran her fingers through his thick hair. It reminded Angela of Speranza's glossy long hair. Her sister-in-law's family was falling apart. She surveyed the children's appearance. Her assessment reinforced what she had concluded several years ago: Salvatore's wife was ignorant and cared only for her own children.

"Can't I go home tonight?" Alicia asked. She chewed gum and blew a bubble while Nunzio tried to pop it with his gun.

"Alicia, that is unladylike," Angela said. "Take that gum out of your mouth. It will ruin your teeth."

Other than chocolate, Angela did not approve of candy or soda. These were substances detrimental to good health.

"Aunt Angela, will you show me how to make ravioli?" asked Joe. He looked up at her with soft brown eyes that were not only shaped like Speranza's but suggested her presence. *Those eyes will charm many*, thought Angela, *but it's what lives behind those eyes that will captivate people*. Angela had learned that it was best to look beyond what you saw. If you looked deep enough, something or someone else came forward.

"I will do that on a Saturday. Tonight we will have dinner, and then I will tell you a story."

"I don't care about old stories," Alicia said. She folded her arms across her chest. "I want to eat and go home."

"I want a story," said Joe.

Angela was carrying an apron for Alicia to prevent her from soiling her clothes during the meal. She looked at Alicia's blouse and saw a brown stain in the front.

"Alicia, you need to change your blouse," Angela said. It was a blouse she had made for her not too long ago. "How did that stain happen?"

"I was helping Ma feed the boys. Ma only washes for the boys, so I have to wash our clothes."

Tomorrow Angela would walk the children home and would confront Immacolatta. She was determined to put a stop to this neglect.

"I'm hungry," Nunzio said. "I didn't have any lunch."

"No lunch?" Angela asked. "Why not?" Angela knew the answer. Immacolatta did not make lunch for them to take to school.

The children ran to the dining room table and took their seats. Angela had designated a certain place for each child so when they came to visit, they knew exactly where they were to sit. This gave them a stability that they badly needed. Franco sat at the head of the table with Angela on his right. Joe sat next to Angela, Nunzio sat on Franco's left, and Alicia sat next to Nunzio. It was important that they had a place at her table.

"I'm going to sit at the head of the table someday," Joe said.

"Sissies don't sit at the head of the table," Nunzio laughed. "You're always whining, you sissy."

"Shut up! He's always calling me names." Joe pressed his hands to his ears to block out Nunzio's voice.

"They fight a lot," Alicia said.

"Sissy," said Nunzio. He pointed his toy gun at Joe's head.

"Stop using that language," Angela demanded. "Give me that gun. You cannot have that at the table."

She took the gun away from Nunzio and placed it on the fireplace mantle.

"Leave him alone," Franco said to Nunzio. Franco favored him, but he tried not to show it.

"He acts like a girl," Nunzio said.

Joe lowered his head as tears descended, laden with sorrow. Angela put her arms around Joe and patted his back. The other two children giggled.

"If you keep it up, you two will eat in the kitchen in silence."

Franco felt the same way about his youngest nephew. He didn't understand why Joe was not interested in his tools or activities that should interest a boy. In Franco's mind, he was a misfit—an aberration of what a boy should be—and he needed to be toughened up.

"Everyone pass me your plates," Angela said.

"Me first," said Nunzio. "Boys before sissies and girls."

"You need to stop that," Angela said. "You will eat in the kitchen alone."

Angela consistently followed through with her punishments, so Nunzio became quiet. He did not want to eat alone.

"They're always mean to me," Joe said. He sniffed and wiped his nose on his shirt sleeve.

"That is all right, my dear," Angela said. "They will stop now."

She shot the two older children a look that said if they continued this behavior, they would regret it.

"Now dry your tears, and we will eat."

Franco found it strange that the only time his wife said grace before a meal was the Blessed Mother's Assumption day. Even after 22 years, she still did things that amazed and surprised him. She never insisted he go to mass with her, even though the other wives were accompanied by their husbands. Angela respected that he had no use for prayers or God.

"Tell me about school," Angela said.

"Well, sometimes Nunzio doesn't go," Alicia said. Angela had heard that the kids at school dubbed her "The Tattle Tale."

"You skip school?" Angela asked.

"I don't like being teased about having midgets for brothers."

"Who teases you?" Angela asked.

"The other kids," said Nunzio.

"Alicia, are you being teased?" Angela asked.

"Stop talking about it," Franco said. He waved his hand as if to erase the conversation. He did not want to hear about Salvatore's deformed children. It enraged him to think that Salvatore had remarried so soon after his sister's death.

"Well, everyone knows that William and Anthony are freaks," Alicia said.

"God made them that way, and I do not want you to use that word to describe your brothers," Angela said. She was not a proponent of Salvatore and Immacolatta's marriage, but no child should be called a freak.

"Why can't we have a normal life?" asked Alicia. She began to whimper as tears rolled down her cheeks. "I wish my mother was here to take care of us."

Angela walked over to Alicia and put her hands on the side of Alicia's face and looked directly into her eyes.

"Alicia, dear, I will always take care of you, as I took care of your mother. This I promise I will do until I am gone."

Alicia was grateful for her aunt Angela and looked forward to evenings such as this. Her life would be sheer drudgery if it were not for Angela, but it was difficult for her to express her appreciation. Her bitterness and shame regarding her home situation overshadowed any good in her life.

"And we will find a clean blouse for you tomorrow," Angela said. "Everyone eat. There is dessert."

* * *

The next morning, Angela walked purposefully toward Immacolatta's house with the children following behind. Her heart pounded, and she began to hyperventilate.

"You didn't have to walk us home," Nunzio said. "I can get us home."

"I want to talk to your stepmother," said Angela.

He aimed his cap gun at a squirrel and pulled the trigger.

"Someday I'll shoot a real gun."

"You should stay in school and get an education," Angela said. "Stop shooting that gun. I will throw it away."

Joe walked up beside Angela.

"Why do we have to run?" Joe asked.

"I am sorry, dear," Angela said.

She slowed her stride to regain her composure. Every time she thought of Salvatore's audacity in marrying his niece, his sister's daughter, it sent her mind into a tailspin.

"Please don't tell her what we said," Alicia said.

Angela did not like that Alicia was afraid to speak her mind in her own house. She picked up her pace again. She no longer had patience with the neglect of Speranza's children. What Angela thought was most dangerous was that they were accepting ill treatment. In her mind, she considered their situation slavery. She would never tolerate that in her own life, and when children were treated like chattel, it was time to confront the source of the problem.

She opened the front door and found Immacolatta feeding three-year-old William while two-year-old Anthony played at her feet. She held a spoonful of eggs as William opened his mouth like a baby bird in a nest. Because of their enlarged heads, they often found it difficult to hold their heads upright. Both had difficulty walking and shifted their weight from side to side like a seesaw.

"You brought them home already?" Immacolatta said. "I thought they were going to stay with you all day."

The children stood behind Angela as if waiting to be invited into the room.

"I have clients coming," said Angela. "Besides, the children live here. Why would they have to know? This is their home."

Immacolatta held William's enlarged head in one hand and fed him with the other.

That boy should be feeding himself, thought Angela. *These poor children will never be normal, and my nephews and niece must live with this.*

"Alicia," said Immacolatta, "now that you're back, please feed Anthony."

Alicia looked at Anthony with disgust and loathing, and Angela saw how unhappy her life was. She remembered washing floors at the convent as an undesirable activity, but she also received an education, clean clothes, and nutritious meals prepared by a cook. This was no way for a young girl to be raised.

"I think that the children should come and live with me and my husband," Angela said. She had no right to take Salvatore's children away, but Salvatore and Immacolatta had no interest in them once William and Anthony came along.

"What am I supposed to do here without help?" Immacolatta asked.

"They are not your help," Angela said. "They are Salvatore's children, not your servants."

Angela remembered her mother saying that the people in northern Italy treated the Sicilians like slaves. Her mother and her women friends often talked about the rebellion that was brewing between the upper and lower classes. The lower classes tended to be suspicious of the church and its priests, while the upper classes controlled the priests and used them to keep the peasant classes down. She remembered how irate her mother would become when she told Angela about the class situation. In the recesses of her mind, Angela felt that it was not the complete story. Her unseen friends encouraged her to keep her distance from local priests who taught children about the necessity of following Catholic doctrine. They conveyed to Angela that she should follow her gut feelings about everyone she met, including priests.

"You need to ask my husband if the children can come with you," said Immacolatta.

"I want to stay here," Joe cried. "I want to stay home, please don't take me away."

Joe lay on the floor and cried.

"No one will take you away," Angela said. She knelt beside him.

"I don't wanna live here anymore," Nunzio said.

Since Salvatore married Immacolatta, Nunzio had expressed a vicious animosity toward his father that overflowed into other parts of his life. He had been consistently truant at school and was failing at his schoolwork.

"If Nunzio is going to live with you, so am I," Alicia said.

"Why is everyone leaving me?" cried Joe.

"Come with us," said Alicia.

"No, I want to stay with Ma."

He ran to Immacolatta and clung to her arm. Joe was the sibling closest to his stepmother. She lavished affection on him that she did not show the older children. She did not seem to mind his interest in dressing dolls and his enjoyment in combing his stepmother's long dark hair. He also was comfortable with William and Anthony's dwarfism. There was an unspoken affinity between them. He was more connected to his new siblings than his older brother and sister.

"On second thought," Immacolatta said, "take Nunzio. Leave Alicia here, because I still need help. If my husband wants him back, he'll come and get him."

Angela saw how relieved Immacolatta was to rid herself of her oldest stepson.

"I'm not staying if Nunzio is leaving," Alicia said.

"Please don't leave me," Joe cried.

He ran to his sister and hugged her around her waist and cried.

"All right, Joe, I'll stay for a while," Alicia said.

Alicia couldn't leave her youngest brother on his own. Her father was disdainful of his sensibility, and there was no one to protect him.

"Alicia," said Angela, "you will stay with me on weekends and during the summer if you like. It is settled. Nunzio, pack your things, and bring them to the house later today."

Angela would not take Joe from someone from whom he felt a connection. She did not want to break up the family. If Immacolatta could provide even the smallest bit of mothering, then Angela would acquiesce for the moment. When Angela and her brother survived the earthquake, they were separated and sent to separate Catholic institutions. They corresponded regularly, but she only got to visit him occasionally—even when he was ill and dying of pneumonia. It was one of the greatest pains in her life. Their letters were filled with encouragement and affection and concern for their younger sister, grandmother, and aunt who had perished.

She would frequently ask her unseen friends if her sister was still alive. They would never give her a direct answer. Angela got the sense they wanted her to feel in her heart whether her sister was still on earth. Angela vacillated between her heart and mind. She would access knowledge in her mind and then attempt to verify it through her heart. The information or answer was always different, and this left Angela confused and frustrated.

"God has given me a great burden to bear," Immacolatta said. "Three stepchildren to raise and two abnormal children who require double the work. Why won't you help me like you helped Franco's sister? Salvatore says that you treated her like one of the saints, but that she was a disobedient wife. She was spoiled by you because you made all her clothes and looked after her like a child, even though she was a married woman."

It astounded Angela again and again that people thought decently designed clothes, good manners, and maintaining a beautifully decorated home were tantamount to spoiling someone. The life she and Franco built in this country was through their talents and creativity. It represented a certain sensibility, and it was not meant to be showy. She had passed this way of being onto Speranza and now onto her sister-in-law's children.

Angela wondered what she would have done in Immacolatta's situation. She was a young immigrant at one time herself. It was difficult enough for Angela to learn English and cope with her husband's family, but maybe she would have been like Immacolatta if she had inherited a growing family. The world Immacolatta encountered was in flux. There was no longer the support structure within the community.

Before she left Sicily, Angela had imagined a different life in America. She had envisioned having her own children and a husband who was protective and robust. Instead she was caring for a disabled husband and someone else's children. She wondered if she had been able to have children whether she would be so anxious to care for Speranza's now. Angela had created her life in America—her business and connections—through her intentions, which were coated with culture and charm.

"It is not that I will not help you," Angela said. "I want Speranza's children to be treated fairly. They come to my house with holes in their shoes and dirty clothes. No one is caring for them."

"We do not have the money to care for them," Immacolatta said. "Shoes and clothes are expensive, and I cannot do all the work. If they want to live here, they need to care for themselves—except Joe."

"It's settled, then," said Angela. "Nunzio, I will expect you later today."

* * *

Sadie Malaci sat in Angela's kitchen and sipped her coffee.

"So Nunzio is living with you now," said Sadie.

"Yes. I'm pleased. He has his own space upstairs, and he helps around the house and helps Franco with his projects. It's nice to have someone else living in this big house."

Angela was comforted when she heard Nunzio move around upstairs and the floorboards creaked.

"Does Franco like it?"

"Yes, now that Nunzio's no longer a child. Would you like a sandwich?" asked Angela.

"No, I have to go shopping and drop by Claudia's for a glass of wine. Her husband has just made a fresh batch. It's the best in town. Are you going to 9 a.m. mass tomorrow?" asked Sadie.

"I guess so," said Angela.

"You don't sound certain," said Sadie.

Angela filled Sadie's coffee cup. Sadie plopped three teaspoons of sugar into her coffee along with a good helping of milk.

"I don't pray much when I'm there anymore. I can pray at home."

"Who do you pray to?"

"The Blessed Mother and I talk to people who have passed over," said Angela. "And sometimes I talk to friends I cannot see who help me out."

"You talk to your guardian angels. Sometimes I talk to my mother," said Sadie.

"I understand. You miss her," said Angela.

"She was a real bitch when she was alive," said Sadie. "She's still a bitch, but sometimes I do miss her."

Sadie and Angela sat for a while in silence, both lost in their memories of people who were once here but have moved on.

"You don't think it's strange that I talk to invisible friends?"

"Nah, people can talk to whoever they want, whether they're here or not. I don't care. Sometimes the people we can't see are nicer than the people walking around. That's for sure. See you later, Angie."

Chapter 4

Fall 1935

"Aunt Angela, hello."

In the dining room doorway stood her youngest nephew, a young handsome boy with a full bottom lip and thick brown hair with a tuft of curly hair over his left eye. His knickers buttoned below his knee, and a silk red scarf was tied around his neck.

"Joe, my dear," Angela said. "Would you like to stay for dinner?"

She put her arms around the boy and kissed him on each cheek.

"I would, and I will help you cook," said Joe. He brushed his hair back out of his eye and smiled at his aunt.

Angela noticed a dark swollen area around Joe's outer eye.

"What happened to your eye?" asked Angela.

"Some boys were teasing me, so I fought back," Joe said.

"I will go to school and speak to the principal about these boys," said Angela. "You go to a Catholic School. The nuns should not allow this behavior."

"No, they'll just beat me up again," Joe said. "I can fight."

"It is not in your constitution to fight. You use your head. Those who fight are animals. You look so much like your mother," said Angela. "Don't you think so, Franco?"

"Yes," Franco said, resting his head back in his smoking chair, not looking at Joe.

"I got my report card today," said Joe. He handed it to Angela.

"Latin-A. Mathematics-A. You have a perfect report card," Angela said. "Look at this, Franco." She held the report card out for her husband to see, but he waved the card away. He did not feel academic accomplishment was noteworthy. Joe had no interest in learning how to make furniture or how to fix a pipe, but when Angela baked chicken and made clothes, Joe hung on her every word. He was successful academically and popular socially with the girls, but Franco knew he did not fit into the school mainstream. *That is why he is beaten at school*, thought Franco.

"We will celebrate your report card tonight with cannoli," said Angela. "Come into the kitchen."

"Oh yeah. I will roll the dough," said Joe. "I would like to make cannoli at home."

* * *

Angela reached into the fridge and took out a bowl of dough.

"I have already prepared the dough. You can roll it."

Angela sprinkled flour on the kitchen table and flattened the dough with her hand. She handed Joe a rolling pin.

"It is your job to roll the dough very thin," Angela said. "Start from the center, and roll out. Make a circle."

Joe took the rolling pin, carefully placed it in the center, and deliberately rolled the pin to the end of the dough.

"This is the head of the boys who hit me," Joe said. "I'm pretending that I'm squishing them, and their brains are leaking."

"I do not want you to think that way. These are ignorant children who come from ignorant families. You do not."

"Pa never sticks up for me," said Joe.

Angela did not know what to say about Salvatore. He allowed his wife to run the house and his personal affairs. Salvatore had very little connection or involvement with his children. He expected Immacolatta to raise Speranza's children, and she resented it. Angela tried to make up for the lack of direction and care in their lives as best she could.

Many of the children at the Catholic school were from working-class families. When she first came to America, she lived in one of those neighborhoods. When she would attempt to share her story, she was met with disinterest and distrust. Many thought she was making up her story about the Principessa, and others thought she was bragging. She was relieved when they bought the house on Morning Glory Avenue, surrounded by professional people who found her appealing.

When Franco was in his early 20s, he had purchased his first multi-family home. He rented the apartments to hardworking Italian immigrants while he lived in a one-room flat with a roommate. He saved diligently and was able to purchase two other multi-family homes and rented those apartments. From the rents on those houses and doing all the work himself, he was able to bring Angela to America, sell the houses, and buy the house on Morning Glory Avenue.

After their move, she ran into a former neighbor from the working-class neighborhood.

"Good morning, Mrs. Crawford," said Angela. Anna Crawford was a woman in her late 50s and already had missing teeth. She had led a hard life and was one of the few who appreciated Angela's story.

"How are you doing, Mrs. Crawford?"

"Ah, not bad. I miss hearing your stories," said Mrs. Crawford.

"You were always kind to me," Angela said.

"Why not? You kept me going," said Mrs. Crawford.

"Going where?" asked Angela.

"You let me know there was a world outside of our neighborhood. My world felt bigger because of your story. It felt like I was part of your experience. The women in our neighborhood were jealous, but you kept telling your story. They were born here and will die here."

"Well, thank you. I wish you well."

Angela watched as Mrs. Crawford walked away with her shoulders hunched, as if the weight of all the mistakes she had made in life were pulling her down.

* * *

Angela scooped out a cup of fresh ricotta cheese and placed it in a yellow Pyrex bowl.

"We start the filling with ricotta and goat cheese," Angela said, "carefully folding them."

"How much of each?" asked Joe.

"You estimate. I never measure, because the recipe is my own. Always make the recipe your own."

Joe observed as Angela mixed in fresh cinnamon and orange peel. She folded the two cheeses into each other, deliberately, creating a light smooth texture.

"I love how you do that, Aunt Angela. It makes me feel fuzzy inside. How do you know you're done mixing?"

"You can feel the texture with your eyes," Angela said. "By how it looks. If it looks like a cloud, then you are done mixing."

He looked up at Angela and grinned. She cupped his face and kissed him on both cheeks with a smack. Joe giggled. Her nephew's joy lightened not only how she felt about her day, but also how she felt about life.

"Then," Angela said, "after we fill the shells, we will add bittersweet chocolate and citrine."

"What is that?"

"Candied fruit," Angela said. "I am sure you will like that."

Joe stretched his arms on the table and placed his forehead on it. He turned his head slightly and peeked up at Angela, his eyes glistening in the sunlight.

He knows something, thought Angela, *like his mother*. Angela saw Speranza's face when he acted coy and seductive. Speranza had also intently observed Angela when she cooked. In fact, Speranza was able to go home and reproduce a dish from memory. Deep observance was a quality that echoed through the generations. This watchfulness and the ability to take in information was a quality Angela possessed in abundance. This played a part in her development before the earthquake and her survival in her new country.

* * *

"Aunt Angela," said Joe, pulling on her apron, "you're daydreaming. I was told not to daydream."

"Daydreaming is a good thing. Do not listen to people who say it is not. You come up with good ideas when you daydream."

Angela felt that she had drifted off and that part of her was not present. It was often a sign that her unseen friends were around.

"I've finished rolling the dough," Joe said.

Joe had rolled out the dough perfectly thin. *Delicate*, thought Angela, *like his mother*. "You can stay the night if you like," Angela said.

"Nah, I think I'll go home. William and Anthony need me."

"It is nice that you are kind to your brothers," Angela said, "but you do not have to take care of them."

"It's ok. They're nice to me when I help them."

Angela smiled. *At least he feels appreciated*, she thought.

"You know, you can stay here any time," said Angela.

"You have Nunzio here," Joe said. "It would be crowded."

The tension between the brothers was palpable. They were two markedly different people; this was evident since birth. Joe had to be tough, which was not in his nature, and Nunzio was aggressive and rarely showed a soft side. Nunzio's friends were the tough boys at school, while Joe's associations were with the girls. Both were blessed with dark good looks. The difference was that the girls liked to talk to Joe but not to Nunzio. Joe was aware his brother was jealous when girls told him their secrets, and Joe's charm was a mystery to Nunzio.

"Why do they like you so much?" asked Nunzio one day after he saw Joe standing among five girls.

"I listen, and I'm interested," Joe said curtly. "I understand. You never do that, you beast."

"Shut up!" Nunzio said.

He chased Joe all the way home.

Angela hoped that Joe would further his education and not get involved with a bad crowd, but given the nature of Nelsonville, that was highly improbable. She decided to continue to nurture Joe's interests in cooking and his academic success. In conversation with some of the neighbors, she had mentioned her hopes for her niece and nephews. She was met with derision, as if hoping to do better would upset some unspoken code. Once when she was in line to buy groceries at the A&P, she overheard whispering behind her.

"I never see her in here," a woman said.

"No, she goes to those expensive Italian specialty stores," said the other. "I'm surprised she lowered herself to shop here."

"I'm not surprised she can shop in those stores," said the other. "She charges plenty for her dressmaking."

Angela's clients came from only a few streets in Nelsonville. They were women who traveled and were educated, while the rest of the town women accepted their fate and circumstances. Recent immigrants to America possessed a drive to improve their situation, whether that would be in business or through education. The general population seemed to maintain the same social and economic position from generation to generation.

"I am shopping here today because I only need milk," said Angela, addressing the women. "Why you care where I shop is beyond me. Those who employ my services expect high quality, and that is what they get. I, in return, can shop where I please."

Angela walked toward the exit and glanced in a mirror positioned over the door. She saw the two women and the checkout girl staring at her, then glancing at each other as if Angela had violated some code of conduct dictated by the inhabitants of Nelsonville. She stepped out in the street and felt she had entered a different time. A few years ago, she would have pretended she didn't hear the women—but now she was ready to own her life and what she had built.

* * *

Franco hobbled into the kitchen. He fixed his cold, expressionless stare on Angela and Joe, and continued to the basement door. Joe was the recipient of that look every time he visited Angela and Franco. Even when Joe smiled back at him, his uncle never reciprocated.

"I'm gonna go home now," Joe said. "I don't think Uncle Franco wants me here."

"No! Why do you say that?" Angela asked. "He has been sick, and that's why he does not talk much. He wants you here. Your mother was his sister. Besides, it does not matter what he wants. I want you here."

Angela tried to smooth things over to create a harmonious spirit in the household so that Joe would feel welcome. At this point, it was clear how Franco felt about his nephew—and at Joe's pre-teen age, he was painfully aware.

Chapter 5

Fall 1936

Joe opened the door to his parents' house and stepped aside so Angela could enter.

"Ma, I'm home," Joe called. "Aunt Angela is with me."

The house was quiet. Angela looked in the living room and found Immacolatta sound asleep on the sofa while William and Anthony played on the floor.

William pulled on Joe's leg and attempted to stand.

"Pull on me and climb," said Joe.

William grabbed Joe's arm and hoisted himself to a standing position. Angela admired how sweet Joe was with his half-brothers. William had obviously done this before. Joe stood firm as a statue, while William did all the work. Angela was incensed that Joe was being treated badly by other children at school.

"I am pregnant with my third baby, and I need extra help," Immacolatta said.

"Again?" Angela asked.

"Why don't you congratulate me?"

"Of course, congratulations," Angela said.

"Joe is such a help, but Alicia does nothing," said Immacolatta.

"She is a young woman," Angela said. "She wants to have a life."

"Well, she is running around with a boy now. That is where her head is. If she wants to get married, she should get married and be done with it."

Angela feared that Alicia would marry too young. She tried to give her niece direction, but Alicia was not responsive to Angela's suggestions. She had tried to encourage her to study, but her home environment did not support education. Angela even introduced her to Gregory, a soft-spoken young man who worked at his father's real estate firm. Alicia did not show any interest in him, but Gregory expressed interest in her.

"What do you mean, marriage? She is 16," Angela said. "Who is this boy?"

"Leo Minuci," Immacolatta said.

"He is not a boy. He is in his 20s. How can you let her do that?"

Leo Minuci was part of the Italian community that ended up as part of Nelsonville's poor. As a teenager, he had dropped out of school and started to frequent local bars. Angela had heard that Leo's father once ended up in jail for domestic violence.

"It is not my responsibility. Salvatore doesn't say anything, so I let her go. There is nothing wrong with Leo."

"He is always in the bar. Does he even work?" Angela asked.

"I do not bother myself with that. I have enough trouble."

Angela decided to have a talk with Alicia about this relationship.

"I did not know she was seeing so much of him," Angela said. "I am sure she will not marry him," Angela said. "Gregory from the real estate office is interested in her."

"You have big dreams for people, Angela. I am not sure that it's worth it. People will do what they will do. You cannot stop them."

Angela was aware that everyone had free will, but she could see a painful future for Alicia if she married Leo. She would try to dissuade Alicia from any further relationship with him.

"I will talk to her," Angela said.

"You will be wasting your breath," said Immacolatta.

"Do not encourage her to think about marriage. She needs to finish high school first."

"High school? She does no school work," Immacolatta said. "She will not graduate."

Angela saw how Immacolatta catered to William and Anthony and that now, with another baby on the way, she would be even more preoccupied with the family she had created and even less attentive to her step-children. This baby would most likely be handicapped as well, so it was clear that Angela would have to step in and correct Alicia's situation. Still, she did have sympathy for Immacolatta, who had been told that if she married Salvatore, she would lead an abundant, luxurious life in America. Angela and Immacolatta shared a disappointment in their American lives.

"I will speak to Alicia. If you rather she lived with me, that would be all right."

"Who would help me?"

"I will, Ma," Joe said. "I don't mind. I want you to be my mother."

"You are a good boy, Joe," Immacolatta said.

Angela said nothing. It was best for her to focus on Alicia and straighten out the situation with Leo Minuci. Alicia could be stubborn and craved attention, as she certainly got none at home. Angela did the best she could to compliment Alicia and encourage her to pursue her dreams, but that only went so far. Angela feared the damage was done and Alicia's fate was sealed.

"I need to start cooking soon," Immacolatta said. "I will have so much more work to do now. Joe is an angel to help."

"I hope he is not ignoring his studies," said Angela.

"You have high hopes for children who are not going to college. He keeps talking about going to New York City. Imagine that? He has a good home here, and instead of getting a job to help, he has dreams of going to New York. Alicia is no help, since she has a boyfriend. I will be stuck."

"Joe has every right to think about his future. If he wants to go to New York City, he should go after high school."

"Ha! What world do you live in? He doesn't seem that interested in school."

Angela had made peace with the thought that none of Speranza's children would go to college. The atmosphere in Salvatore's house was not nourishing for Alicia and Joe, so there would be no advantage to encourage them to stay. Immacolatta wanted Alicia out of the house as soon as she could. It did not matter to her who she married if it was just Salvatore and their three children creating a life. It was a vision that did not include Alicia and Nunzio.

"Joe is just 11 and too young to go anywhere," Angela said.

"I am sure I want to live in New York City when I am older," Joe said.

"Where is Alicia?" Angela asked.

"She's out with Leo," Joe said. "He's too much of a beast for me."

"I told you," said Immacolatta. "She is running around while I have so much work at home."

"Where did they go?" Angela asked.

Angela felt a tug on her blouse.

"I'm learning chess," William said.

"He is very smart," Immacolatta said. "Both my sons are smart."

"I don't know where they are," Joe said. "Sometimes they go to the movies. They're probably making out there." He snickered.

"I do not think you should say that about your sister," Angela said.

"Sorry, Aunt Angela, but all the kids do that." Joe said. "I wouldn't do that."

"That is because you are a good boy," Angela said.

"You are a good woman, Angela, but you live with your head in the clouds," Immacolatta said.

Joe gazed at Angela and smiled.

"Joe has a different nature. He does not like girls."

"Immacolatta, Joe has many girlfriends. They are with each other quite a bit. Isn't that right, Joe?"

"Yeah, we talk about how to dress, and they love the clothes you made me."

Angela believed there was a delicate side to manhood that should be cultivated in boyhood. The roughness boys were taught was not something she supported or thought was necessary. The boys who beat up Joe were headed for disaster if that was how they treated people who had a developed sensitivity. She felt that Joe would do far better in life than his persecutors. At least he had a goal of one day moving to New York City. There were many opportunities there.

"I am going to look for Alicia. Joe, would you like to come?"

"No, she'd get mad at me if she knew I was looking for her," Joe said.

* * *

Angela walked toward town with purpose. Rage was not an emotion that she allowed to take over, but in this circumstance, she had rage for Leo Minuci. He was born in Sicily, and his parents immigrated to America a few months later. Leo was a bully, and his father was a laborer who beat his wife. Angela had no use for Leo Minuci or his family, and she had made this clear to Alicia.

Angela stopped into several shops and restaurants and asked if anyone had seen Alicia. She stood in front of Woolworth's and pondered where to go next, or if she even should. Her chest felt heavy, and her breath was labored. She felt frozen, unable to move. What was she looking for, and why? Her mind began to clear, and Angela felt the presence of her unseen friends. She felt they wanted her to return home. They suggested that Alicia would not comply and return home with Angela and there might be a scene with Leo, and that would be unacceptable. Every time she thought about Leo's rough hands on Alicia, her breath became shallow and her heart contracted.

Angela felt dizzy and started to make her way home. She would call Alicia later and find out where she went. Alicia was not her daughter, but she was Speranza's child—and Angela had every intention of confronting the situation.

Angela collected the mail and unlocked the front door, then went into her bedroom. It was time to light the candles to the Blessed Mother. She lit each votive candle with the intention to gather strength to face the path in front of her. She would keep her commitment to Speranza's children even if they felt she interfered. She was not their mother, but Angela saw herself as their guardian. Maybe confronting Alicia today was not the best course of action. She may outgrow her interest in Leo. Her unseen friends guided Angela to follow her instincts and keep her heart open.

Angela picked up the phone and invited Claudia Cerverci over for coffee and cake.

* * *

"I'm glad you could come," said Angela.

"When have I ever turned down coffee and cake?" asked Claudia.

"Sit in the dining room, and I'll bring it out."

After they had settled at the table, Angela told Claudia about her concerns that Alicia was seeing Leo Minuci.

"That's a bad family," said Claudia. "My husband hired Leo's father for one of his construction projects years ago, and he had to fire him."

"I know about his reputation," said Angela. "I am not happy about this. I'm going to do something."

"What do you plan to do?"

"Well, I would not go directly against this," said Angela. "That never works. I am going to invite Gregory and Alicia to lunch. I won't tell her he will be there. I will get Gregory to talk about himself and Alicia will see he is the better man."

Claudia helped herself to another piece of cake, leaning over to expose her gold cross.

"Well, it could work," said Claudia. "Or you will make Alicia mad, but I think it is worth it. At least you will have tried to do something."

"This reminds me of Speranza and Salvatore," said Angela. "It still makes me angry because I did not do enough to stop it."

"Well, good luck. I hope the lunch works. The Minuci family has too much bad blood."

* * *

"Come home with me, and we'll have dinner," Angela said the next Saturday morning.

"I am going to Leo's house," Alicia said.

"Leo? He is too old for you. You are 16, and he is a man in his twenties."

"I want to get married soon."

Alicia had dropped out of school but had not told Angela. She did not know what to do with her life.

"Someday, but not to him. He is a mean-spirited man. I have heard his parents are the same way. I never invited those people to dinner for a reason."

"I need to have something in my life. Joe wants to go to New York, and Nunzio has you and Uncle Franco. What about me?"

"Gregory is interested in you. He comes from a real estate family and would like to know you better. Uncle Franco did business with his father in the past."

"Why don't you come with me and get to know Leo?" Alicia asked. "He lives near the train station."

"No, that is a poor area. You are a beautiful girl, and you can do much better."

"Why do you have to be superior?" Alicia asked, turning surly.

"I am not superior. Kindness and sensitivity is what I want for you. These people were poor and rough in Sicily, and they have not changed. Your uncle and I built a life by hard work."

"Please come with me? Everyone pays attention to my brothers. I'm always ignored."

Angela understood that Alicia's home life was centered around taking care of her younger brothers and that she had very little social life.

"All right, I will come, but we cannot stay long. I want you to come to my house for lunch, and then I have a client."

"Thank you. You'll see he really likes me," Alicia said.

They walked to a house surrounded by a wire fence with an overgrown front yard. There was a broken step on the front porch.

Angela felt her spine prickle. People who lived in a home like this were not people she cared to visit.

"Be careful of the step. They haven't fixed it yet," Alicia said.

As Angela looked around the porch, she saw an old rusted chair turned on its side. Ripped curtains clung to the inside of the windows.

"Maybe we can come another time," Angela said.

Angela recoiled from any structure that suggested neglect or disarray. She remembered her parents keeping an immaculate house with everything in its place. Most of her friends maintained an ordered home with landscaping that suggested intentional placement without appearing staged. The porch steps sunk under her weight.

"Hello, I'm here," Alicia called.

She knocked on the front door. No response.

"They are not home. It's time to go home," Angela said.

"Wait," Alicia said. "Sometimes he takes a while to answer the door."

Angela heard the locks opening, and the door opened.

In the doorway stood Leo in a white T-shirt and black pants. He looked at Alicia and then directly into Angela's eyes. She returned the gaze.

"I didn't know your aunt was coming," Leo said.

"If you are busy, we can come back another day," said Angela. She touched Alicia's arm to turn her around.

"Wait a minute," Alicia said. "Can we come in?"

"Sure, come on in," Leo said.

There was a sunken couch in the living room and no pictures on the wall.

"Can I get you some wine?" Leo said.

"No, it is too early for wine," Angela said.

"Aunt Angela, this is Leo. You know his parents."

"I have heard of them, but we do not know each other well."

"I'm fond of your niece," said Leo.

He had what Angela thought was a combative stance, legs apart, chest up, and hands on hips.

"What kind of work do you do?" Angela asked.

"He has applied for a job working for the city," Alicia said.

"Well, I hope you get it. A young man should have a trade, so he can always have a job," Angela said.

Angela had heard that Leo's father was in jail for his involvement in the local crime scene.

"Where is your mother?" Angela asked.

"Aunt Angela, you're putting Leo on the spot," Alicia said.

"I am just asking about his family," Angela said.

Angela knew all about his family, but she wanted Alicia to hear it. She also wanted Alicia to see Leo's reaction to her questions.

"Listen, Alicia, I thought we were gonna spend time together," Leo said.

"We are, we are. I wanted you to meet my aunt," Alicia said.

"I can see that I am intruding. Alicia, come to my house by 12, and you can choose a pattern for a new dress and have dinner. I know you wanted something new for next spring."

"Can't we do it another time?"

"I have a very busy week, so I do not have much time. Leo, come by next week to meet my husband. I am sure he would be interested in meeting you."

"Maybe Uncle Franco could help Leo find a job."

"Well, I need to be going," Angela said. "I will see you at home for dinner and the fitting, Alicia."

Angela stepped out into the winter sun and began the walk home. If she were a young girl in America, she would certainly not choose someone like Leo Minuci as a potential husband. She could see his family history would seep into Alicia's life like an insidious inescapable force. There was nothing that she could do to stop it; it was a choice that Alicia was making. She certainly did not have to be happy about it and would continue to express her opinion no matter what. She had neglected to express her opinion forcefully enough when Speranza married Salvatore, but now she had more confidence and strength. Angela no longer got on her knees and prayed to the Blessed Mother, but she communicated with her daily in everyday situations. The same was true of her unseen friends. Now it seemed there was no distance between the past and present. Nothing felt like long ago. It was all happening now, although she had changed, so her perspective was different.

When Angela got home, she called Gregory's real estate office and invited him to mid-day dinner. She would continue to offer alternatives to Alicia until she was engaged. Angela would not be bullied by someone whose only reference in life was living jobless by a railroad station. She opened the door to her workroom and began preparing her clients' patterns for the week.

* * *

Alicia stood on her aunt's porch at noon. She took out a small mirror from her bag to make sure the black and blue on her neck was sufficiently covered with makeup. She took a deep breath and opened the door.

"Hello, Aunt Angela. I'm here."

Alicia went into the dining room where she saw there were four table settings.

"Oh, you are here," Angela said. "I thought you would come earlier so we could choose a pattern."

"I'm sorry. I lost track of time. Leo and I were talking. He doesn't have a phone. Why are there four place settings?" Alicia asked.

"Gregory will be joining us for our dinner," Angela said. "Can you help me bring out the antipasto?"

"I know what you're doing," said Alicia.

"We are thinking about some renovations upstairs, and we needed to talk to Gregory."

"Gregory is in real estate, he's not a contractor."

"Yes, but he can suggest someone. Your uncle can no longer do the work, and I am sure Gregory can recommend the right person. Nunzio is not able to do it."

"I'm embarrassed," said Alicia.

"About what?"

"My family. The way they are. My stepmother is my cousin, and my brothers are not normal."

The doorbell rang. Angela and Alicia stood looking at one another.

"That is not you, and I am sure that doesn't matter to Gregory. Answer the door while I get the antipasto," said Angela.

Alicia opened the door. Gregory was dressed in a navy-blue suit and tie. An abundance of Brylcreem held his hair in place.

"I didn't know lunch was going to be this formal."

"Alicia, it's so nice to see you."

Gregory was confident and sincere and seemed to know where he was going in life.

"Gregory, I am so glad you came," Angela said. "Alicia, do not keep him standing in the hallway. Come into the dining room."

Franco was sitting at the head of the table drinking a glass of wine.

"Mr. Bellini, it's so nice to see you again," Gregory said. He shook Franco's hand.

"Yes, very nice," Franco said.

Franco smiled, and Angela felt hopeful.

"You two sit next to each other," said Angela.

"Alicia, you look very nice," said Gregory.

"I made that dress," Angela said. "I have made most of Alicia's clothes since her birth."

"Your family is so talented," Gregory said.

"How is your real estate business going?"

"Very well. My father has just sold a house on this street."

"Your father sold this house to my husband."

Angela noticed that Alicia seemed to be daydreaming and not paying attention to the conversation.

"Alicia, tell Gregory what you have been up to," Angela said.

"Me? Nothing. I'm sure that Gregory doesn't want to hear what I've been doing."

"Tell him about the classes you like at school."

"I'm interested in anything that you do," Gregory said.

Angela had hoped that Gregory would say something like that, to encourage Alicia to see that she deserved someone like him.

"Well, I don't do much but take care of my handicapped brothers."

It angered her that praise was being forced upon her. She could not bear the burden of it not being true and disappointing everyone.

"Aunt Angela, don't you want to ask Gregory about the upstairs renovations?" Alicia said.

"What renovations?" Gregory said.

"We want to make a functional apartment upstairs. We wondered if you could recommend a contractor."

"I have had many customers use Nelsonville Construction Company. They get the work done on time."

Alicia felt she had nothing to say to add to the conversation. She was never going to own and renovate a home. She would not marry a man who worked in an office and made a living off his intelligence. No matter how she tried to fit into that life, she knew it was not going to happen for her. As the dinner wore on, she felt more and more defeated. Gregory did not hold her attention, but it was not because she did not like him. She felt she would have to put up a charade if she chose Gregory, because she didn't really deserve someone who treated her well.

"I will call them tomorrow," Angela said. "Thank you for your advice. So, your business is going well?"

"It is going very well. My parents own it, but when they retire I will be taking it over."

"That is wonderful. Don't you think so, Alicia?"

"I guess," Alicia said.

"Alicia, I wondered if you would like to come to a few open houses with me. I can show you what I do, and we can spend time together."

"Well, I have a boyfriend."

Gregory's face was overcome with a red glow. "Is it serious?" asked Gregory.

"It is not serious," Angela said.

"How do you know if it's serious or not? I'm sorry, Gregory, but I have someone I'm interested in. I'm sorry you've wasted your time."

"Leave it alone," Franco said to Angela.

"She is not engaged," said Angela.

"I might be soon," said Alicia.

They ate their meal, and they talked about Nelsonville politics. Franco said he didn't like the new mayor because he did not help the people enough. Angela agreed, while inside she struggled with the disappointment on Gregory's face and Alicia's poor choice. Angela saw that she did not realize her worth. After dessert, Gregory drove Alicia home, and Angela pondered why she had lost Speranza's children to a strange Italian-American-culture that was a ghost of itself.

Chapter 6

December 1937

The phone rang.

"Hello, Sadie," Angela said. "Well, yes, come by today and I will measure you." It was nothing short of a miracle that Sadie wanted Angela to make her a new skirt. She had worn the same clothes for years and seemed comfortable with her image. *The world is changing*, thought Angela. *Sadie wants a new skirt.*

A few hours later, Sadie stood in front of Angela's mirror. Usually when Angela looked in the mirror at a client, an elegant form was reflected—someone with curves but who was slim and well groomed. Sadie's reflection told a different story. She was younger and wealthier than many of Angela's clients, but her image reflected a devil-may-care attitude. A show of affluence was never a concern to Sadie, but something had changed.

"What made you decide to have something new?" Angela asked.

"Oh, it's the holidays and I thought it would be a good idea."

"You'll be able to wear your new clothes to my holiday dinner this year."

"I am getting new clothes just in time. Those women always have something to say. This way, I'll shut them up."

Angela and Sadie looked at one another in the mirror and laughed. Angela appreciated Sadie's ability to laugh at herself. It was refreshing in a world where everyone took themselves much too seriously.

"They will certainly be impressed with your new skirt," Angela said. "Let me make you a simple blouse. Then they will know you, and once they recognize you they will not stop talking. They will think you are after a new husband."

It felt good to laugh. At the convent where she grew up, no one laughed very much. Angela's future had turned out to be the brightest of all, and hers was not what she had pictured.

"Is Alicia still seeing Leo Minuci?" asked Sadie.

"Yes, and I worry day and night. I still hope she will change her mind about him."

"He has not proposed," Sadie said.

"No, and that is a good sign," said Angela.

"How are Joe and Nunzio?" asked Sadie.

"Joe is very smart and Nunzio is doing odd jobs and still living with us. He left school, but he will find direction one day…I like the way this looks on you Sadie. What kind of material would you like, and what color?"

"Do you have black material?"

"Black? Why do you want black?"

"That is what I wear. I do not want to change colors."

Angela thought it was a stretch for Sadie to get a new skirt and a blouse, so it was best not to suggest a different color.

"I have some black material," said Angela. "And I have some beautiful pink linen material for your blouse."

"Don't you have any white material for my blouse?"

"Black and white is formal. Don't you want something you can wear every day?"

Sadie's old blouse used to be white, but now it was a dirty grey.

"You should throw out these old clothes," Angela said.

"Throw them out? I can still wear them. They are still good."

"Sadie, your skirt has moth holes in it."

"Well, I can still wear it around the house," Sadie said.

Many of the Italian immigrants used clothing, electronics, and house-wares until they fell apart, regardless of how much money they had. As Sadie's elastic stockings drooped down her legs, she pulled them up and rolled them around her garters. Several holes became more obvious.

"Sadie, you look like a poor person," Angela said.

"That is a good thing. I do not want people to know about my good fortune."

"You dress like this on purpose?"

Angela had thought it was because she was mentally deficient in some way, or she had no sense of style.

"This is for my safety. This way, people see me as a poor lady and expect less. Nobody notices me. I like it that way."

There were certain expectations within the Italian community if you had money. There was an unwritten rule that you were obliged to support the church according to your income. Many of the immigrants gave what they could to the Catholic Church every Sunday. The usual contribution was about a dollar, and people who had more were expected to contribute more.

Angela remembered watching Sadie prepare her contribution envelope one Sunday. She had reached into the bottom of her old needlepoint pocketbook and pulled out fifty cents, a few pennies and a nickel. Sadie said that was how she got rid of the change that fell to the bottom of her bag. She also never put her name on the envelope.

"I will have your clothes ready in a few days," Angela said. "I will make a black skirt with a pink blouse. You need a little color. They will be simple to make."

"Alright, do what you want. Have you heard from the convent?" Sadie asked.

"Every few months. With Fascism taking over, I don't know what will happen to them."

"Did you ever hear from Principessa Giulia?"

"No, I only hear about her through the nuns," Angela said.

"Franco had expected you to keep in touch with her. Maybe he thought you would be gifted a palace."

Angela laughed. "That was a long time ago, Sadie."

"But you see what I mean about expectations."

Franco never expressed disappointment that he did not receive benefit from her connection with Principessa Giulia, but Angela could sense it. She had hoped it would go away over the years, but the resentment was still there.

"We all have expectations, Sadie, sometimes they do not work out."

* * *

Angela decided that she wanted a Christmas tree this year. She was giving a party for her friends this week and wanted the atmosphere to be festive. The people she bought it from delivered it and put it up, and she invited her nephews and niece to help her decorate it.

Decorating Christmas trees was not a tradition in Sicily, but in America everyone did it. She had seen Christmas trees in other houses, and they brought in warmth and light. She felt she needed that in her home.

Franco had disapproved of having a tree, and he disliked holidays—but Angela decided that his disapproval wasn't something that would interfere with her pleasure. This house was her home. She ran the house: made sure the bills were paid, cleaned, and took care of Franco.

As Franco grew older, his outbursts were getting more frequent. He had always been an angry man, but the stroke had accelerated his mood swings.

Joe and Alicia came in carrying boxes of ornaments.

"We got these from Woolworths," said Alicia. "They had a big selection."

"Yeah, it was fun picking them out," Joe said. "Where's Nunzio?"

"He went out," said Angela. "He's too grown up to decorate a tree."

"Great," said Joe. "More for us to do. Let's start with these." He pointed to a box of solid color Christmas balls.

"These have Christmas scenes on them," Alicia said. "I like these."

Angela picked up a box of ornaments and started to place them on the tree.

"First you put the lights on the tree, then you put on the ornaments," Joe said.

"How do you know that?" Angela asked.

"I pay attention," Joe said. "Let's spread out the lights."

They each took a portion of the lights and draped them around the tree. Joe plugged them in, and the multicolored lights glowed. Angela placed an ornament on a branch, then stepped back. She placed ornaments of varying sizes on selected branches so she could achieve balance and harmony. She wanted to be able to look at the tree and feel peaceful. The lighter the better—especially with what was going on in the world.

They worked together to create an atmosphere of reflected light. Angela used purple and gold ribbon she had for dressmaking and wrapped it around the tree. She even wrapped wire around Christmas cookies she had made and placed them on the tree. When they finished, they stepped back and observed their creation.

"We did a good job," said Alicia. "I really enjoyed it."

"Why do you have that?" Franco asked.

Angela turned and saw Franco standing in the hallway.

"I wanted a tree this year," Angela said.

"I don't want it," Franco said.

Joe and Alicia remained silent and moved closer to one another.

"Damn it, take it down!"

"Go home," Angela said to Joe and Alicia.

"We can't leave you," said Alicia.

"It's fine," said Angela. "Go home."

"Let's go upstairs," Joe said. They moved up the steps.

Franco stepped forward toward the tree, and Angela blocked him.

"Do not touch the tree. It is for our pleasure."

Franco hesitated and looked at the tree. Angela was not about to bend to his will, so Franco raised his cane—but Angela stood there and met his gaze.

"Your disappointments and expectations will not interfere with our joy," said Angela. "Believe me, I too have had unmet expectations in this life—in Sicily and here in America—but now I don't care about them. Franco, go in the kitchen and I will be in soon."

Franco lowered his cane, turned and hobbled into the kitchen. She gazed at the floor.

"Is everything all right?" Joe asked. He was sitting on the staircase, leaning against the banister.

"Everything is fine," Angela said. "Your uncle is not used to Christmas trees."

"You're never happy. I want you to be happy," Joe said. "You're good to me." Joe got up and wrapped his arms around his aunt.

"You are like your mother," Angela said. "Never forget that. You will live the life she would have liked to have had."

"As soon as I turn sixteen, I'm moving to New York," Joe said.

"No, that is too young. You need to think about college."

"That's boring," Joe said. "I want more adventure."

Alicia came down the stairs and folded her arms across her chest.

"Is it over?" Alicia asked.

"Do not be too hard on your uncle. He is not well and lives in his own world."

"He doesn't like anything nice," said Alicia. "He's just mean."

Angela could not contradict Alicia.

"He was very kind to bring me to America," Angela said. "I would not have you two if he hadn't."

"I'm going home," Alicia said. "At least there people don't yell because you have a Christmas tree."

She slammed the door behind her.

"I won't leave, Aunt Angela," Joe said. "Let's rearrange the balls on the tree to make it more perfect."

"You start. I will make your uncle's dinner."

"When I live in New York, I will take you out to dinner so you won't have to cook for anyone."

* * *

Angela buttoned the top button of her white silk blouse and put on a diaphanous apron she had made for special occasions. She rubbed her hands in hand cream and went into the kitchen. Everything was ready. She was keeping the fish warm on the stove, and the potatoes were in the oven. A large antipasto sat on the kitchen table: ham, salami, cheese, and olives. She brought it in the dining room and placed it in the center of the table.

Tomorrow, December 28, would be the anniversary of the earthquake. Angela had purposefully organized this dinner to celebrate her victory over the disaster that could have ended her life. There was a time, when December 28 approached, she would have flash backs about her experience of the disaster and live in fear that memories would come flooding back while she was with a client or alone in her house. She no longer had such fears and if memories came back she greeted them with detached observation.

"What are you doing?" Franco asked.

"I'm having my lady friends over for dinner tonight," Angela said. "Remember, I told you. It is nice out. Why don't you go out for a walk around the block?"

Franco nodded and went out the front door.

She lit the red Christmas candles and straightened the white linen tablecloth.

"Hey Angie, how are you?" Sadie asked.

Sadie was the only one who called her Angie. It was a term of endearment. If someone else said it, it felt condescending.

"How did you get in?"

"Franco was on the way out." Said Sadie. "Ooooooh, the table looks beautiful. You have some wine?"

"Not until everyone arrives. Take off your coat," Angela said.

Sadie shed her coat and revealed the new skirt and blouse Angela had created.

"Sadie, you look wonderful," Angela said.

Angela had to agree with Mrs. Einbinder—she was a magician. Sadie's posture was more erect, and her presence suggested a confident, well-put-together woman.

"Won't those old hens cluck," Sadie said.

She wore new stockings that were smooth on her legs, but she carried the same moth-eaten pocketbook.

"I thought I would come early and help in the kitchen," said Sadie. "I was outside talking to Franco for a while."

"He does not talk much these days," Angela said.

She placed red linen napkins with green embroidered edging on each plate.

"I did most of the talking. I told him how lucky he is to have you, and he nodded his head."

"Maybe he did not understand you," Angela said.

"No, you are wrong. Franco loves you."

"He did once," Angela said.

The front door opened and shut, and a voice from the hallway resonated throughout the house. They did not see Claudia Cerverci yet, but her voice preceded her.

"Angela, you have a tree this year. This is the first time I've seen a tree in your house at Christmas."

"I didn't even see it when I came in," said Sadie. "How did you get Franco to agree?"

"There was no agreement. I bought it and put it up. He tried to get me to take it down, but it stays."

"Good for you, Angie," said Sadie.

"I will light it for everyone after dinner," Angela said.

"What are we eating?" Claudia asked.

"You eat enough," Sadie said.

"And you drink more than enough," said Claudia.

Claudia and Sadie laughed so hard that Angela was afraid her glassware would shatter.

"Sadie, you look different," said Claudia. "Let me see, what is it?"

"Oh, for God sake, I have new clothes. Angela made them. You hens are always clucking."

"You look nice, Sadie," Claudia said.

"Thank you, Your Grace," said Sadie.

Sadie bowed while Claudia chuckled and ate an olive from the antipasto.

And these two have not even had anything to drink yet, thought Angela. It would not be a dull evening.

Next to arrive was Immacolatta. She was in a purple flowing dress that concealed her growing waist from having just given birth. Her cheeks were flushed, and she carried a box of chocolates.

"Here, Angela. I wanted to contribute something to our dinner."

"Thank you, Immacolatta," said Angela. "I think you all know Salvatore's wife. I will put the chocolate on the buffet."

"Why don't we have a sip of sherry before everyone gets here?" Sadie suggested.

"I would like a glass," Claudia said.

"I suppose if everyone is having sherry, I will have a glass," said Immacolatta. "I never have such luxury."

"Oh honey, that's too bad if you think sherry is a luxury," Sadie said.

"All right, but just one glass," Angela said.

Angela poured, and they lifted their glasses.

"To Christmas and good food and friends," Claudia said.

Everyone sipped except Sadie, who ingested her sherry in one gulp.

More guests began to arrive one by one. Paolina came with her sister, Nancy Caputo. Amelia Saldi, the tombstone designer's wife, and a heavily made-up Ramina Galluci were in attendance. Elena Domenico, now 91, had become unable to care for herself and was placed in a nursing home a year ago. The Venzetti twins finally found husbands and could not attend.

"Where are we sitting?" Paolina asked.

"Anywhere," said Angela.

The guests looked at one another as if it was a trap.

"Anywhere?" Sadie asked.

"Just sit," Angela said.

The guests chose their seats, leaving the head of the table for Angela. No one would assume that chair.

"Nancy, it's nice you are visiting your family for the holidays," said Angela.

"Thank you so much for inviting me," said Nancy. "You continue to be kind to me."

Nancy held her pocketbook to her chest, and her eyes darted around the room in anticipation.

"No one is going to steal your pocketbook," Paolina said to her sister.

Nancy's nervous condition had worsened over the years, so she spent more time with her sister. She still lived in a rooming house in Manhattan but was becoming more paranoid.

"It's ok, Nancy, if you want to hold onto your bag," said Angela.

"This is unusual," said Amelia Saldi in English. "Being spontaneous is not a quality I associate with you, Angela."

Out of everyone, Amelia spoke the most colloquial English. Sicilian was still the preferred language for these gatherings, but sometimes English was spoken—especially by Amelia.

"How is Nunzio doing?" asked Ramina Galluci. "My daughter, Mary, and Nunzio are good friends. She likes him very much. It would be a good match, don't you think?"

"You would think he would call his father once in a while," Immacolatta said. "He does not like that I married his father, so Nunzio ignores him."

The guests looked at one another, not knowing what to say. Everyone knew about the close familial relation and that it had produced two misshapen offspring and a third who appeared normal but "may be slow." Angela was not going to discuss family business at a social gathering and took control of the conversation.

"Please, everyone, pass the wine and fill your glasses," Angela said.

"Oh, fill our glasses?" Sadie said. "You usually ration it."

"Well, today we are celebrating," Angela said. "It is a festive time of year."

"Sadie, why don't you fill two glasses," Claudia said.

"I will, when you have your second helping of food," Sadie said.

They both laughed, but the other guests remained silent. Then Immacolatta started laughing and the others started to laugh. Even Ramina started to relax.

"We should toast to everything we can think of," Sadie said.

"Why don't we fill our plates first," Angela said.

Angela had made pasta in clam sauce with a caprese salad and homemade cannoli. She picked up the platter and began passing it around.

"Oh, well, Claudia would like that," Sadie said.

"Has anyone heard from relatives in Europe?" asked Ramina. "I hear it's getting worse and there could possibly be a war in Europe. Mussolini is a tyrant."

"Mussolini will eventually fall," said Sadie.

"Why would you say that?" asked Amelia.

"All tyrants have their day, but it always ends badly. You know, during World War I, many girls married enlisted men before they went to war, and if the men were killed they got some money. I have heard that some women do that."

"I hope you're not suggesting that young women marry someone just on the possibility their husbands would be killed," Amelia said.

"Well, if they are going to war," Sadie said, "wouldn't it be better to have a wife waiting for you at home?"

"But you are suggesting they marry someone with the hope of the men being killed," Ramina said.

"No, I am saying if it happens the woman would be compensated. It is better that someone benefits from the man's death."

"I would not allow my daughter to marry a man simply to profit from his death," Ramina said.

"It would be immoral for someone to do that," Amelia said.

"My husband, Salvatore, would join the fight if we had war, but he's too old," Immacolatta said.

"Yes, he would," Paolina said. "My brother would do what is right."

Angela felt that Salvatore would not know the difference between right and wrong if God came down and explained it to him. The way he ignored Speranza's children could not be more wrong.

"Everyone, eat," Angela said.

"You don't have to tell Claudia that," Sadie said.

Sadie's speech was a bit slurred.

"Why don't you stop drinking," Paolina said. "You do this every time."

"Why not drink? She enjoys it," said Claudia.

"Sure, she enjoys it," said Immacolatta. "We should all have our pleasures. Life is hard enough."

"Everything in moderation," said Amelia.

"Angela, as I was saying, I think my Mary and Nunzio make a handsome couple."

"Yes, very attractive, but they are young and have many opportunities before them," Angela said.

"We are lucky to be living in this country and not dealing with a dictator like Mussolini," said Amelia. "God bless this country. I don't think people are patriotic enough. I came to America as a child of six because my parents wanted a better life, and they achieved that."

Angela had heard the same story repeatedly. If her family had survived, she would still be in Messina.

"I am glad to be in this country," Nancy said hesitantly.

Nancy ate very little and kept wringing her hands. She still held her job as an elevator operator at the Park Plaza Hotel, but she found it difficult to interact with people.

"Who would like dessert?" Angela asked. The difference between her clients and neighbors and the present group of friends was immense. Angela saw the repetitive patterns in relationships in the Italian community. The community's insular focus was a barrier to new ideas and different ways of relating. Angela navigated both worlds. It was a skill she had started to develop soon after she arrived in America. She learned the art of communication from her struggle to be understood, even though she did not speak English when she arrived in America. Now she could navigate any social landscape successfully.

Chapter 7

Spring 1938

Angela believed there was nothing like art to revive memory and keep the past and present alive, and it was a path to the future. She thought about her past interaction with paintings in Italy, where there were plenty of old paintings at the convent that she encountered daily. The characters in the paintings became her friends and allies. The figures in the works of art were frozen in time, but they were alive to Angela. When the light changed, they reflected different ideas and feelings. What appeared to be static was pulsing with life in Angela's mind. Her unseen friends had encouraged her to approach the paintings as an alternate universe where beings thrived and interacted. They suggested that she could ultimately step into the interior of the painting and experience the landscape in which the figures lived.

When she and Franco returned to Italy in 1929 to search for her sister, she interacted with many pieces of art that she felt spoke to her alone. Sometimes they communicated to her in words and in body sensations. Franco's cousin, the poet Roberto, was important to her and Franco because he painted with words. Through his prose, they received images of their homeland as it was in the present and where it was going in the future.

Angela opened the mailbox and rifled through the envelopes. There were several bills and advertisements. She came to an airmail envelope addressed to Franco. Roberto was alive. Its postmark was from Paris. Angela quickly went in the house.

"Franco. Franco, Roberto is alive and living in Paris," said Angela. "Franco, where are you?"

She scanned the kitchen but did not fine Franco. She looked out the window and saw him digging in the garden, preparing the soil for planting.

He looked happy to Angela, kneeling on the earth. Every spring, summer and fall they had the most beautiful garden on the street.

"Franco!" shouted Angela. She banged on the window and waved the letter. "It is from Roberto."

Franco dropped the trowel, picked up his cane and hobbled to the back door. Angela had not seen him move this fast since before his stroke.

"I don't believe it," said Franco, taking one stair at a time.

"Let's go into the dining room and sit," Angela said.

Once they were situated, Angela took a deep breath and began to open the envelope with a letter opener. She handled it gingerly, careful not to tear the delicate airmail paper. Like she was cutting a hem, she opened the envelope on a perfectly straight line, took out its contents, and laid the letter in front of Franco. He pushed the letter toward Angela.

"You read," Franco said. He still did not feel confident about his ability to speak in full sentences. Roberto's authority with words made him feel more self-conscious.

Angela unfolded the letter and spoke the first few words.

April 1938

My Dear Angela and Cousin Franco,

How I have thought of you through my turmoil! I am sorry you have not heard from me in over a year, but my circumstances had become grave. Those who speak out against the Italian regime are persecuted, and I am one of the hunted. Presently, my family and I are in Paris living among other writers and artists. We meet in cafes regularly and share information about our craft and the political situation. Even Paris feels uncertain these days, and I wonder what will become of us. There is an underground newspaper where many well-known writers voice their opinions. Some have joined the resistance to the tyranny that is rampant in Europe's cities. Germany is taking over Europe at an alarming rate. I am writing to you to bring news and let you know that I am alive and thriving in the city of light.

Speaking of light, Franco and Angela, I send you much light for I know you both have experienced much loss. America has never interested me, and I do not agree with capitalism, but it makes me happy you are both safe and away from the evil that pervades the fabric of European civilization. My hope is we will see each other again someday when the world is a calmer place and civilized man is no longer enslaved. Please accept the following poem as gift to you both.

With great affection,
Roberto

The Kitten and the Hawk

I have seen the hawk dancing against a clear blue sky;
Its movement graceful but calculated,
Its prey transfixed by its eloquence and freedom.
I would like to be able to fly, thought the kitten.
I would like to be able to spread my wings and have the wind
carry me.
The kitten followed the hawk's movement as it circled over him.
He sees me, thought the kitten.
I am acknowledged, thought the kitten.
Suddenly the hawk swooped down, and the kitten was carried off,
Dancing again a clear blue sky.

Franco and Angela looked at each other, waiting for the other to speak first.

"What do you suppose he meant?" Angela asked.

Franco shrugged his shoulders and picked up the letter. *It could mean anything*, he thought. He never really understood Roberto's poetry—or anyone's, for that matter. He was just glad that his cousin was still alive.

"I will show it to Mrs. Einbinder. I think she would have an idea because she is a playwright."

This confirmed for Angela that the situation in Europe was only going to get worse. Soon there would be war, maybe not now, but in the future. She hoped it would not involve the United States. The evil was expanding into many parts of Europe like an out-of-control infection that was festering.

Many of her clients had, or would have, boys of draft age within the next few years. She did not want to deal with more loss, not from her family or others. It was only a matter of time before America would have to act.

"He is alive. That is good," Franco said.

"Yes, it is."

Angela folded the letter and placed it in the envelope. *Maybe they could go to Paris*, she thought. *It is not occupied by Germany, and they could see Roberto and his wife and children.* She glanced at Franco's cane and was reminded why that trip was impractical.

"I am going to lie down," said Franco. The news from Europe made him sad and tired. He did not understand how one country could have such a major effect on the world. Franco admired his cousin, his courage and his willingness to take dangerous risks. But still, Franco was glad to be out of harm's way.

Franco leaned his cane on the nightstand and lifted his legs onto the bed. He rested the back of his head on the pillow and folded his hands across his chest, feeling his beating heart against his fingers. In his dreams, he saw himself able-bodied and young. Sometimes he dreamed about roaming the Sicilian countryside with his cousin Roberto. His body relaxed into sleep, where his mind was free to roam and imagine. Soon he was in the depths of sleep.

* * *

Downstairs, Angela took out a pen and airmail paper.

May 1938

Dearest Roberto,

Franco and I were relieved to receive your letter. It gladdens our hearts that you and your family are safe. Paris sounds like it is thriving, and we are glad you are living a productive life. Know that Franco and I think of you often and always sleep better when we hear from you. Thank you for your poem. Franco and I were discussing what it meant. We are working people and do not spend much time reading poetry, so sometimes the meaning passes us by.

Angela Paused and read the poem again. She thought she would attempt an interpretation. There was a third party who observed all this, thought Angela. It was the poor kitten, hypnotized by the strength and beauty of the hawk, not realizing he was the prey. The kitten was unable to save himself, because he was awestruck by strength and majesty. This contributed to his demise.

> *Maybe you are commenting on the situation in Europe and how countries let Germany come in and devour them. I hope that will never happen to your precious Paris. It is a city that has offered you refuge before, and I hope it remains free of Fascism. Please let us know of your situation as the months progress. We pray for your safety and a quick return to your homeland.*
>
> *With Deep Affection,*
> *Angela and Franco*

Angela placed the letter in an envelope and sealed it. She would post the letter in the afternoon mail. She glanced at the clock and began to prepare for her next client, Clara Murphy. Angela enjoyed most of her clients, provided they supplied a window to the world or brought an extraordinary point of view. She could tolerate complaining up to a point, but the one client Angela dreaded walking up her porch stairs was Clara Murphy. Clara's family emigrated from Ireland during the potato famine in the late 1800s. She was inordinately proud of being born in America and disliked many of the recent immigrants, even though she lived next to them in a poor neighborhood.

Angela's family's culture was imbued in language, design, and cooking. She felt this was also true of her European clients. American politics was only mentioned if it came up in their discussion of the situation in Europe. Very few in the European immigrant community knew anything about the American Revolution or the Civil War. They had their own history to contend with.

The fundamental issue Angela had with Clara was her huge size: a size 20, and she weighed at least 250 pounds in Angela's estimation. Clara never came to Angela to make a new garment; she only came for alterations. She bought cheap clothes from Woolworth's and expected Angela to transform them into quality garments like the ones she designed for her wealthier clients.

"I do not reconstruct clothes," Angela had told her. "If you want an alteration, I will alter it."

"But can't you take off this collar and put on another?" Clara would whine.

"If you want that, I would have to charge you for a garment made from the beginning."

Angela's mirror was not large enough to reflect Clara's entire body, and when Angela had to pin her hem it was a long way around. Angela had heard that Clara complained her prices were too high. She did not need Clara's business, so today Angela intended to remedy the situation.

Angela flipped the switch to the hall light and pulled the platform away from the mirror so she would be able to see more of Clara Murphy's enormous form. She then went into the kitchen and made a cup of espresso. As she sipped her coffee, she thought about a strategy for ridding herself of Clara. Angela could not abide her whining and small-town gossip any longer, as she talked endlessly about her neighbors and how awful they were and how she was going to move to a better neighborhood soon. Angela knew it was just talk and that Clara would grow old and die in that neighborhood. One needed a skill, trade, or education to change their life's circumstances. Clara and her husband had neither.

Angela finished her coffee, placed the cup in the sink, and went into the dining room. She opened the dining room closet door and began to rummage through hat boxes. Angela would occasionally make hats. Although she was not a milliner by trade, she was a decent hat maker. She had made a few hats to go with suits she had designed for clients. Whenever she had material left over, she tried to make something to accompany the garment to advertise another skill she had mastered. Sometimes she would make something for herself out of the expensive material she had purchased for a client. At times she would have enough for an entire blouse or colorful scarf. The possibilities were endless. Angela was attending a friend's daughter's wedding next month, and she wanted to look the part of a well-dressed European American.

Nunzio came down the front stairs.

"Where are you going?" asked Angela.

"Out to meet some friends," Nunzio said. "I won't be home for dinner."

"When will you be back?"

"Later," said Nunzio.

Angela was relieved that Nunzio lived upstairs. He helped Franco with chores around the house and kept him company. He also accompanied Franco on walks, since his gait was unsteady. Angela worried less about Franco because Nunzio was there for support. Nunzio had not done well in high school and he barely attended classes, so Angela had given up encouraging him to finish. He had dropped out over a year ago.

Nunzio's lack of education was a constant worry for Angela. If it had not been for Franco's guidance, Nunzio would have no focus in life. Franco had taught him how to do household repairs and refinish furniture. He even took Nunzio out to see houses that Franco had once helped build. Nunzio did not seem enthusiastic about what Franco had to teach, but he listened politely and seemed to take in some things. He never outgrew his fascination with guns, and he had started to collect them. *At least he had a role model beyond Salvatore*, thought Angela.

She heard someone on her front steps and went to look out the front window. Clara Murphy climbed the stairs one step at a time, pausing on each stair to catch her breath. *That woman is going to have a heart attack one day*, thought Angela. She thought about going out to ask if she was all right, but that seemed disingenuous.

Clara wore a garment that resembled a tent. Angela wondered how someone that young could end up in such a condition, and she was ashamed to admit that she was embarrassed by Clara's presence in her home. She opened the door for Clara.

"Hello, Mrs. Bellini," Clara said. She blew air through her pursed lips, as if she were blowing out a candle.

"I hope the stairs were not too much for you," said Angela. "You know, there are other dressmakers in town who are on the ground floor. It would be easier access for you."

It was true, Clara's neighborhood was only a few blocks away, but it might as well have been as far as Constantinople. Clara's streets were populated with a mixture of the poor and working class. It was not that Angela disliked them, but she found their conversations trite and limited. They did not discuss style or concepts, but they instead engaged in small-town gossip about how a certain neighbor thought they were better than anyone else because they had purchased a new couch.

Angela believed that culture should be shared with those who value and understand it and not with those who draw a blank when you mention Caruso or paintings in Europe. No matter how poor you were in Sicily, you were surrounded with culture and an appreciation of the past.

Angela wanted to cut her time with Clara short, because she had Mrs. Sweet coming for a fitting. She was the wife of Dr. Sweet, a well-respected physician. Angela had known Dr. and Mrs. Sweet since she emigrated from Sicily. They were the first couple she had entertained who were not part of the Italian community in Nelsonville. Mrs. Sweet had sent many of her friends to Angela for alterations and dressmaking, so every week when Angela made Italian rolls, she would send some to Mrs. Sweet. In fact, anyone who sent customers her way received a gift of fresh homemade rolls. This built her reputation as someone who truly appreciated their business.

"I have several dresses to be altered, and I wondered if you would take the sleeves off this one," Clara Murphy said. She lifted the garment to show Angela. It was a navy blue dress with white trim that looked like it came from the Salvation Army.

"Mrs. Murphy, I do not think it is worth it. This is a poorly made garment. You would be better off buying a new dress from Woolworth's. It would cost you the same as I would charge."

"But it is an alteration," Clara said.

"No, it is a reconstruction. I would have to redesign the shoulders. It is that poorly made."

"Well, that is too expensive." Clara put her thick fingers on her huge hips as if she were in a schoolyard fight.

"I am awfully sorry, Mrs. Murphy, but that is my estimate. As I have said, there are other dressmakers in town who would suit you better."

Clara Murphy picked up her bag of clothes and stormed out of the house.

Angela watched with satisfaction as the large woman held on to the railing and slammed each foot on the stairs, wobbling from side to side. Angela breathed a sigh of relief and was comforted that she would never have to contend with her again.

Angela smiled and thought how, 20 years ago, she would never have done that. If a client was rude or requested a payment plan, she would accept it. Now she no longer had to put up with that behavior, and she felt free to choose the people with whom she wanted to work. When she first arrived in America, she wanted to make money so her husband would feel he had gotten a good deal by marrying her. There was a sense that she had to be worth the effort of Franco traveling to Europe and paying for her hand in marriage.

When she started working as a seamstress at St. Mary's Episcopal School making vestments for the priests and dresses for the students, she had encountered jealousy from the other seamstresses. Angela was meticulous about the quality of her work, and the other women felt it made them look bad. Angela could not understand English, and at lunch the others sat amongst themselves and talked. Sometimes Angela would hear her name, and the seamstresses would glace in her direction. She continued to produce high quality work, and gradually the students and their parents took notice and asked her to make dresses and suits for social occasions.

Now, Angela enjoyed using her talents for creating quality garments— not inferior dresses. She had wanted to dismiss Clara Murphy for over a year, and now she had done it. She not only felt stronger on a professional level, but personally as well.

* * *

Angela had returned from grocery shopping when the phone rang.

"Mrs. Bellini?"

"Yes?"

"This is the principal at Sacred Heart School. You visited my office a year ago. Your nephew was not at school today. I tried calling his home, but the woman who answered was not very responsive."

Dread engulfed Angela, terrified that Joe had been beaten up again.

"Hello, Sister Collier," she said. "Is my nephew all right?"

"Well, I don't know. He has not been at school for three days. Has he been with you?"

"No. Are you sure he has not been there?"

"I will have to report him for truancy."

"No, please, I will talk to him. He has a difficult home life."

"Mrs. Bellini, I know his home life is not ideal, but I am obligated to report this."

"I will find him and come to the school with him tomorrow."

"All right. One more day, but no more," the nun said.

Angela called Immacolatta, but she said Joe was not at home and that he had left the house every day to go to school and returned when school was over. *New York City*, thought Angela. *That is where he goes.* She checked the train schedule and went to meet the train that was close to the dismissal time at school.

Angela stood on the platform, arms folded, as the train pulled into the station. Joe stepped off the train wearing a fedora. When he saw Angela, he stopped and then moved toward her.

"Where have you been? Sister Collier called me. She said that you have not been in school for three days."

"I don't like it there. I'm tired of kids making fun of me, and I'm bored."

"But you are too young to go into the city by yourself, and Sister Collier said she was going to call the truant office."

"I'm sorry, Aunt Angela, but I had the best day. I went into stores and looked at buildings and that made me happy."

"You are only 13. It is dangerous, and where did you get the fedora?"

"I saved up the money you give me for delivering bread to your customers and bought it on the street. Doesn't it look good?"

"Joe, you have to stop this. Tomorrow I will take you back to school myself. We will talk to Sister Collier about the boys who hurt you. Remember, you graduate from eighth grade next month, and then you go to public school."

Joe fished in his jacket pocket and pulled out a chocolate bar and handed it to Angela.

"I know how much you love chocolate."

Angela took the chocolate bar and put her arm around her nephew. As they walked off the platform, a car drove up and out stepped Sarah Einbinder. She was wearing a navy blue suit Angela had made, accessorized with gold earrings.

"Mrs. Bellini, have you just come from the city?" asked Sarah.

"Hello, Mrs. Einbinder. No, I was meeting my nephew, Joe."

"You are a handsome young man," Sarah said to Joe.

"Thank you so much, Mrs. Einbinder," Joe said.

"Are you going to the city?" Angela asked.

"Yes, in fact I have a meeting with families whose relatives have disappeared in Germany."

"What happened to their families?" Joe asked.

"Joe, Mrs. Einbinder has to catch her train. Nice to see you, Mrs. Einbinder."

Angela took Joe's hand and quickly moved away from the station.

"What's wrong?" asked Joe.

"You are too young to know about those meetings," Angela said.

"I'm 13, you know. In three years I can live in New York."

"You have to graduate high school," Angela said. "You will be too young to go to New York City, and you would be on your own. You would be scared and lonely."

"I won't be scared," Joe said. "At least people won't beat me up."

Angela was 13 when Mt. Etna erupted, and she had roamed Messina's broken streets. The profound loneliness and fear she had felt, she did not want Joe to experience.

He looked up at Angela with smiling eyes.

"I will never be lonely, because I have you," Joe said.

She pinched his cheek.

"You are sweet like your mother, and you have her adventurous thinking—but I want you to finish high school."

Angela could not blame him for wanting to leave Nelsonville. He did not have much of a home life, and as he grew older there would be very little for him here. Regardless of his choice, she would make sure he had everything he needed. It saddened Angela to think that he was being abused at school. Maybe New York would give him a fresh start.

"I don't know what finishing high school will get me," Joe said.

"I promised your mother. We can talk about this another time. Tomorrow morning, we will go see Sister Collier."

"That old hen," Joe said.

"Be careful of what you say," Angela said.

Angela waved to Mrs. Einbinder.

"Good luck with your meeting," called Angela. She held Joe's arm as they moved away.

* * *

"Remember to let me talk," Angela said.

Angela made sure that Joe had dressed appropriately for their meeting with Sister Collier. She adjusted his collar and slicked back his hair. Angela knocked on the principal's door, then softly opened it while Joe lingered. Sister Collier motioned for them to come in, and they walked toward the nun's heavy desk.

"Mrs. Bellini, Joseph," said Sister Collier.

"Thank you for seeing us, Sister," Angela said. "My nephew appreciates that you will give him a second chance."

"I did not say that, Mrs. Bellini, I said I would talk to you."

"Well, Sister, my nephew is sorry that he skipped school, but it is very close to graduation and he is high-spirited. His grades are excellent."

"We have had this discussion before, Mrs. Bellini. I want to talk to Joe to see if he is going to apologize and comply with our rules."

Joe and Angela looked at each other. Angela motioned with her chin for Joe to talk.

"I'm sorry that I skipped school, and I really want to graduate," Joe said.

He looked Sister Collier in the face and smiled.

"I am sorry, *who*?" the nun asked.

Angela looked at Joe and widened her eyes. His sassy attitude was becoming tiresome even to her.

"I am sorry, Sister Collier," Joe said. "And I will not be truant again."

"He will not do it again. I will make sure of that," Angela said.

"Joseph, as principal of this school, I need to discipline you. I cannot let this go unpunished. It is a privilege to attend school here, and truancy is not tolerated. As punishment, you will stay after school each Friday and wash all the blackboards in the school until graduation. Do you think that's fair?"

Joe looked at Angela. She nodded her head.

"Yes, Sister Collier," Joe said.

Angela could see he had his fingers crossed behind his back.

"I also suggest," said Sister Collier, "that you encourage Joseph's step-mother to be more involved. Maybe she could learn to speak English with less of an accent. After all, English is the language of our country, so it goes without saying that it is an obligation to communicate better. She would fit in better."

"Fit in?" Angela asked.

"Yes, to fit in America. You speak English quite well because you wanted to fit into American culture. You did not expect others to speak your Sicilian dialect, and outside of your community, it is useless. That is commendable."

At the convent, the nuns would make the girls kiss the floor if they spoke the Sicilian dialect. They were to speak Italian always. Those nuns were a French order, and French was also often spoken. Angela developed an ear for the language and could understand when it was spoken.

"Sister Collier, I speak both Sicilian and Italian, and now I speak English. I also speak a little French. That is the mark of a cultured person."

Angela could have continued in Italian and been much more descriptive. She spoke English, but to her it was a utility language. If Sister Collier spoke Italian, she would have told her that her ability to speak three languages made her universal and that it helped her navigate between two worlds. Americans would do well to listen and understand the world better and consider what is brewing in their own backyards.

"I am sure it is," said the nun. "That will be all. Joseph, you may go to class, and since today is Friday, you can begin with the blackboards in the Kindergarten classroom. Good day."

Angela and Joe closed the door behind them.

"I am glad that is the last time I will have to speak to that woman," said Angela. "I saw your fingers crossed. I am sure you will do as Sister Collier says."

Joe was silent.

"Tell me I haven't wasted my time."

"I was just expressing myself with my fingers," said Joe. "I'll clean the blackboards."

"I am sure you will," Angela said.

Chapter 8

June 1938

Angela finished kneading the dough and put it in the back stairway to rise. She would make pizzas and bread later in the day. The pizza would be dinner for Franco and Nunzio. They were trimming trees in the yard and would be hungry when they finished. Sadie was also going to drop by today for a light lunch and a chat. She did not have clients scheduled today, so it was a day of rest.

"Hey, Angie, I'm here," Sadie called. "You left the door unlocked."

"Oh, I have a lot on my mind," Angela said.

"I locked it for you. What's for lunch?"

"Pasta and a salad," Angela said.

"You have a little eggplant?"

"No, pasta and a salad."

"Ok, fine," Sadie said.

"Franco and Nunzio are almost finished trimming trees," said Angela.

Sadie peered out the window and waved to the two men who were wiping their brows.

"He is sure good looking, your nephew."

"I hope he marries someday and lives upstairs. I would love to have children in the house."

"I never liked children," Sadie said. "It was never something I wanted to do. I know you wanted them."

"God wanted me to raise Speranza's children."

"I like to come and go as I please. That's why when my second husband died, I never remarried. I'm free as a bird," Sadie sang.

"Your stockings are too tight," Angela said. "Your ankles are swollen."

"Yeah, the doctor said my heart is slowing down. I don't pay any attention. He tells me I shouldn't eat salt."

"There is nothing more important than your health," Angela said. "You have to have your health."

"Good health, yes, but you have to enjoy yourself," Sadie said.

Angela took out a bottle of red wine.

"Yes, now that is what I would like. You know me very well, Angie."

"Everyone does."

"You don't make me ask. You accept me."

Angela hoped she was an accepting person, but one thing she would never accept was crudity. Respect was the most important quality that Angela looked for in people. If someone got a little drunk but was still well mannered, she ignored it.

The phone rang.

"Eat your pasta, I'll be right back."

As soon as Angela picked up the receiver, she heard Alicia's excited voice.

"Getting married? Leo? What does your father say? Isn't anyone opposing this?"

Angela's voice became louder and more forceful. Sadie came into the hallway and stood by Angela.

"I do not think this is a good idea. Leo is not a good man for you."

"Oh, oh," said Sadie.

"Let me speak to your stepmother."

"Immacolatta, what do you think of this marriage?"

Immacolatta said that it was none of her business and that if Alicia wanted to get married, she should. Angela's voice held back rage. She started to tremble. It reminded her of Speranza's decision to marry Salvatore.

"This is not going to end well. Leo Minuci is not a good man, and he has no respect for anything." She paused to catch her breath. "Put Alicia back on the phone. Well, where did she go?" Angela hung up.

"Not good news, huh?" Sadie stated the obvious.

"That fool Minuci has proposed to my niece, and she has accepted."

"Nothing you can do about it," said Sadie.

"I am accepting up to a point," Angela said.

"You don't want to push Alicia away. Just be nice to her so she can come to you if she needs advice."

"I will not be able to sleep tonight," Angela said. "Wait until I tell Franco."

"Have a little wine with me. You'll sleep. You want me to tell Franco? I'm good at delivering bad news."

They laughed. Angela depended on Sadie's irreverent sense of humor that was lacking in the rest of the Italian community. There was no pretense with Sadie, and Angela could be honest with her. She appreciated her other friends, but she was most relaxed with Sadie.

"Maybe it's not as bad as you think," Sadie said.

"What do you mean? You have heard about the Minuci family, haven't you?"

"Here and there. I haven't met Leo."

"Well, he has no sensibility. And I can see he is violent."

Sadie took a sip of wine and thought about what Angela said.

"If any of my husbands ever hit me, I would have knocked his teeth out," said Sadie. "When I walk on the street in the evening, I put rocks in my pocketbook."

"Rocks?" Angela asked.

"Rocks, so I can hit anyone on the head if they bother me. Sometimes a woman isn't safe walking around when it's dark. Didn't you know I have a lot of unhappy suitors?"

"Since when?" Angela asked. "You have been drinking too much wine."

"See that, Angela, I can always count on you to say what you actually think. The rest of the crowd would have disregarded me and talked about me behind my back. Sometimes I like to give them material for gossip."

Sadie poured Angela a glass of wine. They lifted their glasses and drank in silence.

"So, what are you doing this afternoon?"

"Today I have no clients, so I am working on some alterations. I will need to tell Franco about Alicia's engagement."

"Good luck. If you need to talk, call me," Sadie said.

"Thank you, Sadie."

"Don't mention it. You have been kind to me in ways no one else has, and I appreciate it."

Sadie got up to leave. Angela watched as she walked away; she swung her old pocketbook.

* * *

"Alicia is engaged to that horrible man, Leo Minuci," Angela said.

"What?" Franco sat in his smoking chair, cleaning his pipes.

"That man is going to marry Alicia. She is a beautiful girl, and she is marrying that ugly man. I do not like him."

"That can't be. Call Salvatore," said Franco.

"They do not seem to mind," Angela said. "Immacolatta has wanted Alicia out of the house for a while now. She resents her being there."

"These people make no sense," said Franco.

"Our Speranza's daughter is going to make a big mistake, and there is nothing we can do about it. She is 18 and will ruin her life."

Angela cried. It was hard for her to let go of her sadness around this relationship. She could see what would eventually happen, and it created a deep sadness that she could not transcend.

Franco stood up.

"Stop crying," said Franco. "There is nothing you can do about it. Stop it."

"You talk to Alicia!" shouted Angela. "You should have stopped Speranza from marrying Salvatore, but you didn't. Your mother and Salvatore's sister arranged that match, and you said nothing."

She picked up one of Franco's pipes and threw against the wall. Franco stepped back. Angela continued to sob and blame everyone for Speranza and Alicia's decisions. She needed someone to blame, but she felt her influence was never noticed.

"I worked so hard with Speranza and Alicia so that they would grow up and make good choices. It doesn't seem to have mattered. No one supported me in what I was trying to do."

Franco disliked the Minuci family as much as Angela, but he believed there was nothing he could do about it.

Angela was determined not to suppress what her intuition clearly told her, and she would speak her mind regardless of who liked it and who didn't.

Angela dried her tears and went into her bedroom to write a letter to the Mother Superior at the convent. She had received notice that the nun would retire soon, and Angela wanted to congratulate her and tell her how much her influence had meant to her. She sat at her writing desk and took out a fountain pen and paper. She dipped her pen in the ink and filled the barrel.

June 1938

Dear Mother,

I am writing to wish you well on your retirement. I think of you and the sisters often, and I want to let you know how grateful I am that you gave me a home after the earthquake. I think of those times with fondness and a sense of possibility. That is what youth is about, I suppose; the feeling of infinite possibilities. Even though my choices were limited, I try to hang onto that feeling, but I am not always successful. I find my life here trying at times, but I remind myself that I had a home with you with the feeling of infinite possibilities. That has made all the difference.

I am concerned about my niece, Alicia. She is only 18 and is engaged to a man whom you would never allow to marry any of the girls at the convent. His father is violent and a criminal. My heart breaks that her life has come to this. I have done my best to discourage her from such a union, but I have failed. I pray that she finds her way.

Please write and tell me how you are doing. I hope the Prince and Principessa are protecting the convent from the unrest in Europe.

All My Affection,

Angela

She sealed the envelope and put it aside to mail. As the nuns grew older and passed away, she wondered if there would be anyone who still knew her. Who would she write to then? She would be a shadow who once lived at Palazzo Butera convent. Many of the girls had married and moved out of the convent, and a few became nuns. Her past was gradually disappearing. The only part left of her former life was her unseen friends, and she had gained strength from the individual care she had received from the Mother Superior.

She thought about Alicia's wedding gown and how she would create it, regardless of how she felt about Leo. Joy did not go into Speranza's gown, nor would joy be part of making Alicia's gown. Her unseen friends had explained that free choice was available to everyone, but Angela believed a choice could also be unchosen. When she created Speranza's gown, she had pretended that Speranza was marrying a professional man who would be considerate and take care of her. She thought about refusing to make Alicia's gown, but it was not a choice she was comfortable in making. Alicia was her niece, and she would make the effort.

* * *

The next morning, Angela lit candles to the Blessed Mother. She knelt and prayed for her nephews, niece, and husband. She asked for Mary's help in navigating the changes in her life. Speranza's children were beginning to make their own lives, and she asked Mary to watch over them. She asked Mary to look after her sister, wherever she may be. Angela requested that if her younger sister were still alive, that she let her know that Angela was alive and living in America. She prayed for her to especially watch over Alicia and to keep her safe. Tomorrow she would fit Alicia for her wedding gown, and she called upon Mary to give her strength.

Angela gazed at her reflection in the dresser mirror. Now in her mid-40s, her hair was rapidly turning grey, and her olive skin had few wrinkles with no evidence of sagging. She still had a slim figure and stood with shoulders back with her chest lifted.

She had bought several wedding gown patterns that would flatter Alicia's figure. She would fill the bodice with faux pearls and sequins. Angela did not believe in plain wedding dresses. Making a statement with sparkle was what a wedding gown should do. Gowns should not be solemn but radiate a glow that would match the bride's energy. This was the state inside that the designer had to access before she could begin work on the dress. The act of creating a wedding gown was a declaration of the bride's intentions as well as a memory marker: before marriage, after marriage. Angela chose a pattern that would accentuate Alicia's slim waist.

* * *

Alicia and Leo wanted to marry in the fall, and it arrived quickly. Today would be Alicia's last fitting. Angela hung the gown on the hall mirror. She had used yards of chiffon silk to create the train. Faux pearls were embedded throughout the gown. The V neckline was trimmed with Italian lace that extended down the sleeves.

"I am so excited about this dress," said Alicia. "Thank you so much for making it. I know you don't like Leo."

"Whether I like Leo or not is not the point," said Angela. "You are Speranza's daughter and my niece, so of course I would make your gown."

Alicia looked like she had just stepped off a fashion runway when she put on the gown. The reflection of the silk glowed in the fall sunlight.

"You look beautiful," said Angela.

"Do you think my mother would love it?" asked Alicia.

"I think she would," said Angela.

"Leo got a job at the fire station as a custodian. He's hoping to become a fire fighter."

"Don't you have to have a lot of training to do that?"

"Yes, they have to accept him into the program. It's good money."

Maybe Leo is turning his life around, Angela thought. *Maybe he won't become his father.*

"Well, that is good news," Angela said.

"I know, isn't it?"

Alicia stepped down and kissed Angela on both cheeks. Angela had never seen Alicia so lighthearted. It made Angela think that she had worried for nothing and that this wedding embodied the promise of a new beginning. She felt that the Minuci family history did not bode well for Alicia's marriage, but maybe things would be different for Leo and Alicia.

* * *

Alicia stood in the vestibule of the church, surrounded by her brothers.

"You make a beautiful bride," said Angela. Alicia's light skin, blue eyes, and auburn hair sparkled under the off-white veil. She had a generous bosom and small waist. Angela stepped back to view the gown she had created.

"You have made an amazing dress," Joe said.

Joe was wearing a dark suit and a white tailored shirt. The sweet aroma of cologne wafted from his clothing.

"You look really nice," said Nunzio. He did not like Leo either, but he was involved in his own life and he had not spent much time with Alicia; they had grown up in two different households.

Angela asked the photographer to take a photo of the siblings.

They stood arm in arm, heads bent in toward each other, as the photographer snapped the photo. This was the moment in time that Angela wanted to remember: her niece and nephews looking beautiful and happy. Angela smiled and was content that they could be together and share this moment. Even though she resisted the marriage, Angela was pleased she had helped shape this moment through her sewing talents.

Fortunately, Leo's father was still incarcerated and could not attend the wedding. Leo's mother was a short overweight woman and wore a knee-length floral dress. Angela thought she looked thrown together, and that was never a good sign.

"Hello, Mrs. Bellini," said Gina Minuci. "It's a great day."

"Yes, we are blessed with good weather," said Angela.

"Yeah, I mean that they're getting married," said Gina.

"Yes, Leo is a lucky man."

"And so is Alicia," said Gina.

"Well, we will see how lucky she is," said Angela. "When does your husband get out of jail?"

"Huh," said Gina. She walked away.

Angela wanted to set boundaries with the Minucis before the wedding took place. Their connection would be limited. Angela spread Alicia's veil, and Salvatore took his place to walk his daughter down the aisle.

* * *

After the bride and groom danced, Alicia danced with Franco and her brothers. Alicia was relieved that her father decided not to dance with her due to his limp from infantile paralysis. She was grateful she was saved from that embarrassment. Leo sat for the rest of the evening drinking and talking to his friends. He did not seem to have much interest in socializing with his new in-laws or with anyone connected with Alicia. Angela saw that he had difficulty standing.

"It looks like Alicia will be going to bed alone tonight," said Sadie. "Thanks for inviting me. I enjoy weddings. They always come with free wine."

"He is such a fool. He's ignoring his own mother," said Angela. "I'm glad you and Claudia came."

Leo went over to Alicia while she was dancing with Joe and grabbed her arm. She shook her head and he pulled her. Angela went over to see what was going on.

"What's the matter?" asked Angela.

"She's my wife, and I want her to come with me," said Leo, slurring his words.

"It is too early to leave," said Angela. "You have guests."

Angela folded her arms across her chest. Leo looked around the room and saw guests staring in his direction. He backed away from Angela and returned to his friends. Gina Minuci saw that Leo demurred to Angela and got up and left the reception hall.

"What's wrong with him?" asked Joe.

"He's just tired and doesn't socialize much," Alicia said.

"He should learn to be more social and not be such a beast," said Joe.

"Enjoy yourselves," Angela said. She walked purposefully back to her table.

"Remind me to never cross you," said Claudia.

Angela nodded her head and sat next to Franco.

"I settled it," Angela said.

Chapter 9

Angela rifled through the mail and saw a letter from Palazzo Butera. The Mother Superior had finally answered her letter. She had thought with all the trouble in Europe, that something had happened to the convent.

February 1939

Dear Angela,

I am sorry it has taken me so long to respond to your letter, but Europe is in such turmoil with the war that we have had to do with much less than we are used to. Our food is rationed, and the cloth we import for our sewing is no longer easy to obtain. Principessa Giulia has been generous as always.

Thank you for your well wishes upon my retirement. In a few months, Sister Elizabeth will become the Superior of the convent and will take over my responsibilities. She will be leading us through trying times indeed. I have told her about you and your experience with the convent and that you were one of our more celebrated students. I am saddened about leaving my post as Mother Superior, but I look forward to less responsibility as I grow older.

I am sorry to hear about the choice of a husband your niece has made. Sometimes we try to influence people to make positive choices in their lives, but in the end, they make their own decisions, right or wrong. We can only be there when they need us. I hope your nephews are doing well and in good health. I fear there will be a war in Europe soon, and I hope your nephews will not have to fight. Please continue to write as the years unfold. I am infinitely interested in your well-being and happiness.

With Respect,
Mother Superior

Angela was sure that Italy would enter the war at some point. She hoped America would stay out of the war. Leo was fired from his job at the fire station because he took too many days off, and he and Alicia were forced to live at Leo's parents' house down by the railroad station.

Angela had made an abundance of Chicken Parmesan and decided to bring some to Alicia as a surprise. She put on her coat and slowly walked to the house by the railway station. As Angela was about to knock on the door, Leo ran out of the house.

"Where are you going?" Angela asked.

She heard Alicia crying and found her face down on the floor, covering her head. Angela turned Alicia's head. Her face was bruised, and she had a bloody lip.

"Is that fool drunk?" asked Angela. "You're coming home with me. You need to see a doctor."

Angela went into the kitchen and got some ice.

"Can't the doctor come here?" asked Alicia.

"Leo is an animal, and you should not be here. Pack a few things right now."

Angela and Alicia walked to Morning Glory Avenue. When they arrived, Angela called her neighbor, Dr. Martens. He went upstairs to see Alicia.

Franco pounded the table.

"This is no good!" yelled Franco. "Someone should take care of Leo."

"Alicia will stay with us," said Angela. "Leo can go to hell."

Dr. Martens came down the stairs. "Well, she's resting now," he said. "Why would anyone do that? Her husband should be in jail."

"Thank you, doctor, for coming," said Angela. "We will take care of Alicia and her husband."

Chapter 10

Summary 1940

Angela was in the dining room, working on a new pattern for a client. She was working with a white Italian wool fabric purchased from a high-end fabric store in Manhattan. She loved the process of fitting the pieces together and creating a final product. This was one area of her life that she could control. The outcome was always beautiful and harmonious. She knew her clients' bodies so well that very little alteration was necessary once she constructed the garment.

"Hello, Aunt," said Nunzio as he came in from the kitchen, tossing an apple in his right hand. He took off his jacket and hung it on a chair.

"Please do not put your jacket there," Angela said. "Hang it in the closet."

"I joined the Marines," said Nunzio. He bit into the apple.

"What? What are you talking about?"

"I've joined the Marines."

"You did not discuss this with me and your uncle."

"We are probably going to war at some point, and I want to be a part of it. I leave for basic training next week in San Diego."

"War has not been declared."

"Oh, it's only a matter of time. Italy is in the war now, and I know a few guys who signed up, so I did too. I'll be in California for four months, and then who knows where."

He took a handgun out of his pocket and presented it like it was a toy.

"Put that away. You have no idea what you are doing. This is not a game."

Angela had had a taste of a war zone and knew that her nephew was a follower and would not protect the truly vulnerable. She'd observed over the years that Nunzio had a strong body, but his mind was limited in its scope. She felt that he had inherited Salvatore's way of thinking. Nunzio did not see beyond himself, did not empathize with others, was easily swayed, and lacked inner conviction. Like his father, Nunzio believed that all vulnerable and weak humans who allowed themselves to be dominated, especially those not able to make it in America, deserved ill treatment.

"I have signed up, so I have to go," Nunzio said.

"Do not tell your uncle. I will do that."

The day Angela had feared was descending on her like a stone building. Her life had not gone as she had wished, and the lives she had envisioned for those she loved was not going the way she had intended.

* * *

Maybe if Nunzio got married, he would become a more sympathetic human being, Angela thought. Ramina and Gianni Gallucci's daughter, Mary, had an eye for Nunzio. Why wouldn't she? He had Hollywood good looks with a well-toned body and a sly smile. Her parents had encouraged the match, but Angela did not understand why. She loved her nephew, but he was prone to immature behavior. If she opposed the match, the Galluccis would think that Angela felt her nephew was too good for their daughter. In the Italian community, that would be a grave insult—so Angela remained neutral. She often cautioned Nunzio to treat Mary with respect. If he did not, word would get around the Italian community that Angela had raised someone with the manners of a hooligan. This, she stressed to her nephew on occasion, would reflect badly on her. Nothing was worse to Angela than a tainted reputation, especially among her own community. Her mostly non-immigrant clients were more sophisticated in their approach to life, so she did not mind conveying her fears and doubts to them, especially regarding family.

Nunzio had been reluctant to get involved with Mary. He knew that her parents treated her well and that she was used to getting her own way. She did not work and was clearly looking for a man to take care of her. This he was not prepared to do. Angela was surprised about how quiet he was around Mary. He was not his usual boisterous self.

Angela wondered how she would get on without Nunzio. Franco could no longer perform certain tasks around the house. Who would mow the lawn and do the yard work?

"I will be proud to wear the Marine uniform," said Nunzio, lifting his chest.

"I am grateful to this country," Angela said, "but I do not agree with war on any account. "I wanted you to get an education."

"The Marines accepted me. It is too late," Nunzio said. "What else would I do with my life? I didn't finish high school."

"You could learn a trade," Angela said.

"I want to wear a uniform and be somebody," Nunzio said, raising his voice.

He turned and walked out of the house.

Angela felt demoralized, not knowing which way to turn. She had done her best to instill sensitivity into her nephew, but she had failed. After all that she had survived, she could not let others' decisions destroy what she wanted to create in her own life. Whenever she felt bewildered, she would read the letters her brother had written to her while he was in the orphanage. She was so grateful that he had survived the earthquake. While she was at the convent, she had visions of them living together one day. She dreamed that once she was 18 and on her own, she would collect her brother and they would return to Messina to look for their younger sister. She tried to convince him that they would continue to look for her, but he did not share her sentiments. His death ended that hope.

Angela went into her bedroom and opened the top dresser drawer. She took out a stack of letters wrapped with red ribbon. She pulled on the bow and selected a letter.

Palermo, 8/2/1910

My Dearest Sister,

I hope this letter finds you well. I am suffering with a cough, but I am feeling better today. I am writing to you to say, my dear Angela, that authorities say it is impossible for our sister, Maria, to still be alive. Please do not think about her any more. Do not torment your mind, because you will need a clear mind for your future. You must keep an open heart so that you can go on with your life in a happy manner. My hope for you is that you will find peace.

With Affection,
Your brother, Enrico

Angela had read this letter so many times that it was falling apart. She knew it by heart. Holding the letter and reading the words on the page, she could almost feel that he was still alive. After he died, this letter was a reminder for her to follow her heart, regardless of outside circumstances. How was he so sure their sister was dead? Why would he give up so easily? She never got the chance to ask him. His cough got worse, and he had died of pneumonia not long after she received this letter.

* * *

Angela heard her husband coming in the front door.

"Franco," said Angela.

Franco was more than familiar with that tone of voice. It meant she needed his undivided attention so that she could present her opinion on some grave matter and, if he did not agree, she would take matters into her own hands. He noticed this tendency was manifesting more frequently every year. She was an American now, coupled with a strong cultural presence based on an arcane past. Most likely Angela would tell him about a situation with Nunzio and what she intended to do to alter any unseemly outcome.

"Why do you think Nunzio joined the Marines without our permission?" sked Angela. She helped Franco off with his coat.

"That is all right. He will serve his country." He shuffled into the dining room.

"He is so young. What if he goes overseas and is killed?" asked Angela.

Franco sat in his smoking chair and lit a cigar, thinking of how she had babied all Speranza's children. She always wanted to know where they were, as if her knowing would keep them safe. Nunzio had enlisted several days ago, and she was still talking about it as if she could change the outcome. It was time that his nephew grew up. The Marines would take care of that. As he blew smoke, he imagined he was forming clouds. God was not the only creator in the natural world. Humans could form clouds by their own means.

"Franco, did you hear what I said?" Angela asked.

Franco had heard Angela, but he did not have anything to say. He withheld a response, because he did not want to have a conversation. She wanted him to discuss issues important to the family, but he did not have energy or the language.

"I don't understand how calm you are about this," Angela said. "We may never see him again if he goes to war."

"It's done. No more talk," Franco said. He walked into the kitchen and went down to the cellar. It was the only way to avoid a heated discussion.

* * *

Angela stepped off the steps of the Sacred Heart church.

"Hello, Angela," said Ramina Gallucci. "How are you doing? It was such a beautiful mass."

"Yes, it was," Angela said. "I always enjoy Father Barberino's sermons."

In Angela's mind, she was not being disingenuous; she was telling a friend what she wanted to hear. *This is how you get along in the world*, Angela thought. Pretending to adapt to someone's opinion, she believed, saved many arguments.

"It was very nice of you to invite us for dinner tonight," said Gianni, dressed in one of his impeccably designed suits.

"My husband and I enjoy your company," Angela said.

Most of the husbands in Angela's circle of friends attended mass with their wives. Franco had never attended mass, even in his healthy days. He felt that the church did everything it could to control people. Angela would tell the wives that he was working, or later, that he was not feeling well because of his stroke. She felt that Franco was right on many levels, but this was one concession she was willing to make so that her standing in the community would not be diminished.

"Mary will be coming with us," said Mrs. Gallucci. "We cannot leave a young girl at home alone."

"Wonderful. I will be glad to see her."

Angela hoped Nunzio would be on his best behavior.

"My daughter is very interested in your nephew," Ramina said.

Ramina Gallucci wanted to make it clear that Nunzio had an obligation to court her daughter and that an invitation to dinner included Mary. "Nunzio seems immature, but I am sure when he enters basic training he will change. You must be proud he is willing to fight for his country."

Most parents were proud of their sons when they joined the Service, but Angela was not willing to lose her nephew to war, regardless of the conflict's legitimacy. Parents of enlisted men were willing to sacrifice their sons for freedom. Angela was not willing to do that for the kind of superficial freedom the government offered. She remembered her parents' attitude toward the Italian government; any law instituted by the government was suspect. Sicilians were not patriotic by nature. They held a deep-seeded belief that the people who controlled the population were not only the politicians, but an unseen entity that permeated every aspect of life. She had thought that America would be different, but she felt she had been wrong.

"Well, I would have preferred that he did not join the military, but it is done now."

"Noooo," bellowed Gianni. "Every young man wants to join up these days. It makes them feel important, and they become stronger physically and mentally."

"Well, I look forward to seeing you both tonight," Angela said. "And Mary, too."

Angela began her walk home. She would have to tell Nunzio that Mary would be coming to dinner and that any plans that he made would have to be canceled.

* * *

Angela would usually start entertaining in the spring and progress throughout the summer. She placed candlesticks at each end of the table and two in the middle. She stepped back to take in her tablescape. *Perfectly balanced*, she thought. The crisp, white linen tablecloth, combined with white candles and glass candlesticks, created a light, inviting look. So much white could create a sterile feel, but with the twilight summer light coming in through the windows, yellows and reds bounced off the linen and glass. She moved the chairs out just enough from the table for guests could slip into their seats easily.

A sharp ring of the doorbell snapped Angela to attention. Before she could step out of the dining room, it rang again.

"Come in, the door is open," Angela said.

The front door swung open. Mary Galluci stepped into the vestibule with her parents behind her.

"Mary," Angela said, "how nice to see you. Come in, come in."

Mary's dress was a floral pattern with reds, blues, and oranges. She wore a hat with the same pattern and white gloves. Her red lipstick was artfully applied.

"Angela, it is so nice of you to invite us," Ramina said.

"Where is Franco?" asked Gianni. Gianni was dressed in another blue suit.

"He will be in the dining room in a minute," Angela said. "Please go in."

Gianni left the women to chat in the hallway.

"Mary, you are so stylish. Your dress has a lovely pattern." Angela thought the material was too loud. It was not a pattern she would ever use for her clients, and it was not appropriate for a quiet dinner.

"I love your home, Mrs. Bellini," Mary said.

Mary circumambulated the spacious hallway like a cat marking its territory. As she walked past Angela, the aroma of her perfume brushed Angela's nostrils.

"The high ceilings make the hallway feel bigger," said Ramina. "Nunzio lives upstairs, doesn't he?"

Angela walked over to the bottom of the stairs.

"Nunzio, the Gallucis are here," Angela said.

No response.

"Nunzio."

"Ok," Nunzio said, "I'm coming."

"He will be down for dinner. Come and sit in the dining room."

Angela liked Mary, but she was not so sure she and Nunzio were compatible. Mary walked over to the bottom of the staircase.

"Nunzio, come down," Mary said. "It's time for dinner, and I have not seen you in a while. I would like to see you before you leave for California."

She sounded like a songbird calling for its mate.

Nunzio bounded down the staircase in a jacket and pressed pants.

"You look so handsome," Mary said. "Doesn't he, Mama?" She gazed at Nunzio approvingly.

"He certainly does," Ramina said.

Nunzio walked over to the mirror on the mantle, straightened his collar, and pulled on his jacket sleeves. Angela thought how much he looked like his mother. His deep brown eyes were Speranza's, peering into world she had left long ago. Nunzio was a fine example of male Italian beauty. He had a face of delicate, unexpressed emotionality, but his conceited nature kept many of the girls away.

Gianni found Franco sitting in his smoking chair reading a newspaper. The headline read, "Luftwaffe raids on channel shipping. President Roosevelt asks Congress for increase in Military preparations."

"Franco," Gianni said, "I see you are keeping up with war events."

"Yes," Franco said. "How are you?"

"You must be very proud Nunzio has enlisted," Gianni said.

"Yes," said Franco. "He will fight."

"Well, maybe the war will end before he has to go overseas," Gianni said.

Franco folded the paper and moved to the edge of the chair. He clutched his cane with one hand.

"Let me help you up," Gianni said.

He offered Franco his hand. This was the first time, other than his wife or medical staff, that anyone had offered him assistance. Before his stroke, Franco was viewed by the community as a bombastic person with a propensity for unprovoked outbursts. He was viewed as strong and self-sufficient, never needing anyone's help. He placed his hand in Gianni's and lifted himself to standing.

"You all right?" Gianni asked. He patted Franco's shoulder.

Franco nodded and, guided by his cane and Gianni, shuffled to his seat at the head of the table.

Angela escorted Ramina, Mary, and Nunzio into the dining room.

"Nunzio and Mary can sit together so they can talk," Ramina said. "Tell us, Nunzio, when do you go for basic training?"

"This week," Nunzio said.

"Well, I will be waiting for you," Mary said.

She touched his arm and gazed at the side of his face. Nunzio looked down at his plate, then away from Mary's gaze.

Angela saw what Ramina was attempting to instigate. Memories of Speranza and Salvatore sitting at the same table came back, only it was Paolina who had maneuvered that relationship.

"I will get the lasagna and chicken," Angela said. "Ramina, can you help me carry the food?"

"Of course."

As she went into the kitchen, Ramina looked back at the young couple and signaled to Mary to continue to talk to Nunzio. Gianni poured a glass of wine for himself and Franco.

"Nunzio, I will miss you when you go to basic training," Mary said.

Nunzio remained silent, and the less he responded, the more she talked.

"We will all miss you. Won't we, Franco?" Gianni said.

"Yes," Franco said. He sipped his wine.

Angela saw Mary rub Nunzio's arm. He turned away and looked out the window, unsure of how to respond. Angela felt Mary was after more than he could give. She was happy he would have a sometime girlfriend but sensed he did not want to have to relate to her constantly. Nunzio had joined the Marines because all young men wanted to fight for their country and become heroes, but she knew he also saw the war as an opportunity to get away from everyone and everything familiar.

Angela observed the interaction between the couple. The Gallucis wanted the relationship to work because they wanted to have their daughter marry an Italian. Angela wanted Nunzio to be happy and not settle for the first girl who showed interest.

"Mary, why don't you start to pass the lasagna?" Angela asked.

She handed the platter to Mary. Ramina came out of the kitchen with the platter of chicken and placed it on the table.

"How is everything going here?" Ramina asked. "Mary and Nunzio, you two look wonderful together. Don't you think so, Angela?"

"Well, they are both good looking people." Angela said. "Nunzio is leaving, so it is nice they get to say goodbye."

"Why don't we eat instead of talk," Gianni said.

Angela was relieved Gianni intervened. Mary was loquacious and often talked without noticing others' behavior around her. *The only good thing about Nunzio going to basic training in California*, Angela thought, *was that Mary would not have access to him.*

"Let us make a toast to all our soldiers," Gianni said. "Soon America will be at war, and our men will end this."

"How do you know America will win?" asked Angela.

"President Roosevelt is building a strong army. We will win."

Angela lifted her wine glass in silence while everyone called out, "To our troops!"

Angela shared a snippet of her deeply held conviction. "I think we are battling a force that has always won, and to best this energy will take more than guns and tanks. We have to look behind the curtain to see who is creating the conflict,"

"What are you talking about?" Ramina asked.

"Like in Sicily," said Angela. "We knew the priests were controlled by the wealthy in the north, but we did not know who they were."

"But this is not Sicily," said Gianni. "You will see. We will triumph." He loaded his fork with lasagna and a piece of chicken. The portion was so large that Angela thought he would not be able to chew.

"This is what is wrong," said Angela. "We feed our bellies while we are all manipulated."

"You have always had quite the imagination," said Ramina.

"I do not see why my nephew has to risk his life for the wealthy," Angela said. "They sell the military to young men. If they don't join, they create a war—so they feel compelled to join."

"That is nonsense. Nunzio, I am sure your father is very proud that you joined the Marines. Aren't you proud of him, Franco?" asked Ramina.

"Yes, he is strong and brave," Franco said.

"I don't really talk to my father much," Nunzio said. Nunzio saw his father and stepmother as flawed, troubled people, and he did not like to be associated with them. When he did not talk about them, in his mind, they did not exist. His father's remarriage was a shame that coated Nunzio's presence like concrete. He thought if he did not acknowledge his father, no one would see or sense it.

"Oh, you are being modest," Mary said. "I am sure he is telling all the neighbors how proud he is."

Mary placed her arm around Nunzio's chair. He leaned forward and wished the Gallucis would eat and leave. They had not finished their entrée, and then there was dessert and espresso. *This could go on forever*, he thought. He glanced at his watch.

"You know I promised a friend that I would help him fix his car. I completely forgot. I really have to go."

"Who needs you to help?" asked Angela.

"Jimmy Sanamo."

"Oh, I did not know he had a car," Angela said. "But if you have to help him, go ahead."

Angela was glad he was leaving, regardless of whether he was telling the truth. She was trying to hold her tongue about Nunzio's father, Salvatore, but was not sure how long she could withhold her opinion.

"I am sure our guests will understand," Angela said.

"Of course," said Gianni. "When a man needs help, he needs help."

"Do you have to go?" asked Mary. "I wanted to invite you to a party I am having tomorrow evening. It is for a friend's birthday."

"Yes, come, Nunzio," said Ramina. "We would love to see you before you leave."

"Ok," Nunzio said. He kept his gaze down as he left the table.

"At five o'clock tomorrow," said Mary. She turned and saw his back as he left the house.

"Did I say something wrong?" whimpered Mary.

"No, Mary," Angela said. "My nephew if very young. He is not ready for marriage."

"I think once he goes into the service, he will be more mature," Ramina said. "You need to be patient. He will come around. Keep inviting him."

"Who would like cannoli and espresso?" Angela asked.

"I am ready," Gianni said. "How about you, Franco?"

"Ready," Franco said.

Gianni leaned back and patted his expansive belly.

* * *

Nunzio stood on Mary Galluci's porch in his Marine uniform and knocked on the door.

"Come in," said a voice.

There were young people sitting around the living room with a "Happy Birthday, Alfred!" banner draped between the dining room and the living room.

"Nunzio," said Mary. "I am so glad you're here. You look so handsome. Come and meet my friends."

He looked around for anyone else in uniform but saw that he was the only one. Many of Mary's friends were in college, so they could still get a deferment because it was still peacetime.

"Everyone, this is my boyfriend, Nunzio. He leaves in a few days for basic training."

"Hi, Nunzio," said one of the young men. "We were in the same class at Nelsonville High School. How have you been?"

"Not bad," said Nunzio. He was embarrassed he didn't finish high school, but the Marines didn't care about that. They accepted him regardless. He didn't recognize his classmate.

"I'm Gerry. Gerry Hamilton."

"Oh, right," said Nunzio. He remembered Gerry as a successful student who was part of the student counsel.

Nunzio had floundered after he left school at 16. He helped Franco and Angela and hung out with friends who didn't finish high school. Joining the Marines was the right choice. He was getting out of Nelsonville and would possibly make the military his career.

Mary held onto Nunzio's arm and directed him over to a group of young women who surrounded a man wearing houndstooth jacket.

"Nunzio, this is the birthday boy, Alfred," Mary said.

"Wow, that's quite a uniform," said Alfred. "What branch of service?"

"The Marines," Mary said.

"Mary has generously given me this party." He walked over and kissed Mary on both cheeks. "She's quite a find, don't you think?"

Nunzio smiled and nodded.

"Just finished my second year in college," said Alfred. "Not sure if I will come back to Nelsonville after I'm done. What will you do after you get out?"

"I haven't thought about it. I just joined."

"It's good to have a plan," Alfred said. He lit a cigarette. "If you don't have a plan, you'll end up someplace random."

Growing up, Nunzio never saw anyone plan for their lives. He realized Franco and Angela must have had a plan to build their skills and buy such a beautiful house. He had benefitted from their labors, but he never saw how they were able to become successful. He looked around the room and saw well-dressed young people who seemed to have direction in life with many choices. Maybe in the future he'll have more choices, he hoped.

"I just wanted to drop by and say hello," Nunzio said.

"But we're going to have cake," Mary said. "You haven't met everyone, and I thought we'd spend more time together."

"I'm helping out at the recruitment office tonight, and I have to pack."

"I will drop by before you leave," Mary said.

"Good luck to you," said Alfred. "Quite a mess in Europe. Hope you don't have to go to war."

Nunzio closed the door behind him and realized that his path was very different than Mary's. He didn't know what his path was, but it did not include her.

* * *

Angela had assisted Franco into bed and turned out the lights. The house was silent without Nunzio there, especially at night. Hearing his footsteps had given her comfort. Now she could hear every creak and tumbling of the house as if it had its own language, and she started to understand its expressions. Sometimes she would hear the house moan as it shifted in its foundation and missed its upstairs inhabitant. Angela had forgotten to get the mail earlier, so she went out to the porch to bring it in. There were some bills and advertisements, and then there was a letter from Franco's cousin, Roberto. He was still living in Paris, and his letters were sporadic. She thought about waiting until Franco got up in the morning to read it, but she did not want to wait. Angela sat in Franco's smoking chair and opened the envelope.

June 1940

My Dearest Angela and Cousin Franco,

I am taking this opportunity to write a quick letter to you from a fallen city—a city I have loved almost as much as I love my home-land. It is no longer a city of outward light, but one of cowering souls who walk with their heads down for fear of the Gestapo. Many prominent Jews are disappearing from the city, and writers who speak out against the occupation are being sent to death camps. I am giving this letter to a friend who is making his way to Switzerland and will mail it. I hope it finds you. My wife sends you her best, and we think of you often. Family is important, and I am hoping that I survive this evil so that one day I will be able to visit you in America.

We are hoping that the Allies can do something about this evil soon. There are investors who are profiting from this war. We will never know who they are, but someone is making money. Still, I believe that I will survive with my family and we will one day return home. Please write to me when you can and tell me how you are doing. I know Franco's health is not so good, but I am hoping that you, Angela, are as healthy and strong as ever. I can still remember the day I told Franco to go to the convent and look at the available girls. Since the day I met you through my sister Patricia (you remember her, she was a student at the convent), I have thought highly of you. I am glad Franco chose you. Until next time.

With Great Affection,
Roberto, Il Poeta

The bulk of the letter was addressed to Angela. She held it close to her heart and wondered if she should even share it with Franco. She felt her unseen friends were telling her not to share the letter. Much of the news was the same as the last letters. Franco would never know. Angela put the letter in her pocketbook. Like the letters from her brother, she would read Roberto's letter whenever she needed a heartfelt connection. Tomorrow she would put it in with her other cherished letters.

She ascended the stairs and stopped at the top. A mirror hung on the wall over the telephone table. Angela stared into it. Her reflection had changed over the years, but her cheekbones were still high, and she had no fat under her chin. Her skin was as smooth as the day she arrived in New York. The grey hair was the only sign of her struggles and disappointments. She still held hope that these rooms would one day be filled with children. Nunzio had used the large front room as his bedroom, but it was perfect for a living room. There were also three smaller rooms, a kitchen, and two bathrooms. The children could come and go as they pleased between downstairs and upstairs. Angela walked into the smaller room that faced the street. She went out on the small, enclosed porch that was connected to the room and overlooked Morning Glory Avenue. The streetlights cast sharp shadows on the street.

During these quiet hours, her unseen friends came to mind. They told her not to concern herself about Nunzio and that he would return to her even if he had to fight in a war. It was not his time, they assured her. Since they were able to transcend time and space, she assumed they could see the future—and they saw her nephew in that future. She would have conversations with them in her mind, and she would be comforted that she had someone to listen to her and respond with insight. Tonight, she told them how worried she was about Speranza's children and the difficult start they had in life. Her entire life was not going as she had planned, nor were the lives of Speranza's children.

She went downstairs to the dining room and took out Roberto's letter and read it again. She began to formulate her response. This would be about her and no one else. Angela had never asked Roberto about what he knew regarding her origins and her family.

July 1940

My Dear Roberto,

I hope this letter finds you well and that you are content and safe in Paris. We just received your letter today, and I am sorry to hear that Paris has been invaded by such a terrible force. I felt your letter spoke about me and my journey. You said that I was strong, and you were glad that Franco chose me. I still write to the Mother Superior at the convent, and she passes the information onto Principessa

Giulia. I have not corresponded with the Principessa directly, but she seems to still have an interest in my life. I often wonder why. While I was at the convent, she treated me with great kindness and respect—much more than the other girls. Why she had this interest is unknown to me. So, I ask you if you have any information about why she would show me such favor. Maybe your sister has some information.

I hope you can return to your beloved Sicily as soon as the war ends. I think of you often. Please give our regards to your wife. I will never forget her kindness when we visited Sicily in 1929. Write when you can and may the Blessed Mother watch over you until you return to your homeland.

Forever Grateful,
Angela

This was the first time Angela had asked anyone about Principessa Giulia's connection to her life. She had dismissed it in her own mind as good luck, but she felt like there was more to the story. If Roberto had information, she was hoping he would share it—not that it would make any difference in her life. She had no intention of returning to Sicily, and America was her home now. She was free from Europe's carnage from wars, and she was grateful every day that the Blessed Mother and her unseen friends had guided her to the United States, despite all her disappointments. But even with all her good fortune, there was something missing. There were gaps in her own story. She sealed the letter, went out to the porch, and placed the airmail letter in the mailbox.

* * *

Angela saw Sadie walking up her steps swinging her heavy, tattered pocketbook in her hand as if she were about to swat someone.

"Hey, Angie, how are ya?"

"Oh, hello Sadie. I am glad you dropped by."

"Well, that's something I don't hear often, but I'm glad you feel that way. How is everything going?"

"Nunzio is taking basic training in San Diego. He is there for twelve weeks, and then he will be home on leave. I miss him."

"At least he's not fighting some war in Europe," Sadie said. "Since Italy got into the war, I have lost a few cousins who are fighting with the resistance. At least we're not in the war."

"That is how I feel," Angela said. "We finally have some luck."

"I was on my way into town, so I thought I would stop."

"I will make coffee, and I have just made anisette cookies."

They went into the house as the phone rang.

It was Ramina Galluci. After exchanging pleasantries, Ramina explained that she was disappointed that Nunzio did not call Mary before he left for San Diego.

"I cannot interfere in this," Angela said. "Ramina, If Mary is interested in marriage, she should seek a husband elsewhere. She deserves someone more committed than my nephew. I have company. I will see you at mass on Sunday."

"Ramina is a pain," she muttered to Sadie. "She keeps pestering me about Nunzio and why he does not commit to Mary. It is obvious that he doesn't have an interest in her. She is not vibrant or independent enough."

"I agree," said Sadie. "You would think she'd have given up by now. I have heard about women becoming pregnant so that the men will marry them. Happens every day."

"What do you mean? I hope Nunzio doesn't do that. Then he'd be stuck with her."

"That's for sure," said Sadie. "You better warn him when he comes home on leave. Mary might be getting desperate."

Angela thought she would not like Mary living upstairs with Nunzio. She had had enough of dependent people.

"I will talk to him when he comes home."

"Where's the coffee?" asked Sadie.

Angela poured the coffee and set out the cookies.

"Are things with Alicia the same?"

"Leo got a menial job cleaning floors at the hospital. Sometimes I see marks on her, but she won't leave him. It makes me furious. I won't allow him in my house. Franco doesn't want him here either."

"Maybe she'll realize that it doesn't benefit her to stay with him."

"Salvatore doesn't seem to take a stand, so I just don't know what to do."

Angela invited Alicia to the house frequently and encouraged her to attend her dinners or luncheons.

"Divorce is more common these days," said Sadie. You should encourage Alicia to divorce him. Don't tell anyone I said that. I should get going. I'll call you tomorrow."

* * *

Chapter 11

Summer 1941

Angela was waiting for a friend of Sarah Einbinder's, Julia Steinberger. Mrs. Steinberger was known in town for her flamboyant personality and business acumen. After her husband's death, she had taken on his lumber business and made a great deal of money selling to contractors statewide. This was her first fitting with Angela. Angela had opened the door to enjoy the summer air and refresh the house.

As Angela pulled the sewing machine out of its cabinet, she saw a tall, slim woman a little younger than herself in a red dress and a hat with a multi-colored feather. Angela went out to greet her new customer.

"Hello, Mrs. Steinberger. I am Angela Bellini."

"Hello, Mrs. Bellini. I have heard so much about your talents, and I need them now."

"Let's go inside," said Angela. "I have some coffee."

"Oh, isn't that nice of you," Mrs. Steinberger said. "I am so looking forward to having a garment made by you. This is a beautiful home, Mrs. Bellini. How long have you owned it?"

"For 20 years," Angela said.

"Is it just you and your husband?" Julia asked.

"Yes. My nephew also lives upstairs. Right now, he is in the Marines."

Julia lifted her gaze to the ceiling and strolled around the hall.

"These ceilings are magnificent. How high are they?"

"About 15 feet," Angela said. "Let's go in and have coffee. I am afraid it will get cold. What is it you would like me to make?"

Angela poured two cups of espresso.

"I saw the gown you made for Sarah Einbinder, and I was so impressed that I would like you to make me a gown for my daughter's wedding."

"That is a wonderful idea. When is the wedding, and what style were you thinking?"

"Something modern. Something that does not scream mother-of-the-bride. I have a slim figure, and I want to show it off. The wedding is at the end of January. I hope it's not short notice."

"Not at all," said Angela. "I have several patterns that would interest you."

Angela did not understand the American obsession with youth. Julia Steinberger was the mother of adult children, and no amount of dressmaking could change that.

"What color? I think silk taffeta is a good choice," Angela said.

"I love the idea of silk. Not everyone can work with silk successfully, but I have seen your work. I was thinking of a rose color. What do you think?"

"I think the family of reds is a good start," said Angela. "It will be winter, so I suggest maroon. This way you can accessorize with brighter colors."

"Oh, what a good idea," Julia said. "You are very knowledgeable."

Angela often wondered why Americans chose material and color for dresses that did not suit them. In her experience, when she did not make suggestions to her customers, the results were usually less than ideal. The color often made them look washed out, or, given the customer's figure, an A-line skirt would have been more appropriate. Over the years, she had developed confidence in articulating her opinion, and the proof was in the results. Most dressmakers wanted the money and would give customers what they wanted regardless of how it would look. When customers worked with Angela, their garments flattered their body and skin color.

"Wait here, and I will get the patterns," Angela said.

Angela rummaged around her pattern closet.

"Mrs. Steinberger, here are two pattern choices and swatches of material."

"These are gorgeous. I love this pattern."

"With the elbow length sleeves, you'll be able to wear long gloves."

"My daughter is having such a difficult time finding a wedding gown to fit her perfectly. Have you made wedding gowns?" asked Julia.

"Yes, I have over the years. I made my sister-in-law's many years ago, and recently my niece's—but I prefer to make wedding gowns for family." It was a few years after Speranza's death when Angela had a dream that

Speranza was in her wedding gown asking Angela why Salvatore had married so soon after her passing. After that dream, it was impossible for Angela to make a wedding gown for anyone outside the family.

"Oh, what a pity. I would like her to have a homemade gown. Do you think you might make an exception? Do you have pictures of your niece's gown?"

Angela thought about Mrs. Steinberger's request and decided to bring out the photographs. Maybe it was time for her to expand her creativity. She had had requests for wedding gowns after Speranza died but did not have the heart to make them.

"Yes, and I have a sample of the material."

Angela brought out a photo of Alicia in her gown and a swatch of the material.

"This is gorgeous. Most of the dresses we have looked at did not have this kind of substance. I would like to make an appointment for my daughter to come and see you."

"It doesn't give me much time to make a wedding gown."

"I would pay you handsomely," said Julia. "I would appreciate it. She is having difficulty finding something she likes."

"All right," said Angela. She loved making wedding gowns, but the two marriages she made gowns for did not turn out well. But for whatever reason, she did not feel the resistance she had once felt about making wedding gowns.

"Wonderful, I will tell her to call you," said Julia.

"Ok, come to the mirror and I will take your measurements."

Later that evening, Angela took out Speranza's gown and hung it in her bedroom. She had hidden it away for years. When Speranza died, her husband wanted to bury her in her wedding dress. Angela took it from the house and refused to give it to him. She felt that Salvatore was attempting to bury her memory. Originally, she would take it out and hold it close to her cheek so that she could feel Speranza's softness and fun nature. It was as if a piece of her was still here, and that made Angela happy. She did not think that anyone passed away completely and that those who were dead communicated with the living. Her unseen friends told her this, and since then, she believed those who passed over could leave messages that communicated they were present at times.

One day, Angela had found that the picture of Speranza and herself moved from the left side of her vanity to the right. She was right-handed and always kept her hairbrushes on the right side. She was sure she didn't move the photo. When she was alone, she often sensed Speranza and those who had passed, but she had never experienced earth communication. Maybe Speranza was sending Mrs. Steinberger's daughter to her for a reason.

* * *

Angela opened the door for her three o'clock client.

"I am Alice Steinberger. My mother sent me to talk to you, but I must be honest. I have seen some homemade gowns, and I think they look too homespun for me. I want something modern, not old world."

This was Angela's first encounter with negativity around her work. It was obvious that Alice was not familiar with the quality of Angela's garments, yet she felt this was a new generation that would wear her creations.

"You are an observant girl. Many gowns made today do not look like a professional created them. I have been sewing since I was 15, and I can tell you everyone looks and feels good in my designs. A wedding gown is not a simple dress to make. It must be done with the bride's intentions in mind. You are a modern girl, so we would use a modern theme."

"Well, I suppose I can see what you have done," said Alice.

Willingness was all Angela needed. She brought out Speranza's gown, a picture of Alicia's wedding dress, and some patterns.

"I made this gown in 1929 for my sister-in-law. I know it may look old-fashioned, but at the time it was popular. The picture is a gown I made for my niece a year ago. A combination of vintage and modern would be a nice touch."

"This is very beautiful," Alice said, standing back and looking at the entire dress.

"Your sister-in-law was very thin," Alice said. "Has married life made her heavier?"

"No," Angela said, "she passed away many years ago."

"I am sorry, Mrs. Bellini. I did not know."

"That is all right. Here are the patterns that I purchased. They are modern, but I can alter them so they will have a vintage feel."

"I like the one with the lower neckline."

"Yes, that is a popular pattern. I can make it a little differently if you like. Every bride should put her stamp on her wedding gown."

"How would you do that?"

"I could sew pearls where the train meets the dress and around the bodice, or I could embroider anywhere you would like an accent."

"That sounds wonderful," said Alice.

"If you like, I can put the pattern together and cut it out in white organza without obligation."

"Yes, I would like that. Thank you, Mrs. Bellini, I see why my mother and her friends speak highly of you."

"I will call you when I have the mock-up done."

"I want a gown that my fiancé will love," Alice said.

"What does your fiancé do?"

In America, Angela knew that was what you should ask when meeting someone. This information informed how a person was treated. In Sicily, people were concerned with who the person was inside.

Angela paused and looked at Alice's face. Written on it was the promise of the new world. Speranza did not live to collect on America's promise, but Angela's greatest hope was that Speranza's children would benefit from the new world the way Alice was benefitting. Angela knew a girl like Alice would never be interested in someone like Nunzio. Alice had education, confidence and money, and she would marry someone with the same privileges. If Nunzio, Alicia or Joe had children, she vowed she would make sure they would be successful.

"He is in law school," Alice said. "We are hoping he will be able to set up an office in town."

"As long as he treats you well, that is what is important," Angela said.

"Of course he does. He is like my father. Please let me know when the mock-up is ready."

After Alice left, Angela thought about Alicia and the choice she had made in marrying Leo. She had hoped Alicia's life would be like Alice's, who was marrying a professional man who treated her well. They would never have to worry about money, and they would send their children to college. If Angela persisted, maybe she could help Alicia change her mind about Leo. *Anything can be changed,* she thought, *with persistence and strength.*

* * *

Angela hung Alice Steinberger's dress on the full-length mirror. Alice had chosen one of the modern patterns using the same material Angela had used for Alicia's wedding dress. Alice had been delighted with the mock-up gown and decided to have Angela make her dress with beads and lace around the edges to give it a vintage feel. If Alice had bought the gown at a New York department store, it would have cost more than double Angela's price. Angela stepped back and admired her work. It had taken her three months to complete the dress. She felt that Speranza would have approved.

The doorbell rang.

"Come in, come in, Alice."

"Mrs. Bellini, how are you? I was surprised when you called and said my gown was finished. I thought it would be two more weeks. Oh my, is this it?"

Alice touched her gown and expanded the train so that all of Angela's intricate work was exposed.

"How did you do this? I have not seen anything like it in the bridal shops."

"Would you like to try it on?" Angela asked.

"Right away, please."

As Alice went into Angela's bedroom to put on her dress, Angela remembered the day Speranza had tried on her wedding dress. When Angela looked deeper, she saw that the gown had transformed Speranza into a woman stepping into her future with grace and elegance. It was no longer about her choice of a mate, but the transformative power of a garment made with intention. The alchemy was unmistakable; this was why she sewed.

Alice appeared in the doorway of Angela's bedroom. The intention that Angela held in creating Alice's gown was melding the old and the modern, and it worked amazingly. The bride was the integration of a generation that had immigrated and their offspring. Angela was mindful of honoring the past when creating a garment that transitioned a woman from one stage of life to another. It was a declaration in time that respected the past but celebrated the future. She had made many Baptism gowns, which brought a child from sin into purity. Although she did not hold the belief that babies were born with original sin, she thought it was an opportunity for babies to acquire another set of parents in case they lost their first set.

The sight of Alice left Angela stunned. The garment and the bride expressed everything that she had intended.

"You are a beautiful bride," Angela said. "I wish you all the happiness that the world and the spirits can give. Let me hook you up in the back."

"It's funny that you should say spirits," Alice said. "My grandmother talked about spirits in her house in Poland. She said they told her what to avoid and gave her formulas for medicine."

"Whether we know it or not, we all have spirits who guide us," Angela said. "Even though we think we've lost them, they are still with us. You are starting a new part of your life. Let the world we cannot see guide you."

Alice was a stranger, and yet Angela felt comfortable expressing her inner thoughts.

"How did you come to America?"

"I was at a convent, an orphanage, in Palermo, Italy, and my husband came from America and found me at the convent. A meeting was arranged, and that was the end and the beginning."

"What do you mean?"

"It was the end of my life as I knew it and the beginning of my connection with the new world."

"I'm sorry you were an orphan, but I'm glad you came to America. If you hadn't, I wouldn't have this beautiful dress."

Alice stepped up on the platform. The mirror reflected a fresh and magnetic energy. The gown was ornate enough to suggest femininity and sleek enough to suggest strength and purpose.

"Mrs. Bellini, if you don't mind my asking, if you had stayed in Sicily, what would you have done? Do you think you would have married?"

"I would have become a nun," Angela said. "I had no family, so I would have stayed at the convent."

"I am sure you were beautiful. Surely someone would have proposed."

Angela thought about that possibility. It had never crossed her mind that that would have happened. Maybe someone would have married her if she had stayed.

"I'm sorry, I am being too forward," Alice said. "It is just that I am so happy. I want others to be happy too."

"I think if my sister-in-law were here, you would like each other very much. She liked to think about many possibilities."

"She must have been special."

"She was, to me and to her children," Angela said. "You have to come back next week for the dress. I need to press it."

"What happened to her children?"

"I took care of them, and now they are grown. It was sad for them to lose their mother so young."

"I'm sure it was sad, but they were lucky to have someone like you, like I am lucky to have you create my wedding gown. I will be wearing a dress with a history."

The level of satisfaction Angela felt was enormous. Even with her favorite clients, she had never experienced this kind of satisfaction. The gown was an homage to her sewing history, to Speranza, and to the future.

"Thank you, Mrs. Bellini, for the dress and the conversation."

Angela watched from her window as Alice walked down the porch stairs. Another generation had been changed because of her sewing, and she was certain there would be another generation after that.

* * *

Angela swept the light snow off the porch steps. There had been a dusting earlier in the day, and she liked to have a clear pathway for her customers and friends. The mailman walked up the steps.

"You have a letter from Paris, Mrs. Bellini," said the mailman. "I've heard things are pretty bad over there. It won't be long now until we're in the war."

"That's what they say. Thank you for the mail."

Angela went inside, put her coat away, and sat at the dining room table to open the letter. She heard a knock at the door. She looked out the window and saw Sadie and Claudia Cerverci standing on her porch. It had started to lightly snow again.

"What are you two doing out in this weather?" asked Angela.

"We had nothing better to do, and we figured you could use the company," said Claudia.

"You don't have a customer, do you?" asked Sadie.

"No, not until much later," said Angela.

"Well, then let's have some coffee," said Claudia.

They went into the dining room.

"Let's go in the kitchen," Angela said.

"You got a letter from Paris?" asked Sadie. She picked up the envelope.

"Yes, Franco's cousin, Roberto," said Angela.

"The poet? The one who got Franco to go to the convent?" asked Claudia.

"That's right."

"Wonderful, I would love to hear about what's happening in Europe," said Sadie. "Do you mind reading it?"

"Sadie, I don't think that would be appropriate," said Claudia. "It's addressed to Franco and Angela."

"Nonsense," said Sadie. "Angela, read the letter to yourself, and then tell us the part about what's going on in Paris."

Angela knew that Claudia and Sadie still had family in Italy and were suffering greatly since the war began.

"It would be nice to know what is going on in Paris," said Claudia. "I send packages to my aunt and cousin in Italy, but I haven't received a letter. My mother's sister in Gela is an old woman, and I know there is very little food. I pray they are safe."

Angela saw the anxiety on her friends' faces. Sadie and Claudia were usually easygoing and light-hearted, but today they needed to know about the reality that their families were experiencing.

"All right," said Angela. She opened the letter and began to read to herself. Maybe she should read it all out loud. Who better to share her background with in real time than her good friends? She read it aloud.

December 1940

Dear Angela and Franco,

I am still in this occupied city. There are food and tobacco shortages as well as clothing. Students are beginning to demonstrate, and anti-German groups are popping up all over the city. Jews are forced to wear the yellow star of David badge, and many are being sent to death camps along with others the Nazis consider undesirable.

As for your question about why Principessa Giulia took such an interest in you, I believe it is time for you to know. Europe is in such turmoil, and who knows if I will survive? Here is what I have heard.

Angela looked up and saw Sadie and Claudia, stone-faced, with their mouths open.

"Should I continue?"

"Yes," both women said in unison.

Your father, Mario Lanza, was a distant cousin of Pietro Lanza di Trabia, Giulia's husband. As you know, your father was a silk merchant and spent many months traveling. Pietro's brother, Giuseppe, was a friend of your father's and took an interest in your mother. It is believed you are Giuseppe's daughter. Giuseppe died several years after you were born. After the earthquake, Pietro learned that you had survived and had you brought to Palazzo Butera to make sure you were cared for.

The aristocracy always tries to hide what they consider to be their missteps. Giulia's interest in you was encouraged by her husband, but she possessed a genuine affection for you. In my view, you are not a misstep. I am sure Franco would agree with me when I say he was lucky he married you. I hope this information is not distressing for you and that it explains your experiences at Palazzo Butera. As you know, Pietro passed away several years ago, and I have heard that Principessa Giulia is now in Switzerland in poor health.

"I did not know Pietro passed away," said Angela. "Mother Superior never told me."

"They never told you a lot of things," said Sadie. "Keep reading."

I hope Franco is doing well and that your family is in good health. You are fortunate that America is not part of the war, but I feel it is only a matter of time before your country will have to join us. Please keep writing, even if it takes months to receive an answer.
As Always, with Great Affection
Roberto

"I always knew there was a connection," said Sadie. "What does that make you?"

"It doesn't make me anything," said Angela. "Besides, Giuseppe is dead, and my life is here now."

"But your life could have been a lot different," said Claudia. "It wasn't fair that they kept that information from you."

"Maybe you're entitled to something," said Sadie.

"It is enough that I know more about my background," said Angela. "The Principessa encouraged me with my designs and sewing and made sure I had everything that I needed—and now I make my living from design. I have the satisfaction of knowing that I am descended from the Lanza family in Palermo."

"I suppose you're right," said Claudia. "Europe is such a mess, but from the sound of it, America will have to enter the war at some point," said Claudia. "That means my son will be at risk."

"Things are not good. The war has affected my ability to rent my properties in Sicily by the ocean. I'm losing money."

Angela and Claudia looked at Sadie as if she had just said that God was dead.

"What? I have a business."

"Angela, I am glad you found out the truth," said Claudia.

"Me, too," said Sadie. "I hope you find that you are entitled to a little something."

"Sadie, be quiet," said Claudia.

"Will you tell Franco?" asked Sadie. "He always thought he would be privileged because of your connection to Giulia."

"Not right now," said Angela. "I need to think about it for a while. The two of you need to be silent about this."

Angela knew that if she requested their discretion, they would comply.

* * *

Angela had not told anyone about her possible connection to the Lanza family, not even Franco. The council from her unseen friends encouraged her to keep it to herself until she felt a need to share it. She told herself it was in the past, but it was also in the present since she was Giuseppe Lanza's daughter. Her father was an elusive figure at best when she was a child, so when he passed away on one of his voyages across the sea, she had not missed him very much.

Angela recalled one day when her mother was preparing a special meal.

Her mother told her, "Someone special is coming, and I want you to put on your best dress. It is Giuseppe, your father's cousin."

The guest was a dark man with a beard and pointed features. He was dressed in a tailored suit with a white shirt that buttoned high on his neck. Angela remembered him meeting with her father a few times before. He embraced her warmly and asked her mother if she needed anything. Her mother seemed pleased to see him and poured him a glass of wine. Angela now realized he was her biological father. Maybe if her mother had lived, she would have told Angela the truth—and her life would have followed a different path.

In her mind, she imagined herself telling certain people about her lineage. It might make Franco angry that he was not able to benefit from her connection. Her American neighbors would not be interested in Italian aristocracy, and her Italian friends would think she was trying to be better than they were. In general, she decided her unseen friends were right in their assessment—although there was one more person who would completely understand her struggle and have an unbiased opinion: Sarah Einbinder.

* * *

Joe was just sixteen and had left school, planning to be an elevator operator and live in a rooming house in New York City. "Then I will do something in travel," he declared.

"But you can stay with us if you do not want to live at home," Angela said.

"No, I need to make my way. Nelsonville is not for me. People have made it clear that I don't belong here."

"I want to take you shopping and buy you a coat and shoes. You cannot go to New York without a winter coat. Your uncle and I will pay your rent for two months."

"Thanks, Aunt Angela. I knew you would help me."

Whenever Angela had walked into town with her nephew, she felt strong, proud, and protected. She smiled at passersby and walked with a purposeful step. As she walked, she celebrated her influence on a new generation of Americans. Joe got his style from her, and she did everything she could to nurture his growing sensibility. When she walked alone, she felt exposed.

"Did Uncle Franco agree to paying my rent for two months?"

"I take care of the accounts. You do not need to be concerned."

Angela was confident with her money and was clear about who she wanted to give it to. She had control over that part of her life in America. She had also saved money since she started sewing. Some of her earnings she put in a savings account, and some she kept as cash. The extra money she had set aside to distribute as she saw fit.

Angela and Joe stood in a men's clothing store in Nelsonville. She had done several favors for the owner, and she planned to collect on those favors today.

"Hello, Andrew. I want a coat for my nephew, Joe. Is your wife enjoying the dresses I altered for your trip?"

"Yes, she is. Thank you for setting aside your other work to alter them. And the hat you made was lovely."

"I know you did not ask me to make it, but it was so simple to make. I thought it would look good with a few of her dresses."

"Thank you for giving it to us for cost."

"What sort of overcoats do you have?" Angela asked.

"I have quite selection. This way."

Angela spotted a camel's-hair.

"Joe, do you like this?" Angela asked, pointing.

"Yes, I do, but it looks expensive."

"What would you want for this coat, Andrew?"

"Your nephew is right. It is expensive, but I have others that would be more in your price range."

He started to take out other coats.

"I think the camel's-hair will suit my nephew better than the others. New York City can get very cold in the winter, and we need a coat that will last. Can you take it out, so we can see it better?"

Andrew slowly put away the other coats and presented the camel's-hair coat to Angela. She inspected the lining and the buttons. It was heavy enough for the coldest winter.

"Try it on, Joe," Angela said.

Angela assisted Joe with the coat. He moved his hands over the smooth wool.

"It fits you, but it will be work to reinforce a few things," Angela said.

"What do you mean? This coat is Italian made," Andrew said.

"With that kind of sewing, I am sure it was not made in Italy. The lining will need to be replaced in a year. That is why it is still here from last season."

Angela made it a point to know the inventory of the retail clothing stores in town. She could note what styles were popular with local women and then reproduce them.

Andrew thought for a moment, then inspected the coat.

"I think I can let it go at 25% off," he said.

"I feel that 30% would be the right discount for the coat, otherwise it will be here next year. I have given discounts to your customers when you recommend my services."

"You are good at what you do, I have no doubt," said Andrew. "You are highly regarded by anyone who uses your services, Mrs. Bellini, and you have been generous to my wife, so it would be my pleasure to offer you the coat at 30% off."

"Oh, that's great," Joe said. "Thank you so much, Aunt Angela."

Joe put the coat on and looked in the full-length mirror.

"I look like I'm 20 in this coat. I can walk on the streets of Manhattan as an adult."

"Manhattan? Are you visiting?" asked Andrew.

"I'm moving there." Joe turned from side to side and gazed at himself in the mirror.

"I'm sure you will be successful," Andrew said. "You look young for such an adventure. Did you finish high school?"

"No. For what I want to do, I don't need a diploma," said Joe.

"What is that?" asked Andrew.

"I want to work in travel, and I want to travel."

"I am sure he will get his wish," Angela said. "He will be warm while he gets his wish."

Angela paid for the coat, and they left the shop. Joe put on the coat and threw his shoulders back.

"My friends will envy me in this coat," Joe said.

"You look wonderful in it," Angela said.

Suddenly the town looked different to Angela. Once Joe was gone, she would not have a gentle soul by her side to escort her into town. Nunzio would be home on leave soon, so Angela looked forward to the holidays.

"Will you see me off at the train station?"

"What about your father?"

"He's mad that I'm leaving. He doesn't understand that I need to build a life. I don't think anyone is really interested."

"I will be there," said Angela.

She slipped her hand into his arm and walked along Nelsonville's streets as if all who passed should take notice of their presence and acknowledge the purpose with which they walked.

* * *

The day Joe was officially moving to Manhattan, Angela gathered her coat, hat, and pocketbook and waited for him outside her house. He would come back to visit, but he would no longer be living only a few blocks away. She thought back to Joe's fascination with New York as a child. He just seemed to belong there. Angela hoped that he would find people who would accept him for who he was. She used to think others' acceptance was the key to happiness, but lately she thought that accepting oneself was the path to happiness. She saw Joe wave.

"Aunt Angela today is the day," said Joe. He wore his new coat and a broad smile and carried a brown suitcase.

"Just one suitcase?" Angela asked.

"Everything I own is in here," said Joe. "Most of the clothes you made or altered."

"No matter. I will send you anything more you need."

"Alicia is meeting us on the platform," said Joe.

They walked toward the Nelsonville train station, Angela holding his arm. She wanted to savor the walk to the station. She walked slowly and talked about what he might encounter living in the city.

"Do not allow anyone in your room unless you get to know them first," she said. "So many things happen in the city."

"I will be fine. You worry too much."

They reached the train station and saw Alicia standing on the platform. Alicia and Joe embraced.

"I can't help but worry about your brother alone in the city," said Angela. She took out a handkerchief and wiped her eyes.

"He'll be fine, Aunt Angela," Alicia said. "You worry too much. He can meet other guys like himself and be happy."

"What do you mean like himself? There is not another like your brother."

"I know," said Alicia. "But there are guys who will be able to relate to him."

Alicia and Joe looked at one another as if they agreed about something.

"Joe is very sociable. He gets along with everyone and makes friends easily."

"I know but…" said Alicia.

"Don't worry, Aunt Angela, I will make lots of friends and maybe a few enemies, but I will be myself."

"Do not make enemies, Joe," Angela said. "Approach everyone as your friend, and come home whenever you can. Remember, Nunzio is coming home on leave next week."

"I won't forget, and I'll meet you at Grand Central. We'll have lunch before we go to greet Nunzio."

The whistle blew, and the train pulled into the station.

"Thank you for everything, Aunt Angela," Joe said.

Angela began to cry as Joe put his arms around her.

"Your mother would be proud of you. I wish you the best, and I hope you get everything you want," Angela said. "Everyone should get what they want. I have packed a sandwich for you."

"Please don't cry. I will be fine."

"Your uncle and I will be visiting you soon," said Angela.

Joe hugged Alicia and stepped into the train for the hour's ride to the city. Angela and Alicia walked along the platform waving as the train pulled out of the station.

Angela stood on the platform crying.

Alicia put her hand on Angela's shoulder.

"I offered him a place in my house," Angela said.

"But Nunzio might come back, and he didn't want to live with Joe. Besides, Uncle Franco would not want him."

"I want him."

"You wanted us all," Alicia said. "I know that now. You have made a difference. What would we have done without you?"

"I'm sorry your father married his niece and left you children without guidance."

"It's not your fault," Alicia said.

"Come home with me and have some tea," said Angela. "We'll talk a while."

Alicia nodded.

* * *

Angela and Joe eagerly walked to Penn Station to greet Nunzio as he stepped off the train. For the past year, Nunzio was stationed at the Hingham Ammunition Depot in Massachusetts, a picturesque town on the water about 20 miles south of Boston. He would write Angela and tell her how happy he was to finally find a place he belonged, and Angela was happy that he was not far from New York. He had also started dating a girl from the next town. His letters mentioned her, but Angela was anxious to hear more. They waited on the platform as the train emerged from the tunnel, coming to a full stop.

Angela and Joe scanned the platform for Nunzio. There were many uniformed men with duffel bags looking for their wives and girlfriends.

"Do you see him?" Joe asked.

"Not yet," said Angela.

Nunzio stepped out on the platform and looked right at Angela.

"Nunzio, Nunzio we are here," Angela called.

She waved, and he waved back. Once again, they were connected. He threw his duffel bag over his shoulder and leaned forward as he walked as if an invisible force was attempting to pull him back. As he drew closer to Angela, she could see his face. Angela threw her arms around her nephew and kissed his face. Nunzio had become a muscular and strong man in the last year and a half.

"I am so glad you are home," Angela said.

"I'm glad you are here to meet me," said Nunzio.

"Good to see you, brother," said Joe. "I live in the city now."

"It's what you always wanted," said Nunzio. "Are you coming with us back to Nelsonville?"

"Not today, but I'll come by next week for dinner," Joe said. "I'll walk with you to Grand Central."

"Nunzio, if you can wait, I have made a wonderful meal for your homecoming," Angela said. "There is a train from Grand Central is less than an hour. Your uncle is anxious to see you."

They walked along 42nd Street and took in the activity. Joe walked ahead with confidence and enthusiasm. Angela could see he was swept up with the sights and sounds of the city. Because of the diversity in the city, there was an air of acceptance for differences—and Joe seemed to flourish.

* * *

Nunzio climbed the stairs to the house and dropped his duffel bag on the porch where Franco was sleeping in his recliner.

"Uncle Franco. Uncle Franco, I am home," Nunzio called.

"Oh, you are here," Franco said.

He sat up and hugged his nephew and started to cry.

"I missed you so much," said Franco.

Angela noticed that Franco had less energy since Nunzio left, but now she hoped he would regain some of his interest in life.

"I have invited Alicia for to eat with us," said Angela. "I just have to warm everything up."

"Leo too?" asked Nunzio.

"No, he is working," said Angela. "Besides, it is best that he doesn't come here."

Angela wanted to have a pleasant evening with her nephew and niece without any disruptive influence.

"Let's go inside," Angela said.

Angela set the table and put the veal and potatoes in the oven. She heard Alicia in the hallway.

"Is he here?" asked Alicia as she came into the kitchen.

"He's upstairs getting settled," said Angela.

Alicia went up the back staircase.

"Tell him we're ready to eat."

Everyone took their places at the table.

"How long will you be home?" asked Alicia.

"A month, and then I go back to the ammunition depot and then back to California for extra training and to teach new recruits how to shoot. My commanding officer says I'm a sharpshooter. I'm good enough to teach others."

Angela had never liked Nunzio's fascination with guns, but his interest had turned into a valuable skill.

"Leo would like to see you," said Alicia. "Maybe you can make time to see him. Since you're doing so well, maybe you can encourage him."

"I can't really encourage anyone," said Nunzio. "I found what I wanted to do. Everyone has to find their calling."

Leo is just a dislikable person, thought Angela. *Why didn't Alicia see that?*

"I'm so glad you are home," said Angela. "You will have time to see your friends."

There was a bang at the door.

"What was that?" asked Angela.

"I'll see," said Nunzio.

He looked out the hall window and saw a drunk Leo, staggering as he tried to hold himself up.

"Alicia, come out here!" yelled Leo. "Who said you could leave the house?"

"Who is out there?" asked Angela.

"It's that idiot, Leo," said Nunzio.

"I should go," said Alicia.

"Like hell," said Nunzio. "Wait right here." He went upstairs and came down carrying a gun.

"Nunzio, please don't shoot him!" shrieked Alicia. "He's just drunk."

"They'll put you in jail!" screamed Angela.

"Don't worry, I'll just scare him."

Nunzio went out and grabbed Leo by the collar. He pointed the gun at Leo's head. After a few words, Leo staggered down the porch stairs.

"He's gone," said Nunzio.

"Alicia, you will stay here tonight," said Angela.

Angela felt she had made the right decision in banning Leo from her house, and now she knew he could get out of control when drunk. If Nunzio had not been there, she would have had to call the police. She cringed to think that this could have happened when she had a customer.

"I'm sorry, Aunt Angela," said Alicia. "He doesn't mean it."

"That son of a bitch," said Franco.

"Ok, it's all done, come on back and eat," said Angela.

Angela felt Alicia's situation was untenable, and she wondered how long it would go on. Her unseen friends told Angela to allow Alicia to come to a decision to leave Leo on her own. But Angela felt if it started to interfere with her own life, she would call the authorities.

Chapter 12

A Day in Infamy: December 7, 1941

Nunzio was home on extended leave for the holidays.

"Tell me about your girlfriend," said Angela.

"I met her at a wedding about six months ago, and we see each other a lot," said Nunzio. He lit a Chesterfield cigarette and settled back in his chair.

"Is it serious?"

"Well, I'm not interested in dating anyone else," said Nunzio. "Her name is Felicia."

Angela saw that he really liked this girl. The military and his time away had made him more mature. He seemed to be making clear decisions, and she hoped that Felicia felt the same way.

"I would like to meet her someday," said Angela. "What is she like? Where do her people come from?"

"She's Italian, and her parents are from Calabria. She is fun and loves to figure skate," said Nunzio. "I think it will be long term."

"Engaged?" asked Angela.

"I was thinking about it."

Angela felt that Nunzio finally had an opportunity for happiness.

"That would be wonderful," said Angela. "I am so pleased for you. I'm sure I will love her."

"Don't tell anyone until she accepts," said Nunzio.

"Of course! I don't want you to have bad luck."

She kissed him.

"Does she know about your family situation?"

"I told her my mother had died and that I felt you and Uncle Franco were my parents. That's all."

Maybe if he told Felicia about his father marrying his niece, she would think twice about saying yes, thought Angela.

"Good luck with everything," said Angela. "I hope she says yes."

Nunzio went upstairs, and Angela prepared a dress pattern for Sarah Einbinder. The demand for Angela's services had increased, so she decided to see customers on weekends. She carefully pinned each piece of material onto the pattern she had created. Her familiarity with her customers' bodies made it easier and quicker for her to design for them. Angela could create a simple dress in two days and still have time to work on other garments. The doorbell rang.

"Hello, Mrs. Bellini," Sarah Einbinder called. She entered the hallway in a white wool suit Angela had made several years ago.

"Mrs. Einbinder, please come in," Angela said. It was always a good day when Sarah came for a fitting.

"I see that you are still wearing your white wool suit."

"Yes, of course. I get compliments when I wear it. It is timeless."

Angela reveled in compliments that came from her educated European clientele.

"I am just pinning the material now. I will be right back."

Sarah looked around the hallway.

"I always enjoy your home, Mrs. Bellini. It suggests your culture but is understated."

Many Italian homes were gaudily decorated in a style that shouted Italian culture. She found Angela's home peaceful and in good taste.

Sarah had not written Angela's story. She could not afford the venues for a new play, and she had been busy teaching at a local college. The war weighed heavily on her mind.

Sarah looked up, hearing someone at the top of the staircase. Slowly Nunzio descended the stairs wearing his Marine uniform.

"Well, who do we have here?"

"I am Nunzio, Angela's nephew."

"Oh yes, you live upstairs. And you are a Marine."

"I'm on leave for the holidays," said Nunzio.

"Congratulations," Sarah said. "You look very handsome in that uniform."

"I see you have met my nephew," Angela said, returning with the pattern draped over both arms as if it were a delicate gown made of the finest silk. This was how she treated all the clothing she made, regardless of the material.

"Yes, I have. I wish him all the luck, and hopefully he will not have to go overseas."

"I am ready to fight," Nunzio said. "I have been trained. Aunt Angela, I will see you later."

After Nunzio left, Sarah turned to Angela.

"He is quite a determined young man," Sarah said. "It is a pity his determination will be used against him."

"Used against him? How?"

"Oh, just some items that have appeared in the newspapers the past few years," Sarah said.

Angela handed Sarah the pattern.

"Go in and change, and slip the pattern over your head. I will make the necessary adjustments."

"I think this will be the perfect dress to wear to the National Council of Jewish Women's Luncheon," said Sarah.

She put on the pattern and stepped up on the platform, facing the full-length mirror. When one of Angela's clients wore a dress she had created for a specific function, she often got a few new clients. This was how she built her business.

"I think Mrs. Bernstein will be going to that luncheon," Angela said. "She was here the other day."

"Oh, did you design something for her?"

"No, it was just an alteration," Angela said.

Angela began to slightly re-pin the pattern to fit Sarah's figure. Angela was not sure if she wanted to know why her nephew's determination would be turned against him, because she was afraid of opening Pandora's box. There was something unsettling about the war situation that Angela could not articulate. If Nunzio had not enlisted, she would have dismissed the feeling and carried on with her life—but since it involved Speranza's son, it was disconcerting.

"Mrs. Einbinder, I wonder about what you said about Nunzio's determination being turned on him. What do you mean?"

Angela continued to work on re-pinning the dress.

Sarah turned toward Angela. Whenever Sarah looked directly at her during a fitting, Angela knew she was about to receive information that would change her in some respect. She took a deep breath and told herself that it is better to know than remain ignorant.

"A few years ago, the *New York Times* reported that Henry Ford received the Grand Cross of the German Eagle, a Nazi decoration for distinguished foreigners," Sarah continued.

"Henry Ford from the car company?" Angela responded.

"Yes, and that is not all. During the early 1920s, the *Times* reported that Henry Ford was financing Adolph Hitler's nationalist and anti-Semitic movements in Munich. America's industrialists are somehow supporting this war on both sides. They have no regard for people like your nephew."

Angela thought about her father's and Franco's distrust of the church and its priests. Her father was sure the church helped fund the suppression of the peasantry. In fact, this was common knowledge among Messina's population. No one in Nelsonville was talking about American industrialists' involvement in the war. The evils of Fascism were talked about among the Italian-American community, but the conversation stopped there.

"This is the first I have heard of this," Angela said.

"Of course, it is never discussed. Very few know about it, or they think it is an untruth."

Angela continued to pin Sarah's garment, not sure how far to go with the conversation. She remembered her father saying, 'Never ask what you do not want to know. Once you know it, the knowledge is now yours and you will be obliged to act on it.

"You do not think the government will share this information?" Sarah asked. "How many young men would go to war to make rich men richer?"

"The government knows what they are doing!" Angela gasped.

"How could they not?"

Sarah turned and looked at the back of the dress. "This is a wonderful dress. I will be an original at the luncheon."

"Yes, you will be."

A lighter conversation was emerging, and Angela took a deep breath. She felt she had been overloaded with information.

Angela wondered how well informed anyone was about the workings of government in America. People generally followed blindly and believed what the government told them. It was different in Sicily, where no one trusted the government or Fascism. People knew what to expect, and they were not afraid to fight—even if it meant losing. The treachery was hidden in America like a looming shadow that both obscured the truth and stalked those who found it. Sarah saw the anxiety on Angela's face.

"Oh, I have troubled you, Angela, and I am sorry. But you are such an intelligent woman that I thought you would want to know the truth."

"Knowing the truth is always good, I suppose. I just worry about my nephew."

"I worry about all the young men who will fight this war. They are not told the truth."

"But how do we stop the Nazis?"

"We have no choice now but to stop them through force, because the industrialists have funded the war."

I am finished. You can get dressed," said Angela.

"Angela, you have worked your magic again," said Sarah.

Sarah turned from side to side and admired Angela's work in the mirror.

"It will fit like a glove," Sarah said.

"This is not the only truth I've learned," said Angela.

"What is it?"

"Last year, I received a letter from Franco's cousin. He told me my real father was Giuseppe Lanza, Pietro Lanza di Trabia's brother. Pietro was Principessa Giulia's husband. You were right to suggest that Giulia's motivation was more than simple fondness. Two of my friends know, but that is all. My husband doesn't know."

"Well, I am flattered you told me. You must struggle with it, and then you have all your other concerns. Maybe you should have it for yourself for a while longer."

"Yes, I imagine what my life would have been like if they would have acknowledged me."

"The Mother Superior must have known," said Sarah.

"I am sure she did," said Angela.

"I am very sorry, Angela. A person does not have the right to withhold that kind of information. I will go change."

Sarah went into Angela's bedroom to change.

Angela tried to think about the day ahead and the tasks she had to accomplish, but the information Sarah had imparted swam around in her mind; each thought knocking into each other like bumper cars in an amusement park. These thoughts grew and expanded into many scenarios. Some scenes involved death and destruction, and others involved peace and serenity. Angela went over to the antique brass clock on the mantel. It was 2:30 p.m. and time for the world news on the radio. She thought if she listened to the news, the random conflicting thoughts she was having would subside. She would focus on what was currently happening. Angela went into the dining room and turned on the radio. The local news was on, talking about the weather for the next few days. Ever since the earthquake, she wanted to know about the weather to be prepared for anything Mother Nature had in store.

"Angela?" Sarah called.

"I am in the dining room."

"When should I come again?"

"You can come next Monday, on the 15th, for the final fitting," Angela said.

There was an interruption in the broadcast.

"The Japanese have bombed the Navy Base at Pearl Harbor," said the newscaster.

"Oh, Angela, I am sorry, but I am not surprised. I am afraid there is no turning back now. War will be declared."

"I am so afraid of what will happen," Angela said.

The reports started to come in: the casualty numbers, the massive injuries, men being trapped in ships underwater. The hospital was overwhelmed and could not care for all the injured. The fates of the victims were familiar to Angela: people being buried alive, dismembered, or left dying without medical care. The memories came flooding back like a tsunami; she had wandered the barren landscape of Messina alone, begging for help where there was none. She had studiously avoided the dark cavern inside of her that the earthquake had created many years ago. She knew what young men like her nephew would suffer. People called the earthquake a natural disaster, but there was nothing natural about the horror of its aftermath. *The aftermath will be the same for soldiers after the shooting stops, thought Angela. They will be lost without help.*

"I need to get home to my husband," Sarah said. "We have friend a whose son was stationed at Pearl Harbor."

"Oh, bless them," Angela said. "I will pray to the Blessed Mother for his safety."

"We will all need prayers," Sarah said.

"I am afraid that is beyond our control now. War will be declared. Ford will make tanks and other vehicles for anyone who will pay. It is all built on greed. I will see you on the 15th."

Angela sat at the dining room table and stared out the window. When the First World War happened, she had hardly seemed to notice. She was still adjusting to her new life in America. She could not have predicted the hardships that lay ahead. The present disappointment came crashing down like chards of glass, cutting her at every angle. She had hoped for a perfect life in America, free from the turmoil of war and prejudice. Now she would have to tell Franco that he may lose his nephew. She feared losing a loved one again, but this time it would not be to a disease or natural disaster; it would be because of something completely preventable. She heard running water in the kitchen. Franco had come up from his cellar cave, where he went to shut out life and its complexities. He would have to pay attention now.

"Franco, come in the dining room," Angela said.

"What now?" Franco asked.

He walked over to his smoking chair, steadied himself with his cane, and slowly sat down with a sigh. He picked up his pipe and a newspaper.

"Japan attacked our bases in Pearl Harbor. Many have died. Nunzio will probably have to go to war. I don't know what to do. Put the newspaper down. Our nephew could die!"

"What do you want me to do?" asked Franco.

"I want you to listen," said Angela.

Angela started to cry. The large Queen Anne Victorian home had felt hollow since Nunzio had left. People thought it was simply a beautiful home, an inanimate object to house furniture and stay warm in the winter, but Angela felt it spoke volumes about its inhabitants. If the inhabitants were happy, the house felt happy. If there was discord, the house reflected that disharmony in its creaking and night shadows.

"Is war declared?" Franco asked.

"No, but it is a matter of time," Angela said, wiping her tears. "They will need trained men to fight in the Pacific."

"Where is Nunzio? He will be a brave fighter," Franco said. He packed his pipe with tobacco as if he were trying to compress every emotion he had into that tiny space.

"He is probably on his way home. I am afraid he will be killed," Angela said. "He is a young boy. He should not have to go. Besides, he is fighting for rich people. The government does not care about us or the Jewish people, but the Nazis must be stopped."

"He wants to fight for his country," said Franco.

"That is what I am saying. He is fighting for the rich."

"He will fight for his country," Franco said.

He lit his pipe and opened the newspaper.

Watching Franco puff on his pipe and read the newspaper reminded Angela how complacent people had become. *We all accept what the government and the radio news tell us*, she thought.

"Are you going to talk to Nunzio?" Angela asked.

"What for?"

"He is your sister's son. Why don't you have more concern for his life?"

"He is a soldier. Soldiers go to war. He must fight for his country. Now please be quiet and leave me alone."

Franco resumed reading his newspaper.

"That is the problem. Everyone is so quiet," Angela said. "No one speaks their mind. I am done being quiet."

Franco did not respond.

"Where is everyone?" Nunzio's voice sounded from the hallway, exuberant but tense.

"Nunzio, we are here," Angela said.

"Have you heard what happened? Everyone is saying that we will go to war. I just came from the recruitment office, and I must leave in a few days."

"A few days?" shrieked Angela, hugging Nunzio as if he had just said her sister was found. "I do not want to lose you!"

"Pearl Harbor has been bombed. I have to go."

"After the earthquake, terrible things happened to people. You are going to see these things."

"I am not going alone. There will be many of us, and we do not leave each other behind."

"You are a good boy," Franco said. "It is good that you will fight for your country."

Angela thought that she should be more supportive, but Sarah's information would not stop repeating in her head. *It is there, and I do not know what to do with it*, she thought. Franco pressed on his cane and lifted himself out of his chair. He walked over and patted Nunzio's face.

"I am proud," Franco said.

Angela forced a smile. There was no point in continuing to talk. The truth often fell on deaf ears. She would have to carry on regardless of the war's outcome. Angela had chosen life after the earthquake, and she would continue to do so. She remembered times when she was so hungry that she thought she might resort to eating dead bodies like many of Messina's inhabitants had done to stay alive, but she had resisted. She lived off rotting fruit and vegetables until the American ships came. She was grateful to America for helping her to live, but she now had a more realistic view of her adopted country.

"Yes, we are proud," Angela said. "But be safe."

"Everything will be fine, Aunt Angela," Nunzio said. "The Marines will take care of us."

Angela tried to control the tears that dribbled down the contours of her high cheekbones. *After Nunzio lost his mother, he changed*, thought Angela. The young man standing before her would have been completely different if

Speranza had raised him. She and Franco did their best, but Angela felt she had failed. The country she had pinned her hopes on had failed her.

"Just come back to us safe," Angela said. "Write to us every chance you get, and let us know you are safe."

In her mind, Angela prepared for the coming war. The violence of war will only bring back broken men who would take a lifetime to recover, making America a fragile, wounded place. It took Messina years to recover after the earthquake, but they put it back together brick by brick. Society could not do that with someone's shattered mind.

"I have to call some other Marines," said Nunzio.

He went into the hall to use the phone.

"He is a good boy," Franco said.

Tears flooded Angela's face and streamed down her neck.

"This could be the last time we see him. Speranza would be so worried," said Angela.

Franco put his arms around her. He could not remember the last time he hugged his wife. When he entered this marriage, he had hoped that he would benefit from her connections with the Prince and Princess of Palermo. He never told anyone, but before he married Angela, he had asked the Mother Superior what Angela's relationship was to the royal couple.

"What do you mean 'relationship?'" The Mother Superior asked.

The nun had stood up from behind her enormous desk. She crossed her arms across her chest, tucked her hands into her habit sleeves and looked down at Franco. He sat on an antique straight back chair in front of her desk.

"Well, Mother Superior, I thought I should know about Angela's background if I am to marry her. I should know everything. Including her relations."

"'You are not marrying Angela for her relations, are you, Signor Bellini?'"

"Of course not. I am very fond of Angela," Franco said.

Mother Superior came around from the back of the desk and stood over Franco.

"Signor Bellini," the nun said. "Your dowry was quite generous, and we appreciate your giving one of our girls a home, but I do not have any more information for you. I wish you luck."

It had made him angry that Angela did not cultivate her relationship with Princess Giulia after their marriage. They might have had more opportunities come their way. He admitted (to whom?) that his wife's connection with the Princess was what originally intrigued him and that he hoped to gain prestige and money from the relationship. His disappointment had spilled over into their marriage, and his attitude toward his wife was not always kind. *If we had children of our own*, thought Franco, *maybe Nunzio's enlistment would not have been viewed as such a tragedy.* Today, in this embrace in 1941, they were both seeking to heal disappointments.

"I will begin to make dinner," Angela said.

She wiped her eyes.

"Ok," Franco said and returned to his chair.

The phone rang. Nunzio answered.

"Hello," Nunzio said. "Oh, Mary. Yes, we probably will go to war. Ok, why don't you come for dinner?"

"Aunt Angela," said Nunzio, "Mary Galluci is coming for dinner."

"Do you think that is a good idea?" asked Angela.

"She said she wanted to say goodbye. This is better than meeting her on my own. Besides, she is a friend."

"All right. Call your sister to come over as well and call your brother to let him know you will be leaving. And you should call your father and let him know what might happen."

* * *

"Mary, it was so nice of you to come for dinner," Angela said.

"Oh, I wanted to. I want to say goodbye," Mary said.

Mary had on more face powder than usual, and her dark red lips glowed in the evening light. Strong perfume emanated from her, and she wore a hat with a large feather that looked like an antenna.

Mary sat next to Nunzio.

"War has not been declared yet," Mary said. "Maybe we will hold off."

"Unlikely, as we are all waiting for FDR to say the word," Nunzio said. "Word on the street is that he will make an announcement tomorrow."

Alicia sat across from Nunzio. The pink in her cheeks had disappeared, and her life-force was diminished.

"Where will you be? Are you going to be in Hingham or sent overseas?" asked Alicia. "How will we know where you are?"

"I will write to let you know, and mail will be delivered to me."

"What if something happens to you?" asked Alicia. "Will they let us know right away?"

"Don't say that," Angela said. "Stop talking about war. Let's have a pleasant meal."

Franco sipped his wine and waved his hand.

"Let them talk, for God's sake," Franco said.

"Don't worry, they'll let you know," said Nunzio.

"I think we should all pray that we do not enter this war," Angela said. "I don't know why we are fighting anyway."

"Because we were attacked," Nunzio said. "We have no choice."

"There is always a choice," Angela said. "We will make the wrong one."

"Maybe they'll give you a desk job and you won't have to fight," said Mary.

"I don't want a desk job. I'm not a coward. I'm a trained sharp shooter."

Angela placed a steaming platter of Veal Parmesan and pasta on the table.

"Everyone, help yourselves," said Angela.

"If you make the Marines your career, you will have a life of adventure," said Alicia. She would have liked to have a life of adventure, but knew she was destined to live her life in Nelsonville.

Franco raised his wine glass.

"To Nunzio," Franco said.

"To Nunzio," everyone responded.

"Nunzio, maybe we can go out to dinner tomorrow evening," Mary said.

"I will be busy, Mary. I have to get my orders and pack."

Mary burst into tears and ran into the kitchen.

"What is wrong with her?" Franco asked.

"I will take care of it," Angela.

Angela got up and went into the kitchen. She found Mary sitting at the kitchen table crying into a napkin.

"What is the matter, Mary?" Angela asked.

"I was hoping that Nunzio would feel differently about me when he came home. I thought he might want to settle down. He sent me polite letters when he was away, but that was all."

"Mary, I think you are a lovely girl and with fine qualities, but my nephew is preparing to go overseas and has other concerns."

"Maybe you are right," Mary said. "When he comes back from the war, he might be ready to get married."

Angela could see Nunzio's lack of interest in Mary, but Mary still had hope that things would change. She did not want to tell her about Felicia, as she felt that was up to Nunzio.

"I think we should finish our meal," Angela said.

"All right," said Mary.

She blew her nose in the napkin, and they exited the kitchen. When Angela and Mary returned, everyone was eating in silence.

"Would you like some veal, Mary?" asked Angela.

"I'm watching my figure, but because of the occasion I will have a piece," Mary said.

She put her arm around Nunzio, and he smiled his sly smile. She put her other hand on his cheek and lightly kissed his forehead.

* * *

Nunzio stood at the Nelsonville train station waiting for his late afternoon train to New York, which would then bring him to his station at the Hingham Ammunition Depot. War had indeed been declared on Japan, and it was only a matter of time before he was deployed overseas.

"Let us know right away if they send you to the Pacific," said Angela.

"I will," said Nunzio. "The train is coming soon. You don't need to wait."

"Keep yourself safe," Angela said. She hugged and kissed her nephew, fearful that this would be the last time she would see him alive. Franco put his arms around Nunzio and patted his back.

"We will see you soon," said Franco.

Any disappointment or issue about the past seemed trivial to Angela in this moment. Even her lineage seemed inconsequential in the face of war.

Angela held Franco's hand as they made their way off the platform. Franco shuffled along silently. She looked back as the train pulled up, and she watched Nunzio throw his duffel bag over his shoulder and enter the train. He was gone.

"We are going to lose him," Angela said.

"Stop it, Angela," Franco said.

It was difficult enough for Franco to leave his nephew at a train station that would eventually take him to war. He did not want to think about the consequences. People came back from war all the time; his nephew would, too.

Angela tried to redirect Franco to the taxi stand, but he moved away from her.

"I want to walk," Franco said.

"What if you fall? Nunzio is not here to help us."

"Leave me, then. I will walk alone."

Franco increased his shuffle and walked ahead of Angela. He was happy to be out and walking independently, because it gave him time to think. Angela caught up to him and held his arm. Franco put one foot in front of the other and often paused. They walked past old factories and warehouses that had once bustled with activity but were now only remnants of once-thriving businesses. The sun came out, and the December freeze cooled their faces. Franco felt like one of the relic buildings that stared at him as he passed. At least these relics could be transformed into something in workable I the future. Franco knew his body could not be transformed back to when he was strong and sturdy. Silently, they made their way home.

"I will sit on the porch for a while," said Franco.

"Do not stay too long. It will be getting colder," Angela said.

Franco sat in the recliner and pulled the blanket over him. Angela took out her keys to open the front door.

"Maybe you are right," said Franco.

Angela closed the door and walked over to Franco.

"What?"

"I don't want to go in the house because Nunzio won't be there and may never be there again. If I stay here, time stands still. The world is moving like lightening. I can't keep up," Franco said.

"I know. Families are not as close as they once had been."

"My family is gone," said Franco.

Angela remembered how distraught Franco was when his brother and sister had died. She knew he desperately wanted children.

"Write to the Principessa," said Franco. "She favored you. Maybe she can offer us some benefit while the war is on."

This is the right time to tell him, thought Angela. Her unseen friends seemed to be pushing her in this moment to connect with Franco through the truth. She sat on the recliner.

"Franco, I wrote to Roberto asking him if he knew anything about my connection to Principessa Giulia. He told me I am the daughter of Pietro Lanza di Trabia's brother, Giuseppe. He passed away a long time ago. So, I am not a blood relative of Giulia's, and there are no favors to be had."

"Roberto knew this?" asked Franco.

"He can't be sure if it's true," said Angela. "We should forget about it and live our lives without thinking about the past so much. Did you marry me because you thought I would bring you the benefit of Principessa's position?"

Franco looked at Angela and paused.

"No. We thought alike, and you were beautiful," said Franco. "That was enough for me."

Franco touched Angela's hand as the sun began to set and twilight shadows settled over the house. The streetlights illuminated the sidewalk for the shadows to sharpen and become fixed, allowing the unseen dimension to participate in the waking world.

* * *

Angela hung Sarah Einbinder's complete dress on the full-length mirror. She had attached gold-plated buttons on the sleeves and on the bodice of the fine, navy blue linen. She loved embellishing her garments with understated detail.

She glanced out her front window and saw Sarah climbing the stairs dressed in a black wool coat with a fur collar. She opened the door before Sarah had reached the porch.

"Come in, Mrs. Einbinder," Angela said.

"So good to see you, Mrs. Bellini," said Sarah. Upon seeing the dress, she remarked, "Oh, It is so elegant. I do like the buttons."

"The color suits you," Angela said. "Put it on, and we'll see if I need to alter anything."

Angela wondered if she should bring up their last conversation about Henry Ford. She'd thought about it the entire week, and she was anxious to know if Sarah had any more information. Since last week, her view of the world had changed. Nothing was as it seemed; her mother's husband was not her father, and the government was not what she was told. If the story about Ford was the truth, she wanted more of it. Angela was tired of being in the dark and accepting someone else's opinion. Luckily, Angela did not have to ask.

"So, have you been thinking about our conversation about Henry Ford?" asked Sarah. "I am still pondering your lineage. Not knowing one's biological father for decades can be a trying truth to swallow. You seem to be at peace with it."

"I am still thinking about our conversation," said Angela. "Since my nephew left, I haven't thought about much else. The situation with my father seems trivial to me with all that is going on. I even told Franco the truth."

"How did he react?" asked Sarah.

"I asked him if he married me because of my connection to the Principessa, and he told me no. He married me because we are of the same mind and I was beautiful."

"That was brave of you, Mrs. Bellini," said Sarah. "It certainly changes your personal story, like knowing about Henry Ford changes your American story. But knowing the truth must give you peace."

"I will not have peace until my nephew comes home."

"Is he a patriot?" asked Sarah.

"I do not think so, Mrs. Einbinder," said Angela. "What else could he do but join the service? He does not have an education. Maybe he can make a career."

"Have you lost weight?" Angela asked.

"Oh, I have not been hungry lately," replied Sarah. "My sister is missing."

"Missing? What do you mean, missing?"

"I received a letter from friends in Germany. The Nazis invaded my sister's house and arrested her and her husband. They have not been seen since."

"Your sister? That is terrible. You need to find her. I know how you feel. I know everything about having a sister who is missing."

"I am sure you do, Angela," Sarah said.

"What will you do?" asked Angela.

"Like you, there is nothing I can do but wait. But, I can still attend my meetings at the National Council of Jewish Women and find out more about the workings of government."

"I will need to take in the dress. Do you think you will start eating again?"

"I hope so," said Sarah. "Unless I decide to starve myself to death, but that is highly unlikely."

They both laughed. It was a much-needed moment of levity in a world that appeared dismal and on the verge of complete destruction.

"Yes, please take it in, but leave enough material to let it out again. I think it is such a charming dress that I am sure it will send many customers your way."

"Thank you, Mrs. Einbinder. I also would like to be kept busy. I am so worried about my nephew going to war. I do not want him to be killed with a weapon paid for by an American company."

The two women looked at each other. Sarah held her hand out to Angela, who grasped it. They paused for a moment and shared their energy. Sarah gave Angela her defiance, and Angela gave Sarah her strength.

"I am not sure who to talk to about Henry Ford," said Angela. "I feel unsure around patriotic people now. When they say, 'God Bless America' I do not know what to say."

"You do not need to say anything. If they have a son or relative fighting in Europe, it will just make them feel worse."

Angela agreed. Why rub salt in a wound?

"Maybe your sister's neighbors can tell you where they took her?" Angela asked.

"The neighborhood has been destroyed. There is no one left to ask."

"Well, at least you have your children," said Angela.

"Yes, I do. My twin boys are 20 years old now. They also have been brainwashed into blind patriotic thinking. They will probably volunteer."

"I hope your sons do not," said Angela.

"I cannot imagine that they will not," said Sarah. "Besides, there's talk of a draft. Husbands will probably be drafted as well."

Angela wondered about all the widows and women in the Italian community who depended on their sons and husbands for financial and emotional support; they would be left to care for themselves.

"I hope this war ends quickly," said Angela.

"If it is in the government's best interest it will, but they can prolong it for as long as it benefits them financially."

"I am having a little coffee and dessert get-together on the afternoon of December 22nd to brighten the season. I hope you will come," said Angela. "It will be my neighbors, customers, and friends."

"That is a wonderful idea. I am sure I know many of your customers."

Angela could feel her energy lightening.

"Please let me know if there is any word on your sister."

                                    * * *

Angela had decided to have a holiday coffee and dessert event for her neighbors and customers to keep her mind off Nunzio and the precarious war situation. He had not been deployed, but Angela knew it was a matter of time. She walked down Main Street in Nelsonville with a bag of homemade sesame cookies for Sasha Bloomfeld, owner of Bloomfeld's Dress Shop. Today she was shopping for Christmas presents for her niece and nephews. She had a tremendous amount to do and was glad she had taken on extra work. After the holidays would be when her customers considered their spring wardrobes created. She would make the best of the holidays without Nunzio.

"Angela Bellini, how nice to see you," said Sasha Bloomfeld. "Are you enjoying the holidays?"

"My nephew had to return to his post in Massachusetts because of the war. He will probably have to fight. It is a sad time. We think he will have to return to California for further training. These cookies are for you."

When Sasha's customers bought a dress and it needed to be altered, Sasha pinned the dress and sent it to Angela. These were jobs that took very little time and ultimately increased her client base and income.

"Thank you so much, Mrs. Bellini. "It is very nice working with you. My customers are extremely pleased with your work."

"I appreciate the work you send me," Angela said. Angela did not especially like the dresses in the Bloomfeld shop, which catered to an older American crowd that enjoyed floral, loose-fitting dresses, but she was successful in persuading some of the referrals she obtained from the shop to choose a more European look.

"Everyone is talking about the war," said Sasha. "I was fortunate enough to have had girls. You never know when there will be a war. I hope your nephew will be safe."

"Thank you. I am off to shop, Mrs. Bloomfeld. I just wanted to stop by and give you my traditional Italian sesame cookies."

"Thank you so much, Mrs. Bellini, and God bless America. I am sure our country will take care of your nephew. I am sure he will be fine."

"Thank you, Mrs. Bloomfeld. I will see you."

Angela stepped into the street and took a deep breath. She felt a constriction in her chest every time there was discussion of the war. It was as if someone tied a girdle around her breasts so that she could breathe enough to stay alive but not to feel enlivened. It had been cloudy all day, and a light snow began to fall. She took the scarf from her neck, wrapped it around her head, and went to the Italian deli to buy veal cutlets and prosciutto.

"I will have three pounds of veal cutlet," Angela said.

A rotund man behind the counter began to weigh the veal. She heard a familiar voice behind her.

"Angela, how are you?" asked Amelia Saldi. "Are you shopping for our dinner? I haven't heard anything about it this year."

"Because of the war, I am having coffee and dessert on the 22nd and you are invited. My neighbors and customers will also be there."

"Your nephew Nunzio is in the Marines. Has he heard anything about where he will be?"

"Nothing yet," said Angela.

Amelia Saldi wore a fitted camel-hair coat with fur sleeves, collar, and hat. *There must have been quite a few deaths needing her husband's gravestones*, thought Angela.

"Sounds like there will be quite a few people," said Amelia. "I suppose a dinner would be too celebratory, given the state of the world. Will all our friends be there?"

"The usual ladies," Angela said.

Angela assumed Amelia was trying to find out if Sadie Malaci and Claudia Cerverci were among the guests. She knew Amelia disapproved of Sadie's alcohol consumption and Claudia's forward manner. Angela felt Amelia's civility toward Sadie took great restraint.

"The get-together will be on the 22nd at 2 pm. I will see you then," said Angela.

Angela took her veal and left the shop. This December, especially, was not a happy month for Angela, but she tried to be social. The earthquake had happened on December 28, 1908, so the days leading up to the anniversary of the disaster were still anxiety-ridden for her. Here she stood in a small town in America with a soft snow that the dusted the sidewalks. People ran to buy presents and prepare large feasts for their Christmas tables. She stood still in this flurry of activity and thought about Nunzio and how he used to build a fire in the hallway fireplace every Christmas Eve.

People scurried around her, not taking any notice. She closed her eyes and heard her unseen friends say that it was time to create the exact life she wanted. It was time to bring her life together and not compartmentalize. Her first step was bringing her customers, neighbors, and friends together socially.

Chapter 13

December 22, 1941

Angela placed the Italian cheesecake and lemon meringue pie on the dining room table. The cannoli were placed in a circular pattern, with one on top of another. She had started a fire in the hallway fireplace, and the room filled with a cedar aroma. *Nunzio would be proud that I could start a fire*, she thought. She placed chairs in the hallway so her guests could enjoy the warmth. Angela lined the mantle with anisette and sherry and placed a photograph of Nunzio in his uniform in the center of the mantle and on the buffet in the dining room.

She heard the front door open.

"I know we're early," said Sadie. "We thought you might need some help setting up."

"We didn't want you to have to do everything by yourself," said Claudia Cerverci.

"I brought some wine," said Sadie. "I know you always have plenty, but some of us drink more than others."

"You had to say that," said Claudia. "You should have brought your own bottle for as much as you drink."

"You both do well in that department," said Angela. "Get the small folding tables and place one near each chair, said Angela."

"Who is coming to this *festa*?" asked Sadie.

"Some of our friends and the other people you don't know, so don't drink too much."

"Sure, sure," said Sadie.

"Alicia will be coming," said Angela.

"Good. That will get her out of the house," said Sadie.

After they finished setting up, they went into the kitchen and sat down.

"I keep checking the mailbox for a letter from Nunzio, but he hasn't written yet," said Angela.

"I'm sure he'll write as soon as he knows anything," said Claudia.

"I ask the Blessed Mother every day to watch over him," said (who?)

The doorbell rang.

Angela opened the door and saw Alicia beaming.

"Alicia dear, why didn't you just come in?"

Angela hugged and kissed her niece. Angela was pleased to see Alicia looking healthy and happy. Alicia stood smiling at Angela.

"What is it?"

"I'm pregnant," said Alicia. "I'm so happy."

"Oh, that is wonderful news!" exclaimed Angela. "Sadie and Claudia are in the kitchen. Let's tell them the good news."

Angela was delighted that there would be new life in the family. This was an opportunity for renewal. Leo was successful in holding his job, and they were talking about finally getting their own apartment.

"You will love being a mother," said Claudia.

"You do nothing but complain about your kids," Sadie said to Claudia.

"Sure, I complain about them. That's because I love them," said Claudia.

"We should have a toast to Alicia's new baby," Sadie said.

"Just one," said Angela.

They lifted their glasses to Alicia.

"I'll greet the guests as they come in, Aunt Angela," said Alicia. She had a spring in her step as she walked toward the front door.

"Well, this is good news," said Angela.

"Maybe it's time to make peace with Leo," said Sadie. "You want to be able to visit Alicia when you can without worrying if Leo will be there."

"I agree," said Claudia. "I would give him another chance."

"I'll think about it."

* * *

Alicia watched a woman walk up the front steps.

"Hello, I am Alicia, Angela's niece. It is nice to meet you."

"Well, it is nice to meet you, young lady, I am Sally Sweet. My husband is a doctor, and we've known your aunt for years. How beautiful you are! Angela was right about you."

Mrs. Sweet held out her hand. Alicia hesitated but then slowly lifted her hand, which Mrs. Sweet reached out and lightly shook.

"Do not hog the greeter," said Mrs. Gruenberger.

Mrs. Gruenberger's German accent cut the air with her sharp English pronunciation. She moved past Mrs. Sweet and presented her hand to Alicia. Alicia thought that maybe she wanted her to kiss it.

"I am Mrs. Suzanne Gruenberger. My husband is also a doctor, but he only takes cases that other doctors are confounded by. He was a specialist in Germany."

"I am pleased to meet you," said Alicia.

Mrs. Gruenberger shook Alicia's entire arm like a car jack, as if she were about to change a tire.

"Really, Suzanne, must you?" asked Mrs. Sweet.

Dr. Gruenberger had been a respected cardiologist in Germany, but now, because of American Medical Association restrictions, he was a general practitioner.

"Hello," said Angela. "I see you have met my niece."

"Yes," said Mrs. Sweet. "And she is a lovely young woman."

"I think she looks like my sister-in-law," said Angela. "I think they all do."

"Yes, it was so sad she passed so young," said Mrs. Sweet.

"You are truly blessed, Mrs. Bellini," Mrs. Gruenberger said. "I know you have had much tragedy, as most of us immigrants have, but God has compensated you."

Nothing could compensate for the loss of my sister, brother, and sister-in-law, thought Angela. *Even today, if my sister were found alive I would board the next ship to Italy, regardless of the war in Europe or my immediate family situation.*

"Come in and have some coffee and dessert," Angela said. "Make yourselves at home. Alicia, bring the others in please. Join us."

Next-door neighbors Anna Reilly and Mable Martens were the next to arrive. Anna was a quiet, thin woman who often had Angela make her simple dresses with little embellishment. Mrs. Reilly rarely expressed an opinion, and because of her thick wire-rimmed glasses and therapeutic shoes, she looked older than she was. During her fittings, Angela would have to fill in the gaps in their conversation. Anna Reilly gave monosyllable answers.

"Hello, Mrs. Reilly," Alicia said.

"Hello, dear. You look very pretty."

"Everyone is in…"

Mrs. Reilly scurried to the dining room.

"Well, I remember you when you were a little girl," Mable Martens said.

Mabel Martens' husband was the physician Angela relied on most. He had been sympathetic when Franco had an injury from a fall several years ago and when he had his stroke. Mabel often played piano in her living room in the afternoon. She held a box of chocolates in her hand.

"Go right in," said Alicia.

I am good at this, thought Alicia. She could hear the women gushing over Nunzio in his uniform.

"Oh my, what a nice picture," said Suzanne Gruenberger. "He is a catch. Any woman would want him on their arm."

Alicia smiled, knowing that her brother would have been completely humiliated having an older woman gush over him. She saw two women climbing the porch stairs. Ramina Galluci and Amelia Saldi stepped into the vestibule.

"I hope Angela has a pot of coffee made," said Ramina. "I am frozen."

"Hello, ladies," said Alicia. "Everyone is in the dining room."

"Nice to see you, Alicia," said Ramina.

"Yes, it certainly is," said Amelia.

They each pecked Alicia on the cheek. A strong aroma of perfume permeated the air as they walked by.

Alicia could hear Sadie entertaining everyone with her opinions and sharp humor.

"Alicia, come and join us," Angela called from the dining room door.

"Someone else is coming up the stairs," Alicia said.

Angela left the dining room and looked out the hall window. She saw it was Sarah Einbinder.

"Alicia, go in the dining room and make sure everyone has what they need."

Angela stepped out on the porch to greet Sarah.

"You will catch your death," Sarah said.

"It is just for a few minutes," Angela said. "I just wanted to ask you not to mention the conversation we had about the war financing." She did not want Sarah to talk about war funding and Henry Ford. It terrified her that her clients would think she agreed with Sarah's opinion even though she did. She knew many of the women were extremely patriotic, and she might lose their business or be labeled a troublemaker.

"Of course not," Sarah said. "This is a party. It is time to celebrate and forget, if only for a moment."

"Come in and warm yourself," Angela said. Just as she was about to close the door, the last guest climbed the steps.

Mrs. Julia Greenblatt was the wealthiest of the group, with a wardrobe and home to prove it. Her parents were aristocrats from Russia who owned homes in New York City's fashionable East Side and in Nelsonville. Her husband traveled for business, and her penchant for young men was well known.

"Mrs. Bellini, how nice of you to invite me," said Julia. She took off her coat and handed it to Angela. She wore a black form-fitted dress with a low-cut neckline.

"Mrs. Greenblatt," Angela said. "You know most of the people here. Introduce yourselves." After informal introductions, the guests talked about the weather, the latest fashions, families, and the war.

"Who is this handsome specimen?" asked Julia, picking up Nunzio's picture.

"That is my nephew," said Angela. "He joined the Marines. Now he is stationed in Massachusetts." She took the picture from Julia and placed it back on buffet.

"We were just saying how handsome he is," said Mrs. Gruenberger.

"It is such a pity that there will be a shortage of young men in America," said Julia.

"My husband and I had hoped he would marry our daughter, Mary, but that did not happen," said Ramina.

"Oh, he's single?" asked Julia. "Angela Bellini, you have been holding out on us. Many of us have marriageable daughters."

Ramina's face became fixed, and her jaw was clinched.

Sadie got Angela's attention and tilted her head toward the hallway.

"Into the hallway, everyone. Alicia will make everyone a plate and bring it out to us."

Everyone moved into the hall and took their seats.

"Sarah, I hear you're connected to a political organization and that you're well informed," said Mrs. Gruenberger.

"Yes, I am a member of the Women's Jewish League in New York. Next week, I will be delivering a talk on how to assist family members who are still in Germany. You are all welcome to attend."

"Doesn't your husband disagree with you being political?" asked Julia Greenblatt.

"Do you think a husband has the right to do that?" Mrs. Sweet said. "We have had the vote for a while, and women will go out to work once all the men are gone. We should have our voice."

"I have not heard from my relatives in many months," said Mrs. Gruenberger. "We are always worried."

Alicia placed a plate of desserts on each table.

"Please enjoy your desserts," said Alicia. "They're all made by my aunt."

"I think they should kill all those Fascists," said Sadie. "The allies should drop bombs. They have done a lot of damage."

"Be practical, Sadie. You can't kill everyone," said Ramina. "You would be killing innocent people."

Alicia brought out the coffee, filling everyone's cup.

"Alicia dear, please sit," said Angela. "Enjoy your dessert. I will refill everyone's cup."

"I don't mind," said Alicia. "Just enjoy your guests."

"You should be resting in your condition," said Claudia. "Alicia is going to have a baby."

Everyone congratulated Alicia and started to give her advice on everything ranging from labor to child care.

"Tell us about your organization, Mrs. Einbinder," said Mrs. Reilly. "Will you be putting together care packages for the soldiers? Do you do that kind of thing?"

"I suppose we will," said Sarah. "But we are a group of women who monitor political activity."

"I still think once a woman marries, her place is in the home," said Mabel Martens. "I was a nurse and a professional pianist until I met my husband. I gave up both, but I still play the piano daily."

"I think Sarah is doing admirable work," said Julia Greenblatt. "I am concerned about the Nazis and Fascism in Europe myself. As far as marriage goes, I think women should marry well so that they do not have to think about money and can do serious work in the world like Sarah is doing."

"What marry at all?" asked Sarah. "If I had to do it all over again, I would have remained single and joined the resistance in Europe."

"Good for you," said Sadie. "Women can fight as well as men. Only we use our brains."

"If anyone would like to join us for our next meeting, you're welcome to come. We do good work. They are now trying to locate my sister, who was taken away by the Gestapo," Sarah said. "To the concentration camps, of course."

"That is what I have heard," said Julia. "They are taking whole families away and making them work."

"They do more than that," said Sarah.

The women all looked bewildered, as if Sarah was speaking a language they did not understand.

"Yes, I have heard they are killing people," Julia said.

"Why are they killing people?" asked Anna Reilly.

"I would say we do not know what is really going on in Europe," said Sally Sweet. "Reports are conflicting."

"Now that America is involved in the war, everything will come to light. I would suggest that you all attend a meeting with me," said Sarah. "Mrs. Gruenberger, don't you have relatives still living in Germany?"

"Sarah, I hear your husband is a radical professor," Sally said. "I believe he did not get tenure at New York University. My husband is a fellow there."

Angela did not want a political argument at her party; the world was in enough turmoil.

"Ladies," Angela said. "there is sherry on the mantle. Pour yourselves a glass so we can toast to the new year."

"Now that is a very good idea," said Sadie. She was the first one to the mantle. "I will pour everyone a glass. We need to keep our strength up for the coming war years. What better way to do it?"

"I believe you are right," said Claudia.

"Mrs. Bellini," Anna Reilly said. "Mrs. Einbinder is such an informed person. I admire her spirit, and I'm sure she's a patriot."

The fire began to dim, and a cooler air permeated the hallway.

"I assure you everyone here supports the men who will fight," Angela said. "I think we would all be more comfortable in the dining room."

As they settled into the dining room, the winter afternoon sun began to set.

"This is marvelous sherry," said Mrs. Greenblatt.

She had drunk it before Angela could do the toast.

"A woman after my own heart," said Sadie.

"Yes, it certainly is. Where did you get it?" Mrs. Martens asked.

"From the Katz liquor store."

"Oh yes, I think their son is in the Army and will fight in Europe," said Sally Sweet. "They have family in Poland, I believe."

"Let us toast to a peaceful and healthy new year," Angela said.

Everyone was quiet as they sipped their sherry, but a frazzled energy hung in the air.

"If anyone would like a dress made, you will have to wait to put in your request until after the new year," Angela said awkwardly before anyone could speak. "I am very busy this season."

"I am afraid the Katz' relatives in Poland are no longer there," Sarah said. She did not want to ruin Angela's party, but she also wanted everyone to know the truth.

"Please eat as much cake and pie as you like," Angela said. "There is plenty. Please take some home if you like."

Angela felt the afternoon would never end.

"Mrs. Martens," Angela asked, "how is your husband's practice going?"

"Very well, thank you. He will be doing exams for the Army next week. They want to make sure everyone is fit enough to fight."

The war has penetrated every aspect of life, thought Angela.

"It is time for me to go," said Sarah. "I am preparing for my presentation."

"My husband will be wondering where I am," said Anna Reilly.

"I will help clean up," said Alicia.

Everyone got up and thanked Angela for a wonderful and stimulating afternoon. She walked them to the door and helped them with their coats. Sarah Einbinder was the last in line to leave.

"I will see you after the holidays," said Sarah. "You know a wonderful mix of people. I enjoyed them all."

"I'm glad you enjoyed it," Angela said.

She closed the door and breathed a sigh of relief. It was the end of a confusing day. She sat on the steps and contemplated what had transpired. The war would now take center stage in the years to come. This was not something she could control. She thought after the earthquake that God and the Blessed Mother would take care of her as her surrogate parents. She had been through so much that she thought she had built up equity in heaven.

Angela heard a car stop in front of the house and a car door slam, which brought her back. She went to the window and saw Franco getting out of a car. She forgot that he had spent the afternoon with Gianni Galluci. He climbed the stairs one step at a time.

How did we get so old? thought Angela. She had been in America for 28 years, and she wondered where they all went. What had she accomplished in the new world? Angela remembered when she first saw Franco in the convent, when he was young and robust and full of promise. She thought her prince had come and the rest of her life would be free of hardship and uncertainty. She opened the door for Franco, and he shuffled in.

"How was your time with Gianni?" Angela asked.

"Fine," said Franco.

"All the dishes are done," said Alicia. "I have to get home to Leo. Hello, Uncle Franco, I am going to have a baby."

"Wonderful, wonderful," said Franco.

"Maybe you and Franco can have dinner with us next week." said Angela.

"Really?" asked Alicia.

"Yes. We're family, and Leo seems to be doing better."

Franco went into the dining room. That would be the extent of his conversation for the evening.

Angela reflected on how different her life was since she first arrived in America. The gathering she had was proof of that. She had increased her social connections, was considered an interesting and elegant hostess, and had built an enviable dressmaking business. *Franco's attitude during their marriage was disappointing, but,* she thought, *you never know what you get when you marry.* She had even integrated her Italian friends with her clients and neighbors. She looked toward the future for more opportunities to do better, for herself and her family.

Chapter 14

Angela collected the mail and unlocked the front door, then went into her bedroom. It was time to light the candles to the Blessed Mother. She lit each votive candle with the intention to gather strength to face whatever her path held for her. She looked through the mail and found a letter from Nunzio. She quickly opened it.

"Franco, I have a letter from Nunzio. I'll read it."

Franco was sitting in his smoking chair.

February 1942

Dear Aunt and Uncle,

I want you both to know that I have asked Felicia to marry me, and she has said yes. We want to marry in the spring. You will both like her very much. I hope you are well. I am enjoying my work at the ammunition depot. I don't know when I will be deployed to the Pacific war. There is talk of getting more training in California. so maybe I will be getting a short leave at some point. When this happens, Felicia and I will come together to see you.

I worry about the two of you alone in that house. I want you to know that I appreciate everything you have done for me. Alicia and Joe appreciate it, too. I'll write again soon. Hopefully I'll have more information about my deployment.

Nunzio

"I am happy for him," said Franco.

"Yes, I look forward to meeting her," said Angela. "They can live upstairs if Nunzio returns after the war."

"At least he will be in the United States a bit longer," said Franco.

She folded the letter and put it back in its envelope. She would add it to her mound of letters tied with a ribbon dating from 1910 to the present. If someone were to find her letters a hundred years from now, they would have a detailed picture of her life.

"He never should have gone," Franco said. "It will get much worse."

"Too late now," Angela said. "I will pray to the Blessed Mother for his safe return. It sounds like he will be on leave once more."

Franco pounded his fist on the table.

"No praying to people who aren't real," Franco demanded. "Fantasy."

"Say what you want. The Blessed Mother kept me alive so that I could take care of Speranza and her children. I have a purpose."

"It's no good. Stop praying to fantasy."

"You encouraged his interest in guns. I told you that was not good. He was a little boy. Whose fault is it he went off and signed up? He is gone because you encouraged him to act a certain way. It is no longer any concern of mine what you think is fantasy."

"He will be all right. He will come home."

"He seems very happy with this girl," said Angela. "I'm happy he has found someone. That is positive. She sounds different from Mary. I will answer him tonight. Is there anything you want me to say for you?"

Franco looked down at his clenched fist and opened his hand.

"Tell him to come home."

"I told you, he may come home before he goes to California. He is a sharpshooter, so he will be valuable in battle. Once he goes overseas, he won't be back until the war is over."

Franco had thought of Nunzio day and night since he enlisted. He would walk into town with his cane and go into a bar for a drink, but most of the discussion was about the war and how everyone knew someone who was a soldier, so he would have his drink and leave. Franco only spoke when spoken to. His daily walks and climbing the cellar stairs were making him physically stronger, but he needed more of a will to live. Nunzio had given him a purpose. Franco was the direct opposite of Salvatore. When Franco was younger, he had been strong and willful. He was confident in his ability to create and do business.

Angela went to call Nunzio's father to let him know she had received a letter from his son.

"Salvatore," Angela said. "I heard from Nunzio today, and he is engaged to that girl he met at a wedding. He still doesn't know when he will go overseas."

There was silence on the other end.

Angela thought the absence would help Nunzio and Salvatore's relationship, but apparently it had not. Salvatore did not know how to talk about his oldest child. Angela had fulfilled her obligation of letting him know that she had heard from his son. She then called Joe to let him know about his brother's letter and to invite him up from New York for Sunday dinner.

* * *

Joe came into the house on Morning Glory Avenue with his winter coat looking as new as when Angela bought it for him. When he took it off, he was wearing a crisp white shirt and black pressed pants. His black shoes were so polished that the reflection of the ceiling light glowed and pulsated on the leather. As Angela put his coat away, the aroma of French cologne emanated from the material. She smiled. It was a dramatic change from his upbringing, and she felt proud that she had supported his vision of moving to New York. *Everyone should have their wish*, she thought, and she was glad that Joe got his.

"You look wonderful and happy," said Angela.

"I owe a lot to you, Aunt Angela," said Joe. "This would not have happened without you."

"I'm glad you're living the life you wanted," said Angela. She hugged and kissed him on each cheek.

"So, Nunzio is engaged," said Joe. "Mary Galluci will be upset and a little crazy." He lit a Fatima cigarette, took a long drag, and held his cigarette in the air.

"You smoke now?"

"Everyone does in New York."

"I'm glad Nunzio found someone," said Angela. "Mary wasn't the girl for him. Maybe you can find a nice girl someday."

"I'm not interested in getting married," said Joe. "It's a plus that she's from an Italian family. She'll be familiar with all the drama."

"Just remember it's not good to be alone all the time," said Angela.

"I'm not alone," said Joe. "I have plenty of friends. Who else is coming for dinner?"

"I invited your sister. Leo is helping a friend fix a few cars for extra money. Your sister has an announcement."

"She's pregnant," said Joe. He flicked his ashes in the ash tray.

"Who told you?"

"No one. In Nelsonville, what else could it be?"

Alicia arrived, and Franco sat at the head of the table. They ate Eggplant Parmesan and pasta with an arugula salad. The eggplant dish was cooked with tomatoes Angela had canned from the garden and fresh mozzarella. The sweet aroma filled the dining room. Alicia talked about preparing for the new baby and her search for an apartment for her growing family. Joe talked about his adventures in New York and his prospects for a job at American Express. Franco even seemed to be at peace. Angela sat back and watched her niece and nephew talk and laugh. She missed Nunzio, but he was doing better than she had thought possible. Her unseen friends always urged Angela to embrace change and stay in the moment. That is what she decided she would do.

* * *

A few days later, Angela walked with a quickened step toward Alicia's house near the railway station. They were having lunch together, so she carried a cake she had made for dessert. The serenity and connection she had experienced at the Sunday dinner stayed with her, and she was hopeful that Alicia would be happy in her marriage. Everything seemed to be finally falling into place for the better.

When Angela reached Leo and Alicia's house, she heard crying. The front door was wide open. Angela froze at the front door and started to hyperventilate. *Not now*, she thought, *when everything was going so well.*

She couldn't seem to breathe until she used her voice. It was as if her voice thawed her fear and anger.

"Alicia, tell me where you are!" screamed Angela.

She frantically looked around and heard cries for help coming from the bedroom. Angela found Alicia on the floor with blood covering her face. Alicia looked like Speranza, and what Angela saw sent her into a tailspin. Both of Alicia's eyes were swollen, and her nose appeared flattened. She ran to get ice, but there was none.

"I have to call the doctor."

Angela ran to the nearest phone booth and called Doctor Sweet. Her hopefulness had collapsed like so many shards of glass, and she vowed she would make sure that Leo stepped on them. Things are never what they seem. Her unseen friends would say that occasionally, but in this situation, she did not use that discernment. They would often stress feeling through a situation or person to uncover the truth.

Angela would never turn her back on the truth again. She allowed the anger to rise to the surface and flood every cell of her body and beyond, into the non-visible world where her unseen friends resided. The communication she received back from her unseen friends was for her to assist her niece as much as she could and not be fooled again by Leo's seemingly good behavior. She ran back to the house.

"Dr. Sweet is on his way," said Angela.

In the meantime, Angela wet towels with cold water and cleaned Alicia's face.

"He's a son of a bitch," said Angela. "He needs to be in jail like his father."

Alicia could only moan. Angela felt her niece's jaw and realized it was broken.

* * *

Angela moved Alicia into Morning Glory Avenue to heal. Alicia eventually got a waitressing job in town, and Angela prepared for a new baby. Nunzio and Felicia's wedding was set for April, and he had obtained a short leave in late February.

"It's a good thing the baby wasn't harmed," said Sadie on one of her impromptu visits. But aren't you tired of taking care of everybody? You raised Speranza's children, and now you have to care for a baby."

"I need to help her get on her feet," said Angela. "But I won't be fooled again."

"I suppose," said Sadie, "but don't get your hopes up. I doubt Alicia will stay."

Angela's unseen friends counseled her to make clear choices. She had made a choice to help Alicia, but she knew she had limited power about the outcome.

"I'm so happy Nunzio is engaged," said Angela. "I believe that he will live a happy life now. He is bringing his fiancé next. I am hoping they will eventually live upstairs."

"Good luck with that," said Sadie. "Children don't live with their parents anymore. They want their own house."

* * *

"My dear, I am so glad you are here," Angela said. "Nunzio speaks highly of you."

"I have heard so much about you, Mrs. Bellini," Felicia said.

Franco extended his hand to Felicia and held it for a moment. She was impeccably dressed in a faux fur coat, gloves and hat. She was petite, slender, and pretty. There was a sparkle and excitement to her presence. Nunzio had told them he'd first seen Felicia in Hingham, where she was dancing the jitterbug with a serviceman. During their high-spirited dance, the serviceman had twirled Felicia and flipped her over, making Nunzio impressed with her energy and boldness. They'd met again at a wedding of mutual friends, and he ended up driving her home.

"Your brother, Joe, would like to meet Felicia," Angela said.

"We can go to the city and see him," said Nunzio.

"That would be very nice," Angela said.

Nunzio and Felicia told them they would marry in April and would have the wedding in the bride's hometown of Cohasset, Massachusetts. Nunzio would wear his dress uniform, and the bride a formal gown. Nunzio planned for Angela and Franco to travel by train to Boston. Aware that Italian-Americans usually married someone from their hometown, Nunzio was relieved that he had chosen someone from outside of Nelsonville.

"Felicia, you can freshen up in the bathroom," said Angela. "Walk through the kitchen, and it's the door facing you."

Felicia excused herself.

"Well, she is everything you said she was," said Angela. "Independent and energetic and certainly well-dressed."

The next day, Nunzio took Felicia into New York City.

They got off at Grand Central Station and walked to the American Express office, where Joe had secured a job booking travel arrangements. Nunzio went up to Joe's desk, and Felicia stood behind her fiancé.

"Hi, Joe," Nunzio said.

"Hello, I'm glad you came into town," Joe said happily. "I thought Felicia was coming with you. Don't tell me she's dumped you."

Felicia stepped out from behind Nunzio. Joe would describe that moment in the future: "I fell in love immediately."

"Oh, you are charming and petite," said Joe. "I am glad you will be a part of the family. This is so important."

"How long have you worked here, Joe?" Felicia asked.

"About a year," said Joe.

"While you show Felicia around, I am going next door to the Marine recruitment office to see their setup."

"I'll take good care of her," Joe said.

Joe felt that he had met a kindred spirit in style and sensibility. He saw how strong she was, and that quality was something he admired in women.

"Our wedding is in April in Cohasset. You can take the train with Angela and Franco."

"A train ticket to Boston is beyond my means. Rent is very high in New York."

"I am sure Nunzio will help you," Felicia said.

Felicia flashed her wide smile and touched Joe's arm. Joe wondered how much she knew about his family. He wondered if she saw that he was different. She didn't know yet that Joe would never ask his brother for money because he felt that Nunzio was ashamed of him.

"We'll see when the time comes," Joe said. "In the meantime, I think you're beautiful and my family is lucky to have you."

"I have not met your father and stepmother yet. Nunzio does not seem to be anxious for me to meet them."

"How much do you know about my father and my mother?"

"Just that your mother died when she was very young, and your father remarried."

"You'll meet them. I should tell you about my stepmother…"

"Hi," said Nunzio returning, "I hope my brother didn't bore you."

"I was just going to tell Felicia about our stepmother," Joe said.

"We have to get going. We're off to buy a coat," said Nunzio.

"Nunzio will tell me about your stepmother."

"No need for that," Nunzio said. "I don't have much to do with them. I live my own life— and besides, Angela and Franco raised me. You have already met my parents."

Felicia sensed heaviness in Joe's silence and observed that Nunzio could silence Joe. Before they walked away, Felicia planted a kiss on Joe's cheek. Joe smiled and thought it best not to bring up any more family history. He sensed that Felicia was open-minded and easy to talk to, and he looked forward to more connection with her in the future.

Felicia and Nunzio walked toward the door. At the exit, Felicia turned around and waved goodbye. He returned the wave and hoped that after she learned about his father marrying his niece, she would still marry his brother—not for Nunzio, but for himself.

* * *

On a chilly March morning, Joe sat on his bed in his rooming house and rifled through his mail. There was an envelope with Felicia's name and return address on it. He opened it and found a check with a note: "I want you to come to our wedding. Here is the money for the trip, and you can stay with my parents. This will be our secret. Don't worry about a present. I will need a dance partner. Bring a friend if you like."

He felt he was an embarrassment to his family, but here was a future member of his family reaching out. She must also see him as a kindred spirit. Angela had offered to pay for his ticket, but he refused, saying she had done enough for him. He jumped up and opened his cardboard suitcase and began to pack even though the wedding was a month away. He would wear the suit he wore to Alicia's wedding.

* * *

The wedding went off in the typical 1940s fashion. There were many men in uniform and young women looking for husbands. It seemed that the entire town showed up at the church. At the wedding reception, Joe sat with his aunt and uncle. Alicia's doctor suggested she not travel because of her pregnancy.

"Look at how pretty Felicia's sister is," said Angela. "She makes a wonderful maid of honor. Joe, you should talk to her."

"I'm not here to find a girlfriend, Aunt Angela," Joe said. "I'm here to celebrate Nunzio's marriage and to get to know Felicia."

After dinner, the band began to play, and couples found their way to the dance floor. Nunzio had awkwardly attempted the first dance with Felicia, but he did not know how to dance, so Felicia had to lead. Joe asked Felicia to dance, and they took the floor. The band played a waltz, and they glided over the dance floor.

"Thank you for the money, Felicia," Joe said. "Without your help, I never would have been able to come and celebrate with you."

"I told you I needed a dance partner," Felicia said. "Besides, I'm sure Nunzio wanted you here."

Felicia's background was Italian, but she was raised in New England among Yankees—people who were fiercely independent. Family was important but not all consuming. Yankees stood a stand regardless of what others thought. Her father had been born in Italy, but her mother was born in New England, so Felicia's upbringing was more free-flowing.

"Thanks for keeping it a secret. I feel like we're partners in crime."

"You should have brought a friend," said Felicia.

"I don't think you want my friends here," said Joe.

"It would have been nice for you not to be alone."

"I have you to dance with, so I'm not alone," said Joe. "My aunt suggested I become interested in your sister."

"You will find someone someday," Felicia said. "You don't have to pretend with me. You are of a different persuasion. That's all right."

"I knew that I had found a friend for life," said Joe.

The band then played swing music, and Joe and Felicia began to jitterbug. The guests gathered around and clapped. Joe swung Felicia around from one end of the room to the other, moving toward and away from each other. Angela was delighted to see such vibrant energy. She saw Nunzio and Felicia's marriage as adding to a family who needed fresh energy and a different point of view.

* * *

Nunzio left for the Pacific a few weeks after the wedding. Angela kept in contact with Felicia, who remained in Cohasset with her parents and continued to work at the ammunition depot. Angela prayed every day for her nephew's safe return from war. She sent him care packages with socks, chocolate, cigarettes, and encouraging words. His letters were frequent at first, and then they were occasional.

August 1942

Dear Aunt and Uncle,

We have landed on Guadalcanal. While we suffered casualties, it was not as bad as the Japanese. Our orders were to secure an air strip, which we did successfully. There are many more battles ahead. There are rumors that after the battles on Guadalcanal are over, some of us will get leave. I'm hoping I will be able to come home for a while.

I had never seen a man die before. Now I have, and I don't care to see it again. I know I will. There are many more islands we must take, so more of our soldiers will die. If I am one of them, please stay connected to Felicia. I hope we win the war soon, so we can all go home.

Nunzio

Angela folded the letter and put it in her dresser drawer with the letters from Franco, her brother, and the nuns from the convent in Sicily. They were a map of her life. She watched over them as if they were important documents that would one day shed light on the times in which she lived. She placed them in chronological order and read them occasionally, from the earliest date to the present, like a novel. She was born in the previous century and was nearly halfway through the 20th Century. The modern world was changing rapidly, and Angela navigated between the two centuries.

Angela had gently placed the letters in the drawer when the doorbell rang. A wave of fear engulfed every cell of her body. She wasn't expecting company. What if it was the Marines with news that Nunzio had died or was missing in action? If she didn't answer the door, Nunzio would still be alive in her mind and life would continue. If she found that men in uniform stood at her door, then her life would be once again changed forever. Angela felt frozen in time and called on her unseen friends, who encouraged her to answer the door and welcome in whoever stood on the porch.

This was an aspect of her life that would not be found in her letters. The connection she had with formless beings not only had no evidence, but there was no one who knew. This experience of her life on earth was internal and difficult to explain to anyone—friend or family.

Angela felt like she had weights on her legs as she crept to the hall window and reluctantly moved her gaze to the front door. She kept her eyes on the porch floor so she could see the person's shoes first. Her unseen friends told her you could tell a lot about a person's journey by examining their shoes; how they walked through life was imprinted in the leather and the sole.

Angela took a deep breath and saw a pair of old brown women's shoes with a small worn heel, the sides and soles worn on each side. Angela breathed a sigh of relief as she quickly opened the door.

"Sadie," said Angela. "I thought you were the Marines telling me that Nunzio was gone."

"Do I look like a Marine?"

Sadie carried a bottled of red wine.

"No, I was just reading a letter from Nunzio, and my mind ran away with me when the doorbell rang."

"Oh, how is he?"

"I think he's doing ok. He says he might have leave once the Guadalcanal fighting is over."

Sadie held up the bottle of wine. "Well, let's celebrate that he is doing ok and will soon be home."

"Everyone says that I drink others' wine and don't contribute. Well, here is my contribution. Are you busy?"

"No, I was going to read the newspaper."

"Forget about the news. Have a drink with me," Sadie said.

They sat at the dining room table and sipped the wine.

"That's what I like about you, Angie. You'll drink wine in the afternoon like a sane person. I find it strange that Nunzio will get leave now. They usually keep soldiers at least a few years unless there is a problem."

"He doesn't say there is a problem, so I am praying for Nunzio to come home," said Angela.

"He has a wife now. He'll come home to her," said Sadie.

"I know, and we're hoping they will live upstairs someday."

"That would be wonderful for you and Franco," said Sadie.

"There will be children here one day, I know it."

"How do you know? Did the Blessed Mother tell you that?" asked Sadie. "I often wonder where you get your information. How you can be so sure there will be children here?"

It was true that Sadie was open-minded and never followed rules or protocol like many Italians, but to speak to her about her unseen friends was different. It would open a conversation that Angela was not prepared to have. Her survival had once depended on her unseen friends, so she felt talking about them would trivialize their relationship with her. Their relationship could not be intellectually understood; it had to be experienced.

"I just know that there will be a family here one day. No one told me."

"Ok, you see the future. I should ask you who will win the next horse race. Can you make me a little money?"

"It doesn't work like that," said Angela.

"I heard Alicia is back with her husband," said Sadie. "I predicted that, and I don't have a crystal ball."

Alicia had had her baby, and Angela was adamant about her staying at Morning Glory Avenue—but Alicia had made up her mind to return to Leo and the house near the railroad station. It angered Angela that Alicia would make the choice to return to a chaotic situation, but there was nothing she could do to deter her niece. Angela had to accept that her influence had its limitations.

"My door is always open to Alicia and the baby. She is Speranza's child, and I will always look after her."

"You're too good, Angie," said Sadie. "You really are."

Chapter 15

Summer 1943

After the many months of Guadalcanal fighting, Nunzio obtained leave and was visiting Angela and Franco on Morning Glory Avenue after he had spent time with Felicia. He was underweight and talked little. He spent his visit lying around the upstairs apartment.

"Nunzio," called Angela. She stood at the bottom of the stairs and waited for a response. "Nunzio."

There was silence. She decided to go and see if he was sleeping.

"Nunzio, are you here?"

"Yeah, I'm in the bedroom," Nunzio said.

"Why don't you come downstairs and have some lunch? I will be going shopping in a while and I will need help with the bags."

He was lying on the bed staring at the ceiling. Angela noticed a glazed look in his eyes. Something was missing from his presence that she could not place, and some of his energy she could not recognize. His behavior had even been different. He startled easily, stayed up at night, and was restless during the day. She wondered if Felicia had noticed the change in her husband.

Angela knew that glazed look well. Messina's residents projected the same expression after the earthquake. Angela did not intrude on Nunzio's reality, she simply invited him to participate in hers. They walked down Morning Glory Avenue and turned into town.

Angela held his arm and nodded to acquaintances. She felt his hand shake.

"Your hand is shaking. What is wrong?"

"Nothing. It's just the result of shooting my gun. It will calm down."

Angela felt that he seemed weak. He had left strong and healthy, but since he had been fighting in the Pacific, his energy had disappeared.

"The military doctors say I'll be fine, especially since I have leave."

"They gave you leave because you're not well?"

"No, they gave me, and other men, leave to rest before the next campaign."

"I need to go into the Bloomfield Dress Shop to see if she has any alterations for me," Angela said. "When we get home, I will call Dr. Martens. I trust our doctor."

"I have seen a doctor, and I don't need another. I'll wait here while you go inside."

"Come in and say hello to Mrs. Bloomfield. She would like to see you."

Nunzio paused and stood facing the shop window. Angela guided him into the shop.

"Good morning, Mrs. Bloomfield. I was just passing by with my nephew, so I thought I would check to see if you had any work for me. This is Nunzio. He's just come back from the Pacific.

"I remember your nephew. We need brave young men like you. You must be so happy to have him home."

Angela smiled. She hoped that the positive response from people would brighten Nunzio's spirits.

"I am so happy, and his wife is relieved. He is just with us for a few days."

"My son is in Europe fighting," Mrs. Bloomfield said. "We miss him every day. I'm hoping he comes home soon."

"I will pray for him. I am sure he will come home."

"I have several clients' garments that need alteration. I will bring them by your house later today."

"Thank you so much. I will see you later. Goodbye."

Angela looked at Nunzio. It was as if he did not know how to interact. He hesitated, then spoke.

"Nice to see you, Mrs. Bloomfield."

As they turned to leave, Nunzio steadied himself on the doorknob.

"Are you sure you are feeling well?" Angela asked. "We can go home."

"I'm fine. Why did you tell her that her son will return? You don't know that."

"It's best to be positive," said Angela. "I was positive about your return, and now here you are. Once the war is over, you will be back—even if you live in Cohasset. You and Felicia are welcome to live with us if you want."

"I want to make a career in the military and travel," said Nunzio.

Angela was not enthusiastic about a career in the military for her nephew, and she was sure Felicia would agree—but what were the alternatives with no education? If Nunzio demonstrated interest in the military, then Angela would support him regardless of what she thought, and no one had to know what she thought—not even Nunzio or Felicia. That was the advantage of remaining silent; no one could criticize or try to argue an opposite position. Besides, the country was at war, and it was not the time to express an opinion outside the consensus.

"How is Felicia?" asked Angela.

Nunzio smiled. It was the first time she had seen him smile since he returned.

"She is fine," said Nunzio. "We're not sure where we will live after the war."

"You need to see your father. He asks about you."

"We don't have much in common," Nunzio said. He looked down as they walked through the town and wiped his brow.

"You are sweating," Angela said. "Doctor Martens will examine you."

"I'm fine. Please stop pestering me."

"A phone call to your father will do. He has been worried about your safety. Besides, you will want to see Joe and Alicia, and there is a new baby."

"You can invite them over. I don't want to talk to my father's wife or, should I say, my cousin."

"I know how you feel about Immacolatta, but she is your stepmother."

"He also has a new family. I don't know how Joe and Alicia can be so accepting."

"They want to have a relationship with their father. It is understandable."

Angela wanted to maintain an equilibrium within the family. Over the years, she had learned diplomacy regarding family matters.

"I won't force you, but maybe you can find a way to talk to him."

"I don't want to talk to a man who would marry his niece. It's embarrassing. He's embarrassed me his whole life, and I don't claim his children as my siblings."

Angela saw his face freeze as if he had been injected with anger and disappointment. She decided she would not bring up the subject again. The concerns of war had taken center stage in his life, not old family problems.

Nunzio left and returned to Cohasset for the rest of his leave. He did not see Dr. Martens, but Angela was comforted that he would spend time with Felicia before he returned to the Pacific. She had feared that her business would suffer because of the war, but the opposite happened. Even with rationing, the America economy was improved by the war. People were working for the war effort, and women who could not afford to have their clothes altered by a seamstress before the war would show up at her door.

Her well-to-do clients were still coming over to order dresses and suits. But when they left, the house was so quiet that Angela sometimes talked to herself out loud or to her unseen friends. They would listen, but they did not have bodies—and what she needed was embodied people with whom she could relate. Angela started to invite her friends over more regularly so that she could practice speaking her mother tongue. As the years went by, she had started to lose bits of her language. Sadie was a regular visitor, but they spoke mostly English. Her language was another reminder of all that she had lost.

Chapter 16

September 1945

Nunzio had returned from the war physically intact and was living in Cohasset with Felicia after his discharge. Angela and Franco were preparing for a trip to visit them. They boarded the train to Boston, where Nunzio picked them up, and they drove to Cohasset.

"Beautiful scenery, coming into Boston," Angela said.

"Yeah," said Nunzio.

"Do you have a job?" Franco asked.

"Yeah," Nunzio said, and stared at the road.

Angela and Franco looked at one another.

"What kind of work?" Angela asked.

"A mechanic," Nunzio said. His face was emotionless and expressed neither relief that he was home nor happiness that he had a job and a wife.

Angela saw that the change in Nunzio's presence was worse than she remembered from two years ago. He stared into space as if he were watching an event unfold. He seemed moody and short-tempered. She assumed it was the shock of living a normal life and that it would pass with time and once he had a family.

"I'm looking forward to seeing Felicia again," Angela said. "We have been writing to each other while you were away. She is looking forward to starting a family."

"Everyone seems to know what is best for me," said Nunzio.

"We don't mean that," said Franco.

"We want you to be happy," Angela said.

"I am happy. We're here," Nunzio said.

"Are you…alright?" asked Franco timidly.

"I'm fine. Come inside," said Nunzio.

The table was set for lunch, and everyone sat down. Felicia passed the pasta.

"I will show you the garage I'm thinking of buying," said Nunzio.

"Here, in Cohasset?" asked Angela, shocked.

"Well, yeah. I would have my own business. I could be more independent than working for someone else. But then I'm also thinking about a military career. We could travel and see the world."

"But Felicia wants to start a family," said Angela. "You cannot do both."

"Listen, don't tell me what to do," said Nunzio.

"We are not telling you what to do, but we are renovating the space upstairs and you and Felicia are welcome to live there. It would be nice to have children in the house."

Felicia looked at her husband and waited for him to respond to Angela's offer.

Nunzio did feel an obligation to Angela and Nunzio because of all they had done for him.

"We will think about it," Felicia said.

"Ok, maybe. I'll think about it," said Nunzio.

"We will take you to see the garage. It's right down the street," Felicia said. "It is a good opportunity for Nunzio."

Angela needed Nunzio to return to Nelsonville. She and Franco were alone without children to care for them as they grew older. Alicia was still having her own problems, and Joe had his own life. Her unseen friends had said she would have children upstairs, and she assumed that Nunzio would provide them. The next few days were filled with family dinners, visits to the beach, and discussing Nunzio and Felicia's future. One evening, Nunzio brought up Angela's offer while he and Felicia walked on the beach with Angela.

"Maybe it would be a good idea for us to return to Nelsonville," he said.

Since his return from Iwo Jima, indeed having been sent back into battle after Guadalcanal, he was nervous and apprehensive about the future. He had experienced chaos and death and felt alone in his experience. His former life with Angela and Franco had brought him stability, and he wanted that again.

"Why? You would have a business here," said Felicia.

"I would like to stay in the military. A friend of mine told me the other day that Camp Smith, across the river from Nelsonville, is looking for someone to teach the FBI to shoot. Besides, I owe Angela and Franco a great debt. They took me in and raised me. Let's try it for a while."

"We would love to have you in our home," said Angela. "It has been waiting for children. Come anytime. The renovations will be completed soon, and you can take your time moving in."

"That would be very nice," said Franco.

"I would be so happy to help with the children when they come," said Angela.

"It would be exciting to live near New York City," said Felicia. "And I would appreciate the help with children."

Angela smiled. Her unseen friends were right, and she knew the children who were to be born were destined to be part of her life. She knew the war had taken its toll on her nephew, but once he started to have a family, she was sure he would become himself again.

* * *

Angela carried linens up the stairs and placed them on the new bed she and Franco had purchased for Felicia and Nunzio, then went into the new kitchen.

"They will be here in a few days," said Angela. "I want to make sure we have everything ready."

Franco was making sure the appliances worked. Since Nunzio had decided to move back to Nelsonville, Franco's mood had lightened and he even seemed younger. She hadn't seen him this enthusiastic since their honeymoon.

"I'm so glad Nunzio survived the war and has a wife," said Franco.

"Yes, we have a new beginning," said Angela. This was the event she had anticipated.

"Is the stove working?" Angela asked.

"Yes, it is all ready," said Franco.

"This is like starting over," said Angela. "Speranza would be so happy."

Angela took Franco's hand, walked down the hallway, and paused at the bottom of the stairs. They both looked back at the house.

"Soon there will be a lot of activity here," said Angela.

Angela thanked her unseen friends that night for their support over the years and told them that she would do her best to influence Speranza's grandchildren so that they would appreciate art, music, and culture.

* * *

"I don't think I'll ever get used to living so far away from a beach," said Felicia.

"Well, there is the Hudson River," said Angela, "but it isn't the Atlantic Ocean."

"I've only been here a few months, but everyone seems so rough here," Felicia said. "There's not much to do, and the town needs a facelift."

"It has needed renovation for a long time," said Angela. "When the men left during the war, it seemed to deteriorate. There was no one here to do the work."

Cohasset was a town that thrived on a summer population of wealthy Bostonians who purchased large homes that could be used year-round. It was picturesque and clean.

"How are you finding living here in general?" Angela asked.

"I miss Cohasset and my friends," said Felicia. "People are different here. I guess it's the city influence."

"You will get used to it," Angela said. "It took me a long while when I first came to this country. Our husbands want to be here, so we make the best of it."

"I guess we just go along with their wishes," said Felicia.

"I have found that to be true of most women. If there had not been the earthquake, I would not be here—but I'm glad I am in America, because the war destroyed Europe."

"Yes, I suppose you are fortunate in that way," said Felicia.

In the spring of 1946, Felicia told Angela she was pregnant. It was almost as euphoric for Angela as the day the Americans rescued her from the aftermath of the earthquake. Full of relief and hope, Angela held a special dinner in celebration of new life.

"Congratulations to Nunzio and Felicia," Angela said, raising her wine glass. "We are looking forward to welcoming this baby into our home."

Nunzio had asked Angela not to invite Salvatore and Immacolatta. Angela felt uncomfortable about excluding them but was also happy that she and Franco were now positioned as "grandparents." Alicia and Leo had moved closer to New York City, where Leo found employment on the railroad, and they rarely visited Nelsonville.

"You can tell them in your own time," Angela said. She had immediately gone out and bought baby blankets and diapers.

The baby was born in January 1947, and they named him Frank. Their family was now complete, and Angela and Franco reveled in spoiling him.

* * *

"It is so nice to see you, Mrs. Einbinder. How have you been?" asked Angela.

"I have just returned from Europe to try and find my family."

"Did you find your sister?"

"I found no one," said Sarah Einbinder. "My family is gone."

"I am so sorry to hear that," said Angela. "I know what you are going through."

"I know you do, Mrs. Bellini."

"Your boys are home and safe," said Angela. "They survived fighting in Europe."

"Yes, they are both safe. They have returned to college. At least I have them."

Angela was grateful that Sarah Einbinder's sons and Nunzio survived fighting in the war. She wondered if her friend's sons had trouble adjusting to civilian life.

"I don't think my nephew is the same person who went to war, but I am thankful he is alive. He's married now with a baby."

"None of the men will be the same, but nobody is talking about the effects of war. It's business as usual."

"What would you like me to make for you?" asked Angela.

"I would like a simple dress with long sleeves. One color. I am sorry I was never able to produce a play about your life, but with the war and the price of venues…"

"That is all right. It was so long ago, and now I'm busy with Nunzio and his family. It's time to look to the future."

"I think looking to the future is where we should all be focusing."

Angela brought out fabric samples.

"Here are a few suggestions. The dark green is pretty, and it will hang nicely. Things should be much better now that we won the war," said Angela.

"The industrialists won the war. They always do. They always win."

There was a resignation in Sarah's voice that she had never heard before.

"What do you mean?" asked Angela.

"We are now set on a trajectory that will be difficult to change going forward, but the Nazis and their horror needed to be stopped. The industrialists made their money, and they will be looking for future wars to make more. Let's concentrate on my new dress."

Angela showed Sarah some new patterns she had purchased. Sarah chose a pattern and decided on the green material.

"As soon as the material comes in, I'll call you," said Angela.

"Thank you, Mrs. Bellini," said Sarah. "I am glad your nephew made it through the war. The hard part is now living a normal life."

Chapter 12

1953

As Nunzio and Felicia's family grew, Angela made sure that all the children were nurtured. They ultimately had four children, Frank (middle name?) in 1947, Robert Joseph in 1949, and Marie Speranza in 1952. Today their last child had been born.

"Another girl," said Nunzio. His face betrayed a depth of disappointment.

"That is nice," said Angela. "Two boys and two girls. That is perfect."

Angela loved the idea of making frilly dresses for little girls. The last time she made a dress for a little girl was when Alicia was a child. It excited her that she would have a chance through her creativity to influence a new generation.

Frank and Robert were sitting at the kitchen table waiting for their father to acknowledge them. Marie was in the high chair. Nunzio went upstairs without another word.

"Why doesn't Dad like us?" asked Frank.

"He doesn't feel well," said Angela.

Angela understood that Nunzio had lost many friends in the war and was not satisfied with the way his life was going, even though he had secured a position at Camp Smith teaching marksmanship to the FBI. He was drinking excessively. She feared there would come a time when he would not keep the balance and energies would tip. She knew he would have preferred to stay in the Marines and travel, but Felicia wanted to have children, so he had gone into the Marine Corps Reserves. His young children made him uncomfortable. Angela sensed it was not the life he had envisioned.

"Frank, take your brother outside and play," Angela said.

"Can we see the baby?" Frank asked.

"When Mommy brings her home. Now go play in the yard and don't worry about anything," said Angela.

Angela was thrilled that there were children in the house. This was what she had always wanted. She had already made a simple pink dress with lace on the hem and sleeves, just in case this baby was a girl. It was identical to the one she had made for Marie.

Angela dialed Sadie's number.

"Sadie, Felicia had another girl," said Angela. "Yes, I am happy. It will be nice to have little girls in the house."

Nunzio came down the staircase.

"Sadie, I will talk to you later," Angela said.

"I'm going out," Nunzio said.

"Are you going to the hospital?"

"No, going for a drink," said Nunzio, a cigarette dangling from his mouth.

"It's the middle of the day," said Angela.

The front door shut behind him.

Angela put on her coat and headed to the hospital.

* * *

She found Felicia sitting up in bed and feeding the baby a bottle.

"Here she is, another princess," Angela said. "I am so glad you have two girls."

"Where is Nunzio?" asked Felicia.

"He had to help Franco with something. He is coming later. Can I hold her?"

Felicia gave the baby to Angela.

"Both the girls remind me of Alicia when she was a baby," said Angela.

* * *

Felicia and the baby came home to Morning Glory Avenue on a cold October morning. Nunzio's mood had lightened, and Felicia held the new baby.

"We have decided to name this baby Andrea Angela," said Felicia.

Angela's heart sang, and she reached to hold her namesake. This was a second chance for Angela to make everything right. She would make Marie Speranza and Andrea Angela her focus going forward. This generation would do well under her guidance, and they would be successful in the new world.

She had not been able to mold her sister-in-law's children into what she would consider successful people—but now she was wiser and felt stronger in her position within the family, so she could be more forceful with her ideas. She now had two great-nephews and two great-nieces, and this was as close to Angela's version of heaven as she could get. Her unseen friends had been right all along. She felt her time had finally come. She gave Andrea to Felicia and picked up Marie Speranza.

"God took my Speranza but has given me you," said Angela.

* * *

Nunzio had chest pain one day while helping Franco, and he went to see Dr. Martens. After careful examination and testing, it was found that he had had a mild heart attack. He retired from the Reserves at age 36 because of ill health but continued his job at Camp Smith. The doctor cautioned Nunzio about his smoking and alcohol intake. Felicia made sure he ate properly and stopped buying wine. Angela attempted to keep Nunzio busy on the weekends with small tasks around the house. As the boys grew older, they spent long hours with Franco learning about woodworking and how to use tools. Angela's time was spent with the girls.

"Tell us about the good angels and the bad angels," said four-year-old Marie. Her younger sister looked on as they played in Angela's sitting room.

"There was an angel who disobeyed God," said Angela. "He was a mean angel and he appeared dark when you looked at him. He was not helping people and was jealous of God's power and His love for the other angels, so God cast him out of heaven."

"What other angels?" asked Marie.

"The angel Michael is one of God's important angels. He likes to wear armor and has a sword."

"He's in the army?" asked Marie.

"I suppose he is in God's army," said Angela.

Marie listened intently while her sister played with a doll. She had her own private seamstress and storyteller, which was better than being read *The Three Little Kittens*.

"Did God kill the bad angel?" asked Marie.

"No, God does not kill angels. He put him in the underworld where there is no light, so he would have no power and could not hurt anyone."

"Then why does he let people die, but not angels?"

"Because He wants us to come home after we are done with our journey on earth," Angela said. "Like your grandmother you're named for. Your middle name was her first name."

"Can you see angels?" asked Marie.

"No, but you can *feel* them."

Angela was careful not to talk about heaven or hell. She wasn't sure she believed in either. Her unseen friends dwelled in a space that was neither. They never talked about heaven or hell, yet they were a real as anyone she knew.

"There is always our Blessed Mother," said Angela. "She helps God make decisions, but she can also intervene on earth and save people. She saved me when I was sick and dying. Keep her close to your heart."

She handed Marie a holy card with the image of Mary clothed in flowing blue robes pointing at her sacred heart.

"If you follow your heart, our Blessed Mother will help you no matter what."

Angela's heart warmed that she had such an attentive pupil. Marie's future would stay bright, and Angela would lead her.

* * *

Angela prepared Marie's dress pattern for Easter. It would be Marie's first fitting in front of the full-length mirror.

"Come up on the platform," Angela said. "You are my first customer of the day. I have sewn for three generations now. You are the third. When I make a dress, people feel what the dress suggests. I have made a petticoat to go under your dress."

Angela slipped the petticoat over Marie's small, thin form. It flared out at the bottom with several layers of lace. She picked up a blue taffeta dress with puffy sleeves and placed it over her shoulders.

"I like the slip better. It's fancier, and it makes me feel fancy. I can just wear the slip."

"You cannot go to church on Easter Sunday wearing a slip. It will reflect badly on the family, and people will talk."

"Yes, but I'm a customer, so I can choose what I want to wear."

"Your mother will not let you wear a slip to church," said Angela. "I would say the same thing to any of my customers."

"You know, I think angels visit me in my dreams," said Marie.

Angela stood up from pinning the hem.

"If angels visit you, you should talk to them."

"Really?"

"Yes, I talk to the Blessed Mother and she helps me."

"In your dreams?"

"No, during the day," said Angela. "Life does not happen with just what we can see. I am done. It fits you well."

Angela stepped back and admired her work. *The blue suits her*, thought Angela. She imagined making Marie other dresses as she grew into womanhood. It would be a way of chronicling Marie's growth.

"They're not around me during the day," said Marie.

"As you grow, you will discover that they are around you when you are awake, along with others."

Marie was quiet and seemed to know what Angela was talking about. Angela was comforted she had found a kindred spirit.

* * *

There was a nagging feel of discontent that had slowly seeped into the walls and ceiling of the Queen Anne Victorian on Morning Glory Avenue, much like the malevolent energy caught between the buildings in Messina.

Nunzio continued to have problems at home; one evening it was the children's bedtime, and Felicia was in a playful mood and invited Nunzio to help her put the girls to bed.

"Nunzio, come and read the girls a story," said Felicia.

"No," Nunzio said.

She put her arms around him.

"Come on. They would like that."

"Leave me alone," Nunzio said.

"Oh, come on, just for a little while."

"Jesus, will you people leave me alone?" Nunzio yelled. "How many times have I told you to leave me alone!"

He got his jacket and ran downstairs, pushing Angela out of the way.

"Where are you going?" asked Angela.

He slammed the door.

Angela called up the stairs. "Felicia, what happened?"

"I don't know. You have to ask him."

Angela went upstairs.

"I can't control his behavior, and I don't want him around the children like that. I don't think he cares for the children at all."

"The war left him deeply scarred," said Angela. "He needs to go to a doctor. It's never been this bad."

"I know he'll never forget what happened during the war, but I can't let it interfere with the care of the children."

"Do you know where he went?" asked Angela.

"I don't know," said Felicia. "I'll call around in the morning if he's not home."

At the very least, Angela thought that Felicia should see if her husband was at any of his friends' homes. Whenever Nunzio acted out, Angela was frightened because she thought Felicia might go back to Cohasset and take the children. The children had become the world to her and kept her going.

Angela went to bed and wondered where Nunzio had gone.

"What happened?" Franco asked.

"Nothing. Nunzio got upset about something and went out."

Nunzio returned about five in the morning, and the next day Felicia and Angela carried on as if nothing had happened. Felicia got the children ready for school. Frank was 11 and Robert nine, Marie six, and Andrea five. All four children went to the same Catholic school where Nunzio had been a student. Felicia had washed the dishes and was drying them when her husband stumbled into the kitchen.

"Where did you go last night?" Felicia asked.

"I went for a drink," said Nunzio.

He lit a Camel cigarette and sat back in his chair.

"You're smoking too much," said Felicia. "The doctor told you to stop."

Nunzio had been having heart palpitations for several months but refused to go to the doctor.

"I'll be all right," Nunzio said.

He sipped his coffee.

"I'm thinking about putting Frank into military school," Nunzio said. "He can have a successful military career."

"I don't know if he wants to do that," Felicia said.

"He'll settle in. I know people at the New York Military Academy, and they'll give him special treatment. It's right in town."

Nunzio soon left for his job at Camp Smith, and Felicia breathed a sigh of relief that she could go on with her day. Having been brought up around Northern Yankees, Felicia had an almost stoic approach to adversity. She would simply carry on until it was time to change things.

"Felicia," said Angela, who had come up the back stairway and into Felicia's kitchen. "Where did Nunzio go last night?"

"To a bar," Felicia said.

"Maybe he should go back to the doctor," said Angela.

Felicia had not wanted a husband who was so fragile. Like Angela's, her vision and dream were entirely different from the reality of her home life. She knew she had to focus on the children and their needs.

"I will mention it, but I don't think he will," said Felicia.

Angela had hoped Felicia would be more forceful with Nunzio to keep him on a positive path, but she could see that Felicia was overwhelmed with her responsibilities. It was easy for Angela to direct her attention solely to Nunzio because she no longer had Joe and Alicia depending on her. Joe was doing well in his America Express job in New York City and found an apartment and a roommate. Alicia was living near New York City and had two more children. She was separated from Leo and occasionally came up to see Angela and Franco with the children.

"I'm going to the market," Felicia said. "The girls will be here before I get home, so can you keep an eye on them?"

"Of course. Take your time," Angela said.

The sisters usually came home from school first and were happy to spend time with their aunt. Angela often played Caruso records for the boys and tried to encourage an interest in music. It opened a door to culture that they would not be exposed to in Nelsonville. Franco taught them practical skills like laying tile and restoring furniture.

The girls came in, and Angela handed them prayer cards with Saint Francis on them. "The good angels are there for us when we have to make decisions so that we make the right decisions," Angela still wanted to instill culture and storytelling into her great nieces' and nephews' lives rather than religion—not just any storytelling, but stories about strong spiritual archetypes with superhuman powers. The girls were old enough now, so their understanding of the stories deepened. She knew Frank did not want a military education, so she encouraged his connection to music. Both boys were musically inclined.

"What did Saint Francis do?" asked Marie.

"Saint Francis loved animals. He is known for his love and care of animals."

"I want some peanut butter and jelly," Andrea said.

"All right, I have to go upstairs to get it," Angela said. "You two behave yourselves and sit at the kitchen table."

As soon as Angela left the room, Marie ran into Angela's bedroom to gaze at her great-aunt's altar to Mary. She felt comforted being close to the altar. The candle rack was like the one found in church where parishioners paid to light a candle. On top of the rack was a statue of the Blessed Mother with her palms open toward the viewer. Marie remembered taking a nap once on Angela's bed, and the last image she saw before she fell asleep was the statue of Mary. In her dreams, the statue came alive and talked to her. She could not hear the conversation, but she remembered Mary was talking.

"What are you doing in here?" Angela asked. "The sandwiches are ready."

"I like to look at your altar," Marie said.

'Well, Mary loves children and likes to have them visit," Angela said. "I am glad you have a fondness for her. She helps everyone."

She told Marie about the time she was very ill and prayed to Mary for help. She told her that she survived the earthquake in order to care for their grandmother and father and now Marie, her sister and her brothers—those who needed her.

"And there is not a day that goes by that I do not think about my sister and whether she survived the earthquake. God took your grandmother away from me, but He gave me you."

Angela served the girls their snack, and then they went out to play in the yard. She watched as the sisters played on the swing set. She felt the gap in her life had been filled, making them clothes and telling them stories. She was glad to be able to pass on what she had learned about making a home wherever she was. It did not have to be in your country of origin. Home had to be in your own skin.

Chapter 17

December 1958

Nunzio had put on weight and had another mild heart attack. The doctor was clear about abstaining from alcohol and cigarettes. Nunzio stopped but craved both.

"Felicia, tell Frank to go next door and ask the doctor if I could have a cigarette," Nunzio said.

"The doctor does not want you to smoke. You have had another heart attack and you still have palpitations."

"I just want one," said Nunzio.

Felicia knew her husband had little joy in life and considered that one cigarette would likely do no harm.

"Frank, where are you going?" asked Angela as Frank came down the stairs.

"I'm going to Doctor Martens to ask if Dad could have a cigarette."

"He is not supposed to smoke," said Angela. "That is a bad idea."

"But Dad wants a cigarette," Frank said.

Angela called up from the bottom of the stairs. "Felicia, do you know that Frank is going to ask Doctor Martens if Nunzio could smoke?"

"Yes, he just wants one," said Felicia. "I don't think one will be a problem."

Angela knew her nephew. One would not be enough.

"Frank, no matter what Doctor Martens says, tell your father that the doctor said no. It is not good for your father to smoke," said Angela.

Frank dutifully went next door and asked the doctor if Nunzio could have a cigarette. The answer was that he could have *one*. Frank was not going to lie to his father. Unknown to Felicia and Angela, Nunzio had given his son money to buy him a pack of Camels. Nunzio opened the pack and lit a cigarette, taking a long deep inhale, settling back in his chair, and blowing the smoke into the air. Immediately his body relaxed, and the world looked better. He hid the pack of cigarettes in his back pocket.

One day, a few weeks later, Nunzio woke up short of breath but felt better after breakfast. It was a week before Christmas. He went back to bed and rested while Felicia cleaned the house and Angela fitted a client with a new suit. During the past week, Angela felt that Nunzio just watched as everyone around him was engaged in the activity of life. She encouraged him to rest on the weekends but on this day Nunzio imploded.

"I have chest pain," shouted Nunzio. "I need some air."

"Frank, stay with your father," instructed Felicia.

She passed Angela on her way out. "Angela, Nunzio does not feel well. I am going next door to get the doctor."

Angela went upstairs and found that Nunzio was gasping for breath.

"Frank, go next door and get your mother and Doctor Martens."

Angela saw Nunzio take his last breath as he passed from this life. It did not seem real to Angela, who thought he would awaken at any moment from that timeless space of the beyond. Angela knelt and prayed to Mary to help him, but this time even Mary was too late. Angela cried and cried that Mary was unable to work her magic. She knew the permanence of death and she despised its grip on the living.

The ambulance and other doctors arrived, and neighbors gathered around the ambulance. Angela ushered the children downstairs. Sadie arrived and knelt with Angela to pray, thanks to phone call placed by one of the neighbors. Angela did not think she could endure another loss, but here she was on her knees saying prayers for Nunzio's soul and everyone she had lost. Her younger sister, her brother, Speranza, and Nunzio were now together in the unseen world. She did not believe in total death, even though she felt death preyed upon the living relentlessly.

* * *

Nunzio had a military funeral and 21-gun salute. Angela observed calmly as Salvatore stood at his son's grave with his wife and shook his head as they lowered the coffin. Angela felt sorry for Salvatore, not because of his son's passing, but because Nunzio had been a phantom to him. There had been no effort on either side to connect. Angela had made sure Nunzio's children were cared for during the wake and funeral.

"Aunt Angela," said Joe several days after the funeral. "Do you think Felicia will stay?"

"I hope so," said Angela. "I want to help with the children, and she will need help."

"I hope she stays," said Joe. "She's part of the family."

Joe stayed close to Felicia during those dark days, having had more of a connection to Felicia than with Nunzio and not wanting to lose it. He could talk to her and feel part of the family. Alicia had seldom seen Nunzio toward the end of his life and was at a loss with his passing.

* * *

The tension seemed to have drained out of the house on Morning Glory Avenue like running water, and as the months went by, Nunzio was not spoken about much. The amount of loss was so profound for Angela that she had given up talking about it. Immediately after Nunzio's death, she saw that the structure she had built within the family was still intact—only now she felt buried under grief. She had known Nunzio was drowning but had been helpless to do anything about it. Felicia had decided to stay in Nelsonville, and Angela was grateful she would not lose the children.

One night, Angela dreamed she was in Messina and a large tower stood looming before her. The tower started to crack, then fell over. The ground was stable and didn't move. She felt the presence of her unseen friends. They told her to think differently about her life and the people in it. They said the old way wouldn't work anymore and that the next decade would be a time of great change for women—with many opportunities for her. Angela awoke with a renewed sense of purpose to nurture the next generation with a re-established strength.

About the Author

Carmela Cattuti started her writing career as a writer for the Somerville News in Boston, MA. She is a writer, painter, and yoga instructor in Boston, MA. After she finished her graduate work in English Literature at Boston College, she began to write creatively and taught a journal writing class at the Cambridge Center for Adult Education. As fate would have it, she felt compelled to write her great-aunt's story. *Between the Cracks* and *The Ascent* have gone through several incarnations and will become a trilogy. The Ascent is the second novel. To connect with Carmela, email her at cattutic@gmail.com or leave a comment at www.ccattuticreative.com/carmela-cattuti-books.

CPSIA information can be obtained
at www.ICGtesting.com
Printed in the USA
FSHW021242010619
58544FS